THE ARYAN

Other Books in the Reg Danson Adventure Series

The Landing Place

The Lost Kingdom

CLINT KELLY

THE ARYAN

THOMAS NELSON PUBLISHERS
Nashville • Atlanta • London • Vancouver

Published in Nashville, Tennessee, by Thomas Nelson, Inc., Publishers, and distributed in Canada by Word Communications, Ltd., Richmond, British Columbia.

Library of Congress Cataloging-in-Publication Data

Kelly, Clint.
The Aryan / by Clint Kelly.
p. cm.
ISBN 0-7852-7960-1
1. White supremacy movements—Fiction. 2. Fascism—Fiction. 3.Racism—Fiction. I. Title.
PS3561.E3929A89 1995 94-49119
813'.54—dc20 CIP

Printed in the United States of America.

1 2 3 4 5 6 — 00 99 98 97 96 95

To those courageous men, women, and children who battle hatred on every front. Be of good courage. He has overcome the world!

Have no fellowship with the unfruitful works of darkness, but rather expose them.
— Ephesians 5:11

Acknowledgments

Special thanks to two very important resources in the writing of this book. The first is attorney Morris Dees and his colleagues at the Southern Poverty Law Center. Together, they have legally challenged the Ku Klux Klan, the skinheads, and other virulent hate groups and effectively slowed their advance. These American freedom fighters risk their very lives to champion the poor and the defenseless, and by their willingness to prosecute racial intolerance, they have saved the lives of many.

Heartfelt thanks is also due the Anti-Defamation League, longtime defenders of the racially oppressed. Their unstinting dedication to the historical facts of the Holocaust will serve as much as any effort to prevent a repeat of that dreadful chapter in human depravity.

CHAPTER 1

He sipped the blazing coffee and stiffened. The menu said "Doomsday Java." No sissy mochas or "double tall skinnies" allowed on these premises. It didn't matter that this was Seattle, espresso mecca. Lattes didn't cut it at Leo's.

Leo Slugitt, amateur philosopher and owner of Leo's Jazz and Java in the district known as Catholic Town, ran his restaurant by one simple creed: "The coffee's black as Hades, final as death!" You hurt Leo's feelings if you didn't order coffee. And Leo's was Reg Danson's favorite place to conduct research—or to lose himself.

The wallpaper at Leo's was circa 1950, but the music was forever. Ten tables and a bare spot west of Reg, Billy Fuller and the Harmonic Can Do's blew a flirtatious rendition of "Peg o' My Heart" on mouth harps big as submarine sandwiches. Eyes squeezed shut, sweaty faces beaming, Billy and his blues brothers blew hot, milking the classic for all it was worth.

Reg Danson took a second tenuous sip from the mug. *Piston grease.* Steam wreathed his handsome features, then curled away from a sickly grin. The bush java kept him awake on a research binge—but tonight it was soup and solitude that drew him in. Homemade stock, crowded with succulent bits of sirloin and a farmer's market of fresh vegetables, the soup was served in a bowl round like a tub and criminally cheap. "What!?" Leo would bristle defensively. "I should charge for hot water?"

Billy's boys slipped smoothly into a Dinah Washington medley, and Reg sighed contentedly. He glanced through yellowing blinds past the orange neon announcing "Jazz and Java" to the massive lighted billboard across the street that airline pilots used to orient themselves on final approach to Seattle-Tacoma International. "Queen of Heaven Speaks to America," it declared. "Call 1-800-ASK-MARY."

"I've called her," said a raspy voice at his elbow. Reg jumped. Leo Slugitt, coffeepot in hand, had poured his way table-to-table, arriving at Reg's usual spot, first table south of the front door, with one cup's worth left. "Sorry, mate," Leo winked, a stringy Popeye in lumpy sailor hat and worn T-shirt. "Didn't mean to give ya a stroke."

A bandy-legged runt of a man, Leo hooked his thumbs in the ties of an ancient apron and squinted through red eyes dimmed by ocean glare. His features had been hammered hard by bad choices and the unrelenting sea. "Seems the blessed Virgin Mother and the blessed Savior himself have been appearing in Long Island, New York, with an urgent message for the world." Slugitt did a little jig. "Wonder if they'll be appearing in Las Vegas next month?" He grinned slyly. "I hear they're the opening act for the almighty Pope!"

Reg said nothing but fortified himself with another cautious sip of Doomsday brew. Leo snorted derisively. "That ain't no way to take your coffee, man! You got to gulp it and chew it and knock it back like a good slug of Irish whiskey. Whiskey's Gaelic for 'water of life,' ya know. For teetotalers like you and myself, God gave us java swill, blessed be his name! Why, the last time my mudder-in-law flew in here on the twelve o'clock broom, I gave her a taste of Leo's fresh ground and she ain't been back since. Nor spoken a word to another living soul. Don't tell me coffee ain't good for ya!" His mirth swept over the restaurant in a flash flood of snorts and hoots. A few customers looked annoyed, but tonight it was mostly the regular crowd. The Harmonic Can Do's lunged into a raucous rendition of a Toots Thielemans standard.

Reg's attention wandered outside again. A chill fall wind shoved the city's debris down emptying streets. Leaves and newspapers collided in a blur like alley cats at war. A light winked off in the second-story office building beneath the glaring billboard and seconds later a man emerged from the entrance, locked it, and moved wearily away until lost in the darkness beyond the sign's reach. Danson cupped the coffee mug, absorbing the warm remains of the liquid, feeling an unbidden pocket of cold deep in his chest. He hoped he wasn't coming down with something.

A body in a blue jacket and knit cap thudded against the window. Startled, Reg dropped the cup with a clatter and knocked his chair back from the window. But the person recovered and stumbled on, glancing back again and again but finally disappearing beyond the searchlight of the billboard.

"Drunk," said Leo's familiar, jovial voice, followed by the comforting gurgle of pungent coffee pouring ebony-dark. But this time there was a note of something else in the glib manner. Something guarded, tight. Was it fear?

"What, Leo?" Reg didn't like the rigid set of Slugitt's jaw. "What is it?"

"Likely nothing," replied Leo, his voice strained. "Just that the poor devil's face looked troubled, that's all."

Suddenly, another person rushed past the cafe, then two more. Shouts of "Don't lose him!" and "Down here! He's this way!" penetrated the club walls. Leo slammed the coffeepot down.

"Sounds like trouble, Leo," said Reg, starting to rise. "We'd better see what's wrong."

"It's just the city, Reg. See it all the time. When ya live this close to the cemetery, ya can't weep for everyone."

The commotion increased, and now people rushed past the cozy confines of Leo's, some of them running, calling encouragement to those behind. Even against the driving sounds of Billy's boys, the anger, the venom in those shouts was unmistakable. Reg planted a five-dollar bill on the table. "Keep the change, Leo. I've got to see if that poor guy needs help."

Slugitt grabbed Danson's biceps in a steely grip and held him down. "Forget it, man! I know these people. They hate for no reason. You'll only get yourself killed!"

Reg gave his friend a lopsided smile of reassurance. "Listen, buddy, I'm a survivor of Leo Slugitt's Doomsday swill. What's a few inebriated kids?" The explorer's face held an undeniable resolve. The firm jaw, steady amber eyes, lean body, and tan skin, baked earthen brown by the African sun, brooked no objection. Leo let loose of Reg's arms. "I thought I was invincible, too, when I was a pup," he said. "Now I get more done with my cooking than I ever did with my fists."

Reg laid a comforting hand on Slugitt's shoulder. "Keep the soup and the band hot until I get back." And he was gone.

He caught his breath in the night chill and was tempted to fall back into the warm womb of Leo's. *Safety first.* Remembering the childhood admonition, he zipped his jacket to the neck. A lifetime of adventure forced him onto the sidewalk, pulled in the direction of the angry shouts.

Wind whipped at his pants legs and turned his breath to fog. His head was bare, sandy hair close-cropped. He'd never liked anything on his head even in the foulest weather; it hampered the senses of sight and sound. His scalp was as brown as the rest of him.

He was part of the wind, propelled along by its push and shove. Across O'Connell, east on Murray, down the alley between Cork and Crofton. Past garbage drifts and Dumpsters, he hurried after the ragged throng. Danger from the alley didn't occur to him. He was part of the human tornado sweeping the lesser dangers of rats and winos aside.

"Dead chink—good chink" was scrawled in red paint down the wall to the right, "Jew swine" across a wooden service entrance to the left. And over that in Day-Glo green, a mystifying "WWRR."

Hatred in a spray can.

Danson burst out of the alley onto the O'Leary Street overpass. The hunters had treed their quarry. A lone figure stood tottering on the railing high above the rushing lanes of Interstate 5. A shaky hand brushed a sign that read "$500 fine for throwing anything from bridge," using it for balance. His tormentors milled about his feet like half-crazed hounds scenting the kill. Their taunts raked the night.

"Jump, you black baboon!"

"Niggers never prosper!"

"You're roadkill, dirty coon!"

The males' heads were shaved like concentration camp internees, their skulls pale and gaunt in the eerie sterile light of the street lamps. Four girls were dressed in the same army-green field coats and black jackboots as the men, their hair partially shaved, the remainder streaked orange or white. Great pendulous collections of metal hung from their right ears. All but one seemed detached from the scene, add-ons, like antsy biker babes waiting for their men to finish the dirty business before moving on. One girl, though, was taller and older than the others, and carried a giant crucifix. She held it like a sword and jabbed it at the man on the railing. "Thieving goon!" she screamed.

The knot of fear tightened in Reg's stomach. The young people had been drinking, a bottle or two still clutched in their hands, but this was no alcohol-induced prank. They wanted to be there; they wanted the man to jump. Their snarled epithets pelted the victim like hot buckshot, and he leaned away from them out over the freeway abyss. Horns honked obscenely at the man's plight.

Danson walked quickly past the girl with the crucifix, noting that the tangle of metal in her earlobe was a collection of tin swastikas. She started to say something to Reg, but it died in her throat. The males, he discovered, were only boys, but there was an ancient hardness in their features. Predators. Their bleak colorless eyes flickered at the intruder. Hands balled into fists. A lead pipe sliced the air and clanged hollowly against the bridge railing, forcing a moan of terror from the man on the edge.

Reg lunged past the mob and grabbed the cold railing in both hands, looking across Lake Union to the winking lights of the Space Needle, willing himself to look neither at the man nor the rushing, honking craziness below.

"Come on, buddy, nothing's so bad to kill yourself over. Talk to me, man, talk to me!" he shouted to be heard above the traffic.

Out of the corner of one eye, he saw the man straighten, take a firmer grip on the pole, and glance warily at Reg Danson. The man had a handsome, gentle face, a face glistening with tears that ran down the collar of a blue ski jacket. Danson judged him to be about thirty years old, 180 pounds.

"I got nothing to live for!" he shouted back. "These people are right—I'm nothin' and nothin' good's gonna come from me stickin' around. I got no education and there's no work for a man with no skills. I end it now and you got less taxes to pay to keep me on the dole. That's what my woman said, just fifteen minutes ago. She said, 'Terrence, you might as well just throw yourself onto the freeway as mope around here feeling sorry for yourself.' So let's just see if she meant it!"

The man tipped forward on the balls of his feet and let go of the sign pole. The crowd shouted its encouragement. Danson threw his arms up, still staring straight ahead. "No! Wait! Terrence, God loves you and doesn't want you to take your life. Believe me, man. Don't do anything so drastic when you're not thinking clearly. Come on down and we'll go over to Leo's Jazz and Java. I'll buy you dinner, and we'll see if we can't figure out some way to find you a job and maybe even some schooling. Billy Fuller's jamming on the harmonica, and you'll see, the place is hopping!"

Terrence grabbed the pole.

"Nigger lover!" spit the girl with the cross. She waved it at Reg as if marking him for dissection. "White nigger!"

But Terrence turned toward Danson, and Reg could detect hope and interest elbowing through the despair. Reg smacked his lips. "Ummm. The soup, man, you've got to try the—"

"Jump, you black devil!" The boy with the pipe growled the command and tested his swing like a batter before the first pitch. Baleful eyes targeted the backs of the black man's legs. He would help Terrence make up his mind.

"Jump! Jump! *Jump!*" The others joined the chant. Whether it was from the man's resolve to jump or the sudden gust of wind that hit them square in the back, the man on the railing pitched forward and let go.

Reg leapt high in the air and threw both arms around Terrence, pulling backward with a mighty jerk. He half carried, half dragged the man into the oncoming path of a city transit bus. Air brakes shrilled in protest. The bus lurched to a halt less than six feet from the pair. Not daring to let go, Reg manhandled Terrence to the bus door.

"Are you lousy drunks lousy insane?!" yelled the driver, throwing open the door. He reached for the heavy, clublike handle of a flashlight fastened to the dash.

"Police!" gasped Danson, stumbling to his knees in the doorway, pinning the black man against the steps. "Radio for the police! A hate crime's been committed!"

The astonished driver wrenched the phone from its hook. Two burly male passengers surged forward and pulled the sobbing, dazed Terrence up into the bright interior of the bus. Reg tried to stand, but his knees shook and he slumped back to the ground.

Someone ran up behind and passed two wiry arms beneath Reg's armpits and hoisted him up. Leo Slugitt's lips were pursed in a grim smile.

Reg returned it weakly. "Leo, anybody ever tell you you've got the face of an angel and the timing of a politician?"

Leo grimaced. "Fallen angel, maybe." He coughed uncomfortably. Brakes squealed. Flashing red lights turned the old sailor's face a ruddy hue. The angry youth scattered like spilled marbles.

Except one. She moved nearer, into the red wash from the police cruisers. Thin, pale face, wraithlike body enveloped in an oversized flak jacket. Isolated from the others, her shaved and tinted head looked especially freakish, a clown gone berserk. The letters "WWRR" were crudely tattooed small on her left cheek. But the eyes were soft, quizzical, never leaving Reg Danson. An officer handcuffed her. Still she stared, wondering.

Leo placed his lips against Reg's ear. "Didn't I tell ya? Ya can't weep for everyone. Lucky for this one ya did, though. Crazy Nazis!"

A news van screeched to a lurching halt. Four people leapt out, one of them turning the intense beam of a spotlight on the scene. Cameras whirred.

Danson groaned.

"What can I do?" Leo whispered, scowling fiercely at the reporters.

Reg smelled the sea in Leo's old Navy pea jacket. "Coffee!" he replied, closing his eyes against the glare.

CHAPTER 2

The car without the muffler roared out of the driveway next door, each snarl another nail in Danson's splitting head. *Either that kid gets a muffler or I move to Bora Bora.*

Reg moaned, lifting his rumpled self from the bed where he'd collapsed fully clothed an hour before. When he had slept, red flashing lights bloodied his dreams, and it was as if a dozen booted skinheads shared the bed with him. They shouted profanities and racial epithets and clubbed one another with lead pipes. When he asked them to be quiet, they swung at him with the pipes and turned into horrifying stand-up comics, their death's head grins identical. If he didn't like it, they leered, he could just take a fast flying leap off the bed. *Jump!*

He'd spent most of the night sorting a growing stack of hate reports from around the world. They were tacked to the walls, taped to the lamp, and formed a wretched patchwork quilt of loathing across the bedspread. The collection had been waiting for him when he'd returned from Africa, inexplicably sent by his boss, Richard Bascomb—no explanation, just the usual cryptic note: "Reg, my boy, a little heavy reading for your idle moments. Tell me what you make of these."

Danson had read the mounting evidence that the world was coming unglued:

> WUPPERTAL, Germany—Two neo-Nazi skinheads and a bartender were convicted of murder Monday and sentenced to prison for kicking and burning to death a man they thought was Jewish.
>
> HEBRON, Israeli-Occupied West Bank—Dr. Baruch Goldstein, an immigrant from New York and a member of the extremist Kach movement, burst into the Ibrahim Mosque Friday and opened fire on the more than 600 Muslims praying there. At least forty people died.
>
> JOUNIEH, Lebanon—A bomb exploded in a packed Maronite Catholic church Sunday, killing nine worshipers and wounding at least sixty as they lined up in front of the altar to take Communion, police and witnesses said. Pieces of human flesh, torn clothes, and shoes were scattered across the blood-soaked carpeting.
>
> NEW YORK, New York—Louis Farrakhan, controversial leader of the Nation of Islam, stood on the steps of his 125th Street headquarters yesterday and called whites "devils" and Judaism "a gutter religion."
>
> NEW YORK, New York—A federal jury on Friday convicted all four of the men on trial in the bomb attack that killed six people at the World Trade Center and caused hundreds of millions of dollars in damage. The cold-blooded act sent a jolt of fear through a nation abruptly aware of its vulnerability to terrorism.

BATON ROUGE, Louisiana—A press release seized from a member of the White Patriot Party warns its members to "beware the black beasts in human form who lust after the chastity of our mothers, wives, sisters, and daughters. This would lead to the everlasting contamination of the very blood of the Caucasian race."

The last report was accompanied by a photo showing one of the press releases nailed to a telephone pole, the cryptic "WWRR!" clearly legible on the fence behind.

Reg held his head and moaned again. Who did the kid with no muffler hate? Should Danson move to the wilds of the Olympic Peninsula and live off the land? His son, Tony, loved the steely crags and primeval darkness of the forest, and they were planning a week's backpacking expedition where cars did not rumble and people did not bomb other people. Tony had decided to finish his archaeology studies at George Washington University and work part-time in Alexandria, Virginia. Reg missed him. They were good for each other.

A hermitage in the wilds. He'd talk it over with Tony. They liked to dream impossible dreams. Reg could wreck coffee as well as Leo. Tony was a fair hunter. He could bag 'em; Reg could cook 'em. Happy ever after.

But could he defend his mountain aerie from all comers? Could he repulse enmity with force? How many skinheads did it take to turn a peacemaker into a killer?

Reg plunged his aching face into a basin of biting cold water and fumbled in the medicine cabinet for aspirin. He closed the cabinet and winced. Still taped to the mirror, survivor of many a steamy shave, were the words of Helen Keller: *No pessimist ever discovered the secrets of the stars, or sailed to an uncharted land, or opened a new heaven to the human spirit.*

"Helen, Helen," he said softly. "Even in your sightless, soundless world, there was little tolerance for despair. I'd say you scaled mountains of prejudice and self-doubt far higher than anything I've encountered. But what about the kid next door?"

The jangle of the phone produced a fresh stab of pain. The wicked thing could just ring its fool self to death for all he cared. He'd taken a personal oath not to answer it for at least another month. He was due a giant Sabbath rest, and he fully intended to take it.

"Hello. You've reached the Danson residence. Accept my regrets at not personally taking your call but there's an alligator in the bathtub. Please leave all the pertinent information and I'll get back to you between adventures. In case of emergency, please call the Enigma Society at 1-800-MYSTERY. Godspeed!" Beep.

Danson buried his face in the sink just as Bascomb's booming baritone filled the house. "Reg, my boy, time is money. Drop whatever you're doing and pick up the phone. I know you're there . . ."

In three strides, Danson snatched the phone off the bedstead.

"Look, Mr. Bascomb, you promised me some time to unwind. To do that, I have to be left alone. I had a rough night—"

"A bit edgy, Reggie?" said Bascomb without slowing in the least. "I don't wonder what with having to fend off gangs and rescue a potential suicide. I'll wait while you fetch the morning paper."

A sinking feeling in Reg's stomach sang duet with the clanging in his head. He put down the receiver and paused unsteadily before the front door. Taking a deep breath, he opened the door, grabbed the folded paper, and slammed the door shut before the cameraman filming the front of the house got too close a look.

The doorbell rang but he ignored it. He stared at a quarter-page photo of Leo whispering something about Nazis in his ear on the O'Leary Street overpass. "Explorer Saves Life of Attempted Suicide" screamed the headline.

The doorbell persisted and so did Bascomb, whose urgent voice buzzed unintelligibly from the phone. Reg ignored them both. He could kiss peace and quiet good-bye. Since last night's little outing, he was big news.

The doorbell's ring became an insistent knock and the buzzing became . . . barking. Reg shook his head, then laughed wearily. A barking Bascomb was not to be denied.

"Under siege, are we?" Bascomb said sympathetically, calming himself with effort

"Apparently," Reg answered, giving the pounding door a worried glance. "The gophers are rather aggressive this fall."

Bascomb laughed, but the sound lacked conviction. Something more was eating him. "When I told you to examine those reports of hate crimes, I didn't expect you to run a field test."

"Believe me, it wasn't planned."

"Well, renown always complicates matters, but that can't be helped. Are you all right?"

Reg leaned back and caught a glimpse of himself in the bathroom mirror. "Nothing some aspirin and a chalet in the Colorado Rockies couldn't cure."

"Yes, yes. We must get you away one of these times, absolutely. The pace of things is becoming positively monstrous. Oh, sorry, no pun intended. That was a pretty piece of work you did for us in the Congo. The Smithsonian has been relentless in its request for a debriefing, but I told them flatly that it would keep, that these creatures you found have been there for millennia and aren't likely to go anywhere in the next two or three months. I said you needed a breather and time to digest everything before locking horns with the fossil boys. Can you believe they threatened *sanctions*? I told them what they could do with their sanctions—all very professional, I assure you—and that if they didn't calm down, we'd simply zipper the whole project tight and they could go back to doing artists' renderings of imagined prehistoric creatures and playing Twenty Questions."

Reg chuckled. Bascomb was flamboyant and pushy, but he was fiercely loyal to his own. He was a good man to have in your corner—and what a spender. "I'm sure a strong case could be made for cleansing humanity of evolutionary scientists," said Reg. "As a race, they're greatly inferior, bad genes and all. But nobody can touch them on the exhibit hall floor. Why, they make the Big Bang theory look like a day at Disneyland."

Something was wrong. Bascomb wasn't in a joking mood. He loved firing shots at their favorite targets, the scientific establishment. But apparently not today.

"Something's come up, Reg lad, and I need you. You must fly to Rome immediately. Pack light—you won't be there long. Tell Tony where you are, but no one else is to know. You are to meet at the Vatican with Monsignor Claudio Andone. It is a matter of the gravest concern. That they have turned to us for its solution indicates just how grave it is." His voice softened. "God is using you mightily, Reg. I know you've been thrown into the fire without having first grown accustomed to the frying pan. But this one nags at me. Time is short, and I fear that if we do not respond now, the earth will suffer some awful agony. Eat at Gianni's. Tell them I sent you. When they have done with you, you'll think you have died and gone to gastronomical heaven!"

The reporters were looking in the windows now. The way they yammered their indecipherable questions through the glass reminded Reg of wooden marionettes run amuck. Rome sounded great all of a sudden.

"And Reg?" Bascomb's voice was faint and tenuous. Fearful. "Note the lead story at the top of the front page. Keep eyes in the back of your head, son. I wouldn't want anything bad to happen to you."

"What?" Reg began. He stopped. The line was dead.

He tucked the paper under an arm and walked around to all the windows, pulling down the shades. Then he turned on the overhead light and walked to the middle of the room. Slowly he unfolded the paper and turned it over. His breath caught.

There, above the story of last night's incident and the photo of Leo and Reg were two other photos. One of a devastated man in a formal frock of the Catholic church standing beside an ornate desk and Tiffany lamp, visibly wringing his hands. Monsignor Claudio Andone, Vatican under-secretary for foreign relations. Beside that photo was another, showing what appeared to be a cloth of some kind bearing the haunting image of a man.

The renewed knocking and doorbell ringing were swallowed by the roar of white noise in Danson's throbbing head. He hurried to the dining room table and spread the paper full. Recognition of the cloth and the banner headline came simultaneously:

"Stolen! Famed Shroud of Turin Seized
in Daring Daylight Heist"

CHAPTER 3

Tony lifted the tight powder wig from his head and set it on the Styrofoam form. He removed the black frock coat, ruffled shirt, brown trousers, and knee-high stockings of "James Earl Hall, citizen of Alexandria" and turned from the two-hundred-year-old contemporary of George Washington back into Tony Danson, nineteen-year-old college student, hustling for the next college tuition payment.

It had been a good lunch crowd. The patrons, mostly tourists from around the world, packed Gadsby's Tavern in Alexandria, re-created as it was circa 1770, where independence and national sovereignty had been vigorously debated and defended by revolutionary patriots. The General and Mrs. Washington had been frequent guests at Gadsby's, and George's favorite duck was still the house specialty.

Tony was tired but satisfied. He'd gotten the prize job through friends of his dad's in the Smithsonian. It was a decent commute from his apartment and from George Washington University. With tips it would make a sizeable dent in tuition, and it allowed him to work with Kathleen Snow, a willowy girl with a dazzling personality. He enjoyed playing lute and exchanging good-natured barbs with the convivial diners. They in turn enjoyed the repartee of this handsome eighteenth-century firebrand who held court on matters of voluntary taxation and the dealings of the Colonial Congress in Richmond.

"Archaeologists like old stuff," he'd told Kathleen, or Miss Snow as she preferred, when asked how he so easily discoursed on matters two centuries past. One night before closing, they'd stolen a dance around the empty ballroom where presidents and high society had entertained and forged a new nation. She was soft in his arms, her hair caught in a tight braided bun at the back of her head. In a blue floor-length serving dress, she'd looked radiant, from another time, a kindness from God—and he'd told her so.

"My dear Mr. Hall," she'd said in her best guest house manners, "you do turn a girl's head!" Too bad she didn't start work until later that evening.

Tony sighed dreamily and smiled at the good-looking guy in the mirror. The tan he'd gotten assisting his father in the Congo stopped at the elbows and neck, "but the sparkle in the azure blue eyes goes on forever!" He snorted at his own conceit and flicked water on the image. Properly chastised, he slipped into slacks and a lightweight tan cardigan for the short walk to his car.

He called good-bye to the maitre d' and went out onto the tavern steps where George Washington had performed his last military review. It was early still, the sun just about to call it quits. He breathed deeply the fresh fall air and descended the steps to North Royal Street. He headed for King's Road, where his "puddle jumper," a '72 four-cylinder Toyota Corona Mark II, waited patiently by the curb. He gave it an affectionate smack on the hood and started to insert the key in the lock. The note on the windshield stopped him.

"Mr. Hall, what are the chances of your coming by Riverside Park before my shift starts? Miss Snow."

Tony's heart did a brief rumba. He'd never seen her handwriting before. It was surprisingly more masculine than he expected, but then she'd probably exaggerated the capital letters on purpose. She was nothing if not spontaneous, and a little feisty.

He smoothed his hair in the side mirror, winked at the idiot grinning back, and trotted downhill toward the Potomac River.

He felt good, lighthearted, not wanting to hit the books just yet. A walk along the waterfront with Kathleen would suit his romantic mood just fine. He cut down the left side of the Torpedo Factory, a World War II munitions manufactory-turned-art gallery, and headed for Riverside Park.

His dad had phoned to say he'd be in Rome for a couple of days. "When Bascomb calls, Dad jumps." Tony grinned ruefully, thinking of the amazing hunts resulting from such phone calls. The one in the Congo, though, had been too close for comfort. Dad didn't always cover his backside. It angered Tony that his father was off again after so short a time at home. Reg Danson needed rest. Maybe he could bunk in with Tony and they'd do D.C. together. Yeah, that was the ticket. They were good for each other.

It was a beautiful evening, the river gliding quietly past the park's benches and meandering walkways in no particular hurry. Two families played beneath the trees, moms tickling their kids until they ran screeching into the rough embrace of their fathers, only to be hoisted aloft by strong arms, then plunged in a dizzying corkscrew dive to end in a laughing, breathless pile upon the grass.

Tony stood on the shore at the rear of the Torpedo Factory looking across the wide expanse to the thin line of trees opposite. They seemed to rise straight from the water, and he could imagine the Union Army in the dusky interior of the woods settling in for a long and bitter winter of killing.

He shuddered. *Where'd that unpleasant thought come from?* Romantics could be endearing or they could be morose. He hugged himself against the coming night chill and grinned away the gloomies. Where was Miss Snow hiding? Had he missed her?

The stern-wheeler *Cherry Blossom* sashayed past, wooden paddles slapping the water in cheery rhythm. Her windows glowed invitingly, candles bathing dinner guests in silky yellow rays. Tony watched the boat grow small in the gathering night and felt sad to see it go.

"'Scuse me," said a voice from behind. Tony whirled to face it.

There stood the fathers he'd seen playing with their kids. He'd been too lost in thought to notice their approach. They were young men, perhaps in their mid-twenties, the age Tony'd probably be when he settled down. Over their shoulders he saw that their families still played beneath the trees. *A little late for youngsters to be out this time of year in short sleeves . . .*

"Gotta light?" the taller, light-haired man asked, displaying a cigarette between his lips.

"Oh, no, no," Tony answered uncomfortably, bringing his arms down to his sides. "I don't smoke."

The two strangers exchanged knowing glances. They were bulky and hard like weight lifters, muscles straining against their shirts. *Why aren't they wearing coats or sweaters? Where are the blankets or lawn toys or food baskets families normally take with them to the park?* Tony wondered.

"Nice night." The light-haired man stuffed the cigarette into his shirt pocket. The shorter man, head closely shaved, said nothing. Tony couldn't quite make out the tattoo on the knuckles of his right hand.

The world seemed suddenly deserted. The closest houses were the brownstones across the street from the Torpedo Factory, a good two hundred yards away. On a Saturday evening, much of upper-class Alexandria was gone to the theater in D.C. or dining in the black-tie establishments along Coronation Boulevard. Tonight, there was a special reception at the Masonic Monument across town, a fund-raiser for the Democratic war chest.

Tony felt the river's chill now, deep in his bones. Something dawned on him. *Miss Snow didn't write that note.* "Well, you fellows enjoy the evening," he said, moving forward to go. They did not move from his path.

"Before you leave," said the taller man, voice flat, "we need to know where your father is."

"How do you know my father?" countered Tony, desperately aware of how little room there was between these thugs and the water.

"Where is he?" demanded the spokesman. The silent one bunched his fists and leaned slightly forward.

Tony bolted but caught a sweeping kick to the shins. On the way down, he took a knee in the chest that felt as if it collapsed his lungs. Flat on his face, he felt the knees again, backed by 230 pounds of beef, grind into the small of his back. A meaty hand gripped his hair and snapped his head back. Hot breath filled his ear.

"I don't wanta have to break anything you might need," the man hissed. "All I need to know is where your old man went and all of us can go home and relax. We dropped by his house and saw the gone fishin' sign, but with all the commotion he's been stirrin' up, I'd say fishin' was furthest from his mind. *Where is he?*"

He screamed the question in Tony's ear, pulling back on the handful of hair until the neck threatened to snap. Tony managed a choking snarl of defiance.

Suddenly the man jerked Tony's head forward and ground his nose and mouth into the dirt. He lifted the head again and said, "Well?!" Tony said nothing but spit dirt and fought for breath.

Again his head slammed into the dirt, then jerked back, nose streaming blood. *God spare me!*

A hard, stinging slap landed on the right side of his face followed by a hard-boned backhand to the left cheek. "Well?"

"I-I'll tell—you!" croaked Tony, and in a sweet rush, the pressure vanished from his spine. They yanked him to his feet. He steadied himself and peered at the taller man through the one eye not yet swollen shut. "I believe he said he was going car shopping. The old clunker's on its last—" He didn't finish before they began to drag him out of sight behind the factory. Mustering every last ounce of strength left, Tony bellowed for help. But when he looked to the trees where the women and children had been playing, the lawn was empty.

They beat and kicked him until he couldn't have said anything had he wanted to. He tried to record everything about their features he could, but soon he took a punch that closed the other eye.

They picked his limp body up and threw it into the Potomac. The only thing he could remember as the dark waters closed over him was the heavy fist racing for his one good eye, the knuckles of it etched with the capital letters "WWRR."

Monsignor Claudio Andone was a man bereft. Though only one of three thousand people employed by the Vatican, he was a man of great importance. The under-secretary for foreign relations was courted by every president, prime minister, and sultan in the world. Not only was the Roman Catholic Church fabulously wealthy, but it held powerful sway over the lives of millions around the globe. Staying friendly with Andone meant bringing its enormous influence to bear in matters of state, be they peasant uprisings, the building of new schools, or feeding the starving masses.

Normally, Andone would not handle matters concerning religious phenomena. Supposed apparitions, weeping statues, miraculous cures, and divine revelations were the province of a special department in the Vatican known as the Investigatory Council. "Club Weird" was how some in the church referred to this body of priests specially trained in all manner of arcane and questionable practices such as demonic exorcism and relic worship.

Monsignor Andone was chief among skeptics when it came to instances of what he considered ecclesiastical voodoo. If it made the people happy and they kept a lid on it, fine. But when it became an international circus and made the church look like a pack of superstitious fools, then it went too far.

Right now there was the devil to pay for what should have been nipped in the bud twenty-five years before at Flushing Meadows, New York. A brisk walk from Shea Stadium was the so-called "Lourdes of America" at the intersection of Grand Central Parkway and the Long Island Expressway. Jesus and Mary were said to speak to the world through seer Veronica Lueken on the grounds of an old Catholic church in Bayside.

More than three hundred messages later, covering everything from the start of World War III to the evils of rock music, the shrine now featured "holy hour" every Sunday, miraculous rose petals dropped from heaven that heal even by mail, and a spontaneous spring of healing waters that appeared on the eve of feast days to cure cancer, diabetes, and AIDS. Thousands upon thousands of pilgrims had made the journey to the site. Many gave glowing accounts of ordinary rosaries turned to gold and the flight of luminous doves. For the benefit of pilgrims caught up in the religious fervor, a system of vigil lights kept them apprised of the Virgin's arrival and departure. A blue signal meant she was present. Christ's arrival rated a red signal. Three flashes of red in a row signified either Our Lady or Our Lord had bestowed a blessing.

The in joke, of course, was that anywhere else in the world, three flashes of anything meant Mayday, S.O.S., save my hide.

The local clergy called it religious hysteria. They refused to seek an official church investigation for fear of fanning the fanatics. The operators of the shrine cried foul and passed along Mother Mary's warning of a chastising comet set to obliterate three-quarters of humankind. The Pope didn't help matters by accepting the dictated messages of Bayside from an emissary to the Vatican in 1979 and then pronouncing the protection of the Blessed Mother on the whole operation. Now the hallowed grounds were the object of bus and air charters by the dozens with special pilgrim discounts from Marriott, Travelodge, and Holiday Inn.

No, normally Monsignor Andone would not be bothered with such goings on. They were for him, as they were for the majority of the church, mere bits of sometimes entertaining, more often irritating, oddities—what one cardinal secretly, albeit facetiously, called "the marketing of the church, tabloid-style."

But now this. Andone was not fool enough to discredit the veracity of the great relics of church tradition. Any sacred object having to do with the Passion of Christ deserved respect no matter how recently it may have appeared on the scene. The crown of thorns, the nails that pierced his blessed hands and feet, the cross itself, were all worthy of meditation, perhaps even veneration. They could, in fact, be catalysts to genuine faith. What harm is a physical representation said to be the very article itself?

Whatever he thought, some things were sacred by default. And now the most sacred relic in all Christendom had been stolen.

For the hundredth time, Andone fingered the white rectangular calling card dissected vertically by a gold lightning bolt and inscribed with the printed letters "WWRR" at the top and the single handwritten word "Kaspar" at the bottom. It was the only thing left in the vault of the cathedral at Turin, Italy, where the great burial cloth of Christ, the famous Shroud of Turin, had once lain.

On the desk blotter next to that card rested two others, identical, each found at the site of a daring theft, each a maddening taunt from person or persons unknown. People had died: innocent priests, researchers, and Vatican security personnel charged with guarding the priceless treasures of the church.

"Why?!" Andone cried, beating softly on the desk with his fist. "Why this madness?"

A hesitant knock at the door forced him to seek composure. He did so before calling, "Enter!"

25

THE ARYAN

Father Piero Vincente opened the door, then stood against it, motioning his companion inside. The priest was a large, stocky man dressed in black Western clerical garb. Folds of skin overlapped the white collar beneath a stern, slightly sour face, lending him the unsettling appearance of an upright bulldog. "Reginald Danson, Enigma Society!" announced the priest with resonant dignity, the overlapping folds of skin vibrating with the announcement. Reg stepped into the room.

The small apartment was in an alcove of the Vatican museum dating from the days of Napoleon. Paintings and rich vestments from many periods adorned ancient halls and marbled walls of the sprawling complex. Some of the oldest scrolls and manuscripts in all of Europe were contained there. The library housed 350,000 volumes and more than 50,000 handwritten texts including Egyptian papyri more than four thousand years old. At the end of the hall was the exquisite statue of a father and his children fighting several huge snakes—a statue from the island of Rhodes so finely sculpted that Michelangelo had called it "the miracle of art."

The spare apartment looked drab in comparison to the king's ransom Reg had glimpsed on the way here. Danson faced the man who'd summoned him to Rome.

"Ah, Mr. Danson. How kind of you to come. I apologize for the abrupt invitation, but I assure you that it is a matter of the gravest importance. Please, be seated."

Andone was a small man, ferretlike in his neat, narrow features. A few strands of black hair survived on his shiny pate. He wore a handsome blue silk suit with a bright red handkerchief in the breast pocket. A large silver ring set with opals graced the ring finger of his right hand. The fingernails were impeccably maintained, not a ragged cuticle in the lot. Reg self-consciously folded his hands, the rough, calloused fingers inside the palms, and met the earnest gaze of his host. The pain of the man's predicament was obvious.

"You have met Father Vincente." Andone's English was as trim and orderly as the rest of him. "He is a chief investigator for the Investigatory Council on Religious Phenomena and not a man easily fooled. But I don't mind telling you, Mr. Danson, this shocking turn of events has us completely baffled and absolutely frantic. We've had small thefts before, even some fairly significant ones, but always we have traced the culprits—disgruntled employees, a mentally unbalanced pilgrim, even a disillusioned priest or two, but never anything like this. And now the Shroud . . ."

Danson threw out a hand to stop the monsignor. "What do you mean, *now* the Shroud? This is not the first theft of an important relic?"

Andone and Vincente exchanged uneasy expressions. "No, signor," replied Andone, heartsick. "It is the third."

Thunderstruck, Reg let out a slow whistle.

Andone nodded to Vincente and the priest continued in a heavy, spiritless voice. "Six months ago, on the sixteenth of April, sometime between midnight and three A.M., the Holy Coat of Treves was snatched from the cathedral in Treves, France. That, as you may know, is said to be Christ's seamless robe of royal hue for which the Roman soldiers cast lots. It had for so long been kept on open display in a glass altar case that no special security precautions were in effect. Treves is but a small town. Why be concerned for the safety of the blessed relic? It is to be revered, not stolen. All that was found in place of the Holy Coat was this card." Andone handed one of the white calling cards to Danson. He examined it with a studious frown.

"We immediately placed all traditional Christian holy sites on cautionary alert," Vincente continued, "but three months went by and nothing more was heard. To be honest, we concentrated the bulk of our attention on the Shroud at the cathedral at Turin. For fourteen centuries it has been revered as the burial winding cloth of Jesus our Lord. Its haunting image of the Christ reclining in death would cause a stone to weep! Between thirty and forty years of age, 1.82 meters tall, about six feet, powerfully built, approximately 80 kilograms—170 pounds—in weight. Bearded, long hair, face bruised, head lacerated by sharp, pointed objects—"

Vincente faltered, his eyes watery with emotion. His voice grew huskier. "Back torn, knees bruised, wrists pierced, the heart—" A tear trickled down the big man's bulldog cheek. He swiped at it with a heavy paw and took a deep breath. "The heart possessed a wound the length and width of my thumb caused by the blade of a lance. But the spear thrust, to hasten death, was unnecessary. The blood on the cloth indicates the flow dribbled from the wound as opposed to bursting forth, as it would have done had he been alive at the time. As the holy Scriptures tell us, he had already given up his spirit." Vincente looked away from the two men. It was deathly still in the room, save for the ticking of a clock and the faraway echo of tourists exclaiming over an ancient work of art.

Andone broke the silence. "Some deranged person broke into the Royal Chapel of the Cloth and attempted to burn the Shroud in 1972. Thank God the asbestos interior of the shrine thwarted the crime. It did serve to awaken the scientific community to the pressing need to authenticate the cloth, and in 1978 we began the most intense scrutiny ever of an ancient object.

"The awesome assignment was to so thoroughly test the physics and the chemistry of the cloth and its image as to verify or refute, once and for all, the genuineness of the Shroud. Twenty scientists and seventy-two crates of instruments began a nondestructive examination that included chemical analysis, thermography, isodensity, infrared and fluorescent spectroscopy, optical and ultraviolet reflectance, photography, x-radiography, and X-ray fluorescence. A pathologist was present as was a medical examiner."

Andone sighed resignedly, the enthusiasm of his tale slacking ever so slightly. "Sophisticated carbon-dating placed the Shroud around the fourteenth century. These men of medicine, of chemistry, of archaeology were forced to conclude that the Shroud perhaps most properly fits under the heading 'Revered Cloth—Origins Unknown.' Just what the church needed, another relic of apocryphal birth!"

The under-secretary brightened some. "It is a divinely blessed forgery, if that is what it is! The extraordinary crucifixion of Jesus Christ is there on all counts from the scourging to the absence of broken bones. The body the shroud covered in no way decomposed, despite burial. It had to have been removed from the cloth by other than natural means as there is no sign of blood clots smeared or broken. Some declare it to be the image of Christ. Others hold to their professional reserve but place the onus on the doubters to prove that it was a forgery. Bottom line, as you say in America, is the vindication of the church's claim that here is a relic of enormous mystery and importance. It is appropriate that the Holy See has not officially declared the Shroud to be the grave clothes of Christ. For what is faith but an individual choice that cannot—*must* not—be legislated?"

Andone rose abruptly, nearly overturning the chair. He placed both immaculate hands on the plain mahogany secretary from which he had addressed the needs of the faithful from Albania to Zaire. Anger rippled the tight jaw muscles. "They *knew* we would focus on protecting the Shroud and so they struck us a blow right under our very noses instead! While the Vatican Guard virtually sealed off Turin and held its poor citizens captive in their own town, the swine came here—right here!—and stole the Veil of Veronica from its marble coffer in the Basilica of St. Peter's, a stone's throw from this room!"

The foreign secretary stood in front of Danson, bitter predicament sharply etched in the imploring eyes. The neat hands tightened into fists and beat against the blue silk suit. "How could I have been so stupid? To expose Pope John Paul to so great a risk was unconscionable."

Reg pitied the monsignor. "How was the second theft accomplished?"

Andone paced, exchanging anxious glances with Father Vincente. "There are a million places to hide in the Basilica. The largest church in the world is not impenetrable despite the thorough combing by security personnel after visiting hours. It was built for worship, after all, not for war!" He gave a bitter laugh. "Someone stayed inside beyond closing and then made his way to the four pillars that sustain the cupola of St. Peter's. Inside one of these huge pillars is the Chapel of St. Veronica and beside it the statue of the saint herself.

"In the base of the statue is a door to the vault containing the cloth tradition says was used to mop the perspiration from Jesus' brow as he struggled beneath the weight of the cross en route to Golgotha. Veronica was a woman of means who took compassion on Christ and wiped his face during the lull when Simon of Cyrene was given the cross to carry the rest of the way. Miraculously, the cloth came away forever imprinted with the portrait of Christ impressed in his blood and sweat." Andone gave a deprecating laugh. "I will leave it to Father Vincente and his detective brothers to corroborate that notion. Regardless, it is a holy treasure that comes to us from the catacombs and has been preserved through fire and flood. But I digress.

"The door to the vault has three locks, the keys kept by three priests trusted to guard the Veil. Sometime around midnight on the sixteenth of July, motion detectors on the walls of St. Peter's sensed unauthorized movement. Alarms sounded and three armed guards rushed to the scene. What they found was the door standing open, locks melted, and the empty display chest of crystal and silver gilt shattered on the floor. When they turned to exit the chamber, they were hit with rounds from a rapid-fire weapon that left two dead and the third paralyzed for life; he remembers nothing but a flash of light and blinding pain. Though the guards wore bullet-proof vests, the ammunition was armor-piercing. A second white card, again inscribed with the cryptic WWRR, Kaspar, and the gold lightning bolt"—he handed it to Danson—"was found between the cold lips of one of the dead. Those men gave their lives in the service of the church. May they rest in peace."

Claudio Andone stopped before a small photograph of Michelangelo's famed sculpture of the Pietà. He touched the glass over the limp body of the slain Messiah held in the arms of his grieving mother. *Such passion. Such sacrifice. Blessed Son of God!*

Andone whirled to face the others, hands clasped in despair. "So we naturally increased security at St. Peter's and *then* they struck at Turin! At three o'clock in the afternoon of this Wednesday past a bakery truck made a delivery to the cathedral staff and a half dozen or so researchers whose ongoing fiber analysis may shed further light on the exact age and origin of the cloth. Fire suddenly broke out in the refectory kitchen and someone shouted the alarm. When most of the staff and the researchers ran to the kitchen to help, they were met by two people in white delivery uniforms and black ski masks, brandishing automatic weapons. The cook and two helpers were dead on the floor. The gunmen began to herd the latest arrivals into a storeroom when Dr. William Branton of the University of Chicago School of Antiquities tried to make his escape. In the ensuing confusion, Dr. Branton, Dr. Lipstadt of the Institute of Holy Land Studies, two priests of the Holy Order of the Shroud, a gift shop worker, and a security guard were wantonly slaughtered. Meanwhile, other swine were stealing the Shroud, and before they left, two more security personnel lost their lives. Fortunately, visiting hours end at noon on Wednesdays and no tourists or worshipers were on the premises. Again, in place of the sacred cloth, was another of these vile calling cards!" Eyes averted, Andone held the third card at arm's length, gingerly pinched between trembling thumb and forefinger as if the little piece of paper might carry the plague. Reg took it and compared the three cards.

The capital letters "WWRR" were printed in black across the narrow width of each card and joined to the cursive "Kaspar," also in black, by a preprinted gold lightning bolt the length of the three-

and-a-half inch rectangle. The handwriting was bold and confident but with an uneven baseline that curved up, then down, slanted to the left. It would bear professional analysis.

"Why have you called me, Mr. Andone?" Reg handed him the cards. "I'm very sorry about the tragedies you have suffered, but this is a matter for the international intelligence agencies. These are obviously no petty thieves. They are highly sophisticated in their methods and utterly ruthless in their execution. Terrorists.

"I'm not trained in police procedures, Mr. Andone. I work with inanimate objects and wild four-footed beasts. Man is just too dangerous for my tastes. Richard Bascomb must have told you—"

Andone held up his hand. "I assure you, Signor Danson, we have conducted our own internal investigation and called upon every friend of the church, but to no avail. We are baffled. Our extensive worldwide network of contacts has turned up nothing of any use. The most virulent anti-Catholic factions in the world have on the one hand expressed their barely contained delight at our loss and on the other voiced sincere regret that they cannot take the credit for it. Believe me, they would boast from the rooftops if they were responsible. And it couldn't be black market profiteers. There's no market for priceless spiritual treasures such as these. You could never place them at auction. As investments, they could never appreciate in value.

"No, the only possible motive to which I can lend any credence—and it is dreadful enough—is that some deranged but wealthy collector is willing to go to any lengths to acquire one-of-a-kind artifacts of great significance for his own private viewing. I don't need to tell you that someone so motivated wouldn't hesitate to destroy those same artifacts in a fit of pique." Andone looked imploringly at Father Vincente.

The big man drew in a mighty breath of air and expelled it in a loud huff. He leaned forward in his chair. "To be frank, Mr. Danson, these thefts are as humiliating as they are frightening. Before the incident at Turin, we tried to conduct as discreet and private an investigation as possible to avoid the glare and loss of face the media attention would bring. And if I've learned one thing in my time with the Investigatory Council, it is that the church gains little from the notoriety of the bizarre. The Coat and the Veil are not, if you'll pardon my saying so, as solid historical links to the blessed events in Jerusalem two thousand years ago as the Shroud. They are by definition among the lesser relics. Their verification is more apocryphal than actual, not having inspired near the scrutiny as that of the burial cloth.

"But as a man who has seen it all from talking crucifixes to levitating communion wafers, my guts tell me there is something much bigger in these incidents than mere robbery for vanity or criminal gain. It will take someone outside the Roman Church to see what may be as plain as the noses on all our faces. Someone tenacious, someone who has proven he can find what no one else can. That someone is you!"

They were looking at him with all the naked hope and desperation of mothers of kidnapped children. They had nowhere else to turn.

Reg Danson stood. For a long moment he said nothing, and in the stillness, the ticking of the clock seemed to accelerate, almost as if racing ahead to some inevitable meeting. When he spoke, he looked only at the Pietà. "Take me to the Chapel of St. Veronica, in the pillar of St. Peter's. I will do what I can."

CHAPTER 4

The ducks drifted lazily in the shallows of the Potomac River. The water was cooler now, signaling the change of seasons. Fluffy white clouds piled the skies with dollops of cream. Each time one obscured the sun, the elderly man walking along the bank walked a little brisker and burrowed a little deeper into a quilted jacket.

Glad for the stout stick he carried, the man avoided the soft mud. At the mouth of a thin stream, he vaulted across using the stick as a brace, wincing slightly—bad hip—but loving the young feel of so cavalier an act.

How he craved the woods in fall, the promising bite of the harsh season to come turning his nose a rosy red. The river smelled different, tangy. There was a crackle and crunch under foot in the dry places where the weeds and grasses were getting ready to die. He thought of the fire and the Dickens classic half finished beside his comfortable old recliner and turned to go home.

And almost tripped over the head of Tony Danson.

The old man recoiled in horror, staggered backward, set to run for the Alexandria police. Then the head emitted a gurgling gasp and the ground behind it shifted. A shoe rose and fell. Then all was still.

The man dropped to arthritic knees beside the head and prayed to heaven he could remember CPR.

"WELCOME, RIDGE DUNSAN!"

The friendly man behind the misspelled sign on yellow poster board stepped forward and wrung Reg's hand in no uncertain grip. His wide, sunny face was missing every other tooth, but the radiance of his greeting more than filled the gaps. A nest of cornrow strands of hair sprang from the merry head and danced about the grinning countenance. Below a brown shirt were bright yellow shorts that matched the sign.

"Wel-l-l-come to Sea-Tac Interna-a-a-tional Airport!" chortled the man, grabbing Danson's carry-on bag. "Ree-chard Bascomb send for you. He say, 'Willie'—that's me, man—'Willie, you pick up my Ridge, take him home, make him take a long, hot bath, then have him call me. Yes? Willie, yes?' I say, 'Is de Pope Catholic or no?' He see my point right away quick!"

In a hailstorm of happy jabber, the unlikely chauffeur whisked the jet-weary Danson down to baggage pickup and out to a battered green Oldsmobile slouching at an expired meter. Willie cheerfully deposited the bags in the trunk, Reg in the backseat, and himself behind the wheel.

Danson was too tired to protest. It was just like the unpredictable Richard Bascomb to send in the clowns when the chips were down.

"You know Bascomb?" Danson asked dubiously, sinking back in the seat with a mighty yawn while Willie coaxed the heater to life with unintelligible threats and two whacks to the dashboard. He practically stood on the gas pedal. The car lurched backward and incurred the instant wrath of the driver of a sleek convertible that narrowly missed their rear bumper. A horn sounded like a southbound freight train screaming through the parking garage. Willie gave the other driver a jaunty wave and drove swiftly for the exit.

"Willie know everybody!" he exclaimed in happy reply to Reg's question. "You won't forget me either!" Reg didn't doubt that for a minute. Bascomb funded expeditions in search of answers to the world's mysteries. He'd never met him but Reg harbored a hunch Bascomb was himself one of the world's biggest puzzles. Was this man behind the wheel a missing piece?

Yet it was good of Bascomb to have Danson picked up at the airport, even by someone so eccentric as Willie. Never look a gift ride in the glove box.

Danson closed weary eyes and rubbed throbbing temples, trying to make sense of all he'd learned in Rome. What did the three stolen relics have in common that would cause professionals to kill for them? All were fabric, two were said to bear Christ's image seared into the cloth. No one was taking credit for the daring thefts, no ransom had been demanded, yet two of the thefts resulted in ten dead and one paralyzed without regard to official rank. Nothing else had been taken, though in the Vatican many valuable items studded with easily fenced gems were within close reach. Nothing else taken, but in each case the same calling card left behind with the Germanic spelling of the word *Kaspar.* A person? A place? A code for something else altogether? And what did the letters "WWRR," which he kept seeing at every turn, mean? And what was the significance of the gold lightning bolt? Something about it, too, seemed oddly familiar.

And the $64,000 question: Were the perpetrators finished or would they strike again, and where? The international press were clamoring for answers, and the alarm was especially acute among the Catholic faithful. Not only had their sacred shrines been brutally violated, but what church could now be considered safe sanctuary? The church was under siege. Monsignor Andone pulled his by now familiar strings and had military and police from several nations placed on twenty-four-hour guard at dozens of Christian holy sites around the globe. Reg Danson wondered sleepily if even the president of the United States could garner that much cooperation in so short a time.

"Hee-hee-hee!" cackled Willie, swerving to miss a stray dog. "You ree-lax and we be to your house plen-ty fast!"

Reg gave it up and lay down on the backseat, knees bent, using his arms for a pillow.

What he knew about the age-old traffic in religious relics was not a pretty picture. Entire cults had formed around the bodies and the bones of the early saints and martyrs. Their tombs became altars, cathedrals, and entire cities where followers flocked to fawn over the skeletal talismans of their fallen heroes. To be physically close to the remains was to appropriate the power and the blessing of those who'd been close to God. The Eucharist was celebrated on their gravestones. Manifestations followed. Claims of miraculous cures, even resurrections, channeled the religious fervor of multiplied thousands.

By the fourth and fifth centuries, the relic controversy raged across Europe. "Idolatry!" accused Vigilantius. "Honor!" rebutted Jerome. The traffic in relics became big business, which prompted laws prohibiting the exhumation, transportation, and merchandising of martyrs. Counterfeit martyrs drew the wrath of Augustine, but by the middle ages, the thirst for relics was insatiable. Hucksters met the demand with vials said to contain a sneeze of the Holy Spirit, the rays of the star of Bethlehem, or the sound of the bells at Solomon's Temple. The catacombs in Rome were reexcavated for more bodily remains to feed the frenzy. By the late 1200s, fully half of the annual income for the town of Canterbury, England, was derived from offerings made to the shrine of Thomas Becket. Duplication of the saints became commonplace. At least nineteen churches at once claimed to have the jaw of John the Baptist.

But not everyone caved in to the relic rush. When King Louis XIV of France made a handsome offer for the bones of St. Thomas Aquinas, he was politely refused.

The decrepit Olds turned onto the airport's perimeter service road and accelerated past air express companies and catering firms. By the time those buildings gave way to open fields and an uninterrupted view of runways and navigation towers, the rumble and sway of the car had worked its soothing way into Reg's weary frame. He dozed a few seconds, then awakened when the car jarred over a section of rough road.

"Hee-hee-hee!" the driver laughed, checking the rearview mirror to make certain his passenger was still lying down. One hand gripped the wheel, the other felt under the seat and found what it was looking for. "Sorry 'bout dat, man!" he sang in exaggerated dialect. "Little bit con-struc-tion mess. Not bad." The voice was light.

But the eyes in the mirror were hard.

Danson turned belly down, feet in the air, cheek to vinyl, enjoying the pleasant tickle of the road vibrations through the seat. His dreamy musings returned to medieval history when every detail of Christ's agony received the highest veneration of all. The reeds with which he'd been whipped, the pillar to which he'd been tied, the sponge in which he'd been given drink, and, of course, the cross to which he'd been nailed supplied his followers with the reputed means to experientially recall events central to their faith. Even the blood and water that flowed from his side became a focal point of religious devotion. His bones, of course, were not available. He'd taken them with him in a bodily resurrection and ascension into heaven.

But the lack of the Savior's bones didn't slow the relic-mongers in the least. You could easily add to your personal sanctity and prestige by making a pilgrimage to holy sites boasting Christ's swaddling clothes, his circumcised foreskin, the boards of his manger bed, the leftover bread crumbs of the multiplied loaves and fishes, the tablecloth from the Last Supper, or the preserved body of the donkey he rode into Jerusalem. Couldn't afford a pilgrimage? Not to worry.

Traveling relics would soon come to a town near you. These venerable road shows—together with the Crusades in all their excesses—actually helped spread Christianity by decentralizing the church, but at a sometimes terrible price.

"Pretty woman, walkin' down de street," sang the driver softly, eyes flicking back and forth from the blinking construction barriers to the rearview mirror. "Pretty woman, de kind I like ta meet . . ." The hand gripping the small caliber handgun rose slowly up the back of the driver's seat.

The car sped on. Too fast.

The vibration against Reg's cheek abruptly changed from the steady buzz of asphalt to the rough irregularity of gravel. He struggled to rise, momentarily confused. The driver swore, swung his firing arm over the back of the seat, and looked behind and down. Gone was jaunty Willie the chauffeur. The man who faced Danson now was cold, operating on reflex.

The car jerked violently left, plowed earth, and pitched sideways toward a freshly dug utility ditch. Reg, hurled face down on the floor, clawed for a handhold. With a roar of protest, he threw his head back and twisted to face his assailant. He was looking up at the barrel of the gun.

He recoiled in terror. The world tilted sharply left and the gun blasted through the car's ceiling. The Olds plunged straight down in a storm of flying glass and screeching metal. Reg felt the world compress. When the world hit bottom, everything went dark.

For the second time in three days, the blood red and royal blue flashes of a police cruiser turned Reg Danson's skin a sickly neon. This time, some of the red was his own blood, trickling from cuts to forehead and right hand. He regained consciousness amid excited shouts and the yanking open of the right side back door, now directly above his head. He was kneeling on broken glass and earth poking through what had been the Olds' back left window. The car's dome light was to his left, the transmission hump to his right, the back of the front seat in his face. The car was wedged tight in a newly opened ditch awaiting the laying of utility lines. Danson's knees felt wet and sticky with blood.

"Hey, buddy, you okay down there?"

Reg squinted up at the swatch of daylight silhouetting a police officer's dark and featureless face and nodded. "Sweet Sophia!" yelled the officer to others behind him. Then to Reg: "Aren't you that famous dinosaur hunter that's been in all the news?"

Reg managed a shrug in what suddenly became very tight quarters. "Guilty," he said, brushing at the glittering beads of broken glass.

"Can you stand?" asked the officer.

"Think so," Reg replied, but he found the simple act difficult. Every muscle ached and his legs felt wobbly. And it required a force of will to orient in the suddenly unfamiliar surroundings.

But slowly he made it to his feet, catching grisly sight of the driver. The man lay on his back against the driver's side door, left hand touching the floor, right hand still clutching the pistol. The brown shirt was torn by the steering wheel, a dark stain spreading across the rib section even as Reg looked on. The yellow shorts were soaked in blood, the man's legs bent double, knees near his chin as if he were about to push off the side of a swimming pool. The cornrow headdress was fake. The wig had slipped forward to cover one eye like a rakish pirate's patch. The face and forehead were severely lacerated from contact with the windshield. The man was as still as . . . death.

"Doubt there'll be much helping that one," said the officer somberly. "Your bones in one piece?"

"Yeah," Danson said, feeling nauseous. "I want out of here."

"Not surprising. Reach up slow like, Mr. Danson, and we'll give you a hoist up."

It was like being sprung from a coffin. He stood in the sun, gulping fresh air. Sweet, fresh air. An emergency aid unit whined to a halt, and two medical personnel jumped from the cab. They were met by the officer. "I doubt the one in the well needs a lot of immediate attention," he said. "But this fellow here needs a going over. Neither one wearing a belt. Front seat saved this one. Still, use extreme caution with the guy in the car. There's a gun in his right hand."

Reg wandered to the side of the road and sat down, head in his hands. His shoulders shook and his stomach churned. He was vaguely aware of men shouting into the ditch, checking for response from inside the car. They were met with silence.

The silence was broken by the squealing of two more city patrol cars and one from airport security. They were followed by a Channel Eight news van. Dazed, Reg shook his head. *Ambulance chasers!*

The first officer on the scene took charge, keeping the media at bay. He ordered the removal of the remaining occupant of the Oldsmobile. Resuscitation began immediately on the man. The gun was bagged and tagged.

In less than five minutes, the attempt to revive Willie the chauffeur ended. Only a medical examiner could pronounce the driver dead at the scene, but each of the living at the accident site knew the pronouncement was only a formality.

The activity swirled away from Reg Danson. Mercifully, it did not center around him until he'd regained equilibrium. A homicide team arrived and assumed the investigation. When the detective in charge came Danson's way, it was cautiously, a look of puzzlement firmly fixed on grizzled features. "Let's have the med boys check you out, Mr. Danson. While they do, if you're up to it, I'd like to hear how you came to be riding in the same car with Lawrence Reinhard. By the way, I'm Detective Bob Burnham, Seattle P.D."

Reg looked at the gurney and the shrouded body being lifted into the ambulance. He shivered. "I flew in just now from a business trip to Rome. That man met me with a sign bearing my name and told me that he had been sent by my employer, Richard Bascomb, to take me home. Said his name was Willie. I should have called and verified, but why would I? He knew Bascomb's name; he knew my flight and arrival; the guy was real disarming. Plus I was tired. . . . I was stupid, okay, just plain stupid!"

Detective Burnham looked sympathetic. "I might have done the same thing. Don't beat up on yourself. Fortunately for you, your guardian angel didn't take the day off. Lawrence Reinhard is—was—a very big fish in the world crime pool. An assassin for hire wanted by every police agency on earth. He's done a lot of work for various hate groups lately. His skin looks black—he's of Caribbean descent—but he's a chameleon, make no mistake. That made him especially valuable to the neo-Nazi nuts. He could infiltrate the black organizations of African Americans or South Africa, do his dirt, and be back in his native Germany before they knew what'd hit them. Wonder why he took a sudden interest in you?"

He looked hard at Danson, sniffing out the tiniest nervous tic or shifting of guilty eyes. He wasn't disappointed. Reg twitched, shifted, and flushed bright red. "It may have to do with my current assignment. There have been a number of thefts of priceless . . . uh, you see the Catholic church is concerned about, uh . . . I think you'd best speak to Monsignor Claudio Andone, the Vatican's under-secretary for foreign relations."

He looked down at the ground and kicked at a clod. "James Bond, your job is safe," Reg muttered under his breath. "They should have hired Mother Teresa!"

Detective Burnham permitted himself a small, pinched smile. "I thought you specialized in ancient artifacts, perhaps a prehistoric mammal or two. I should think you might want to stick with that line of work, don't you? At any rate, please have a seat in the rear of my car. Make yourself comfortable. My partner's name is Lemcio. Brad Lemcio. I'll be back once we've tracked down this Monsignor

Andone of yours. Then we'll want you to have a little visit with us downtown. Best cake donuts in the region. The coffee'll kill you, but the donuts are divine." The detective headed for one of the patrol cars.

Coffee that kills. Did Leo have coffee to go? "When ya live this close to the cemetery, ya can't weep for everyone." "Hey! Detective!" he yelled after the retreating figure.

Detective Burnham stopped and waited.

Reg didn't think twice. He stood. "When you talk to the monsignor, tell him I'm sorry, but I'm off the case!" The detective nodded and walked on.

The county coroner arrived and Reg turned away, a great weight lifted. He was unable to stomach any more of a scene that had almost been his murder investigation. He was through. No piece of allegedly sacred cloth was worth getting killed over.

He heard a clamor and looked up. Lights. Cameras. "Mr. Danson, just a moment, sir, please," said a tall woman rushing at him with a microphone. "Could what happened here have any connection with the suicide attempt you thwarted just three days ago? Are the neo-Nazis retaliating?"

Reg Danson felt a gnawing apprehension. He would reply "No comment," of course, but for once a reporter had asked him a very good question.

It was late when the plain blue sedan turned in at the Danson driveway. Reg felt deep, numbing fatigue. The only satisfaction he'd derived from the whole affair was the begrudging look of respect in Burnham's eyes when the detective returned from his conversation with Andone. From then on, it was Mr. Danson this, Mr. Danson that. They'd arrived at the homicide division, and instead of cake donuts, they'd found sacks of Taco Bell's finest waiting for them in the interrogation room. The house coffee was in fact dangerous, but not so deadly as Leo's.

Danson was free to go. Andone's strings stretched far indeed. He'd only asked that Reg himself call the Vatican. Soon.

The car's headlights pinned the neighbor's cat to the lilac bush, then splashed on the garage before winking out. "Did you notice his hands?" Burnham asked out of nowhere.

"Whose hands?" replied Reg dumbly.

"Reinhard's. The palms. Each had an odd tattoo."

"Oh?" Reg said vaguely, studying the front of the house. Something wasn't right.

"The letters 'WW' in the right palm, and the letters 'RR' in the left. Like some kind of weird voodoo thing. They could only be read right way up when he stood facing someone, hands down, palms out. Maybe it was some kind of password code, the only way inside some secret club or—"

"Someone's in the house!" yelled Danson. "The lights are on! I didn't leave them on!" He lunged against the car door, new life springing from a hidden reserve. *God protect me!*

"Whoa, now," said Burnham, catching Reg's arm. "You've had enough run-ins for one day. Besides," he grinned tightly, "your taxes pay my salary. Let's see if I'm worth it!" With Danson's keys in hand, Burnham and Lemcio hurried to the back of the house.

Reg stayed in the car, suddenly glad for the detectives, no matter how annoying their questions. He was drained.

He stiffened. A figure appeared in the front door, opened the screen, and quickly closed the door behind. Reg's heart raced. He knew that form. *Something wrong. Badly limping. He's hurt. Oh, Lord, no . . .*

He caught his son just as Tony collapsed on the bottom step. Reg cushioned his fall against the stairs, oblivious to the stabbing in his own bruised ribs.

Fear fused with firm resolve in the boy's voice. And pain. Too much pain. "Run, Dad!" he cried, trying weakly to push his father up and away. The pale light from the corner street lamp told the dreadful story. Eyes blackened nearly shut, face swollen and purplish, lips cracked and scabbed, Tony Danson was unrecognizable—except to his father.

Reg wept, burying his face in his son's hair, smelling again the mix of little boy sweat and strawberry shampoo. Fifteen years ago? Only yesterday.

Again the imploring voice. "They're after *me,* Dad! They don't know you're back. Get away before—"

"Shh, Tony. I'm afraid they do know—"

Detectives Burnham and Lemcio yanked open the front door, crouched low, and leveled their weapons at the pair huddled at the foot of the porch. A cat howled two backyards away. Reg smoothed the tousled hair and tenderly felt the strong muscles shift stiffly through Tony's damp T-shirt. He'd been ambushed: the ugly sons of Satan had set a snare for his kid.

Burnham straightened and motioned for Lemcio to sheath his weapon. They quietly returned through the house and reached the car the way they'd come. For a long while they studied the night and waited. The father murmured reassurances to the son that he was all right now. They had not come to finish him. The father would not let them. God would not let them.

Finally, Burnham spoke. "Mr. Dan—"

Reg released a low growl of rage and frustration. "Detective!" he shouted. "You call Andone back and you tell him, Detective, you tell him for me!"

Burnham waited. "Tell him what?"

Reg Danson swallowed hard and gripped his son tight to his chest. He pressed trembling lips against the boy's shoulder and repressed a sob. Then came a loud sigh born of grief and fury. The words were muffled but did not need repeating. "Tell him I'm back in!"

CHAPTER 5

Reg Danson ignored the phone through a dozen messages. Let the answering machine catch them. He'd spent the night at Haborview General with Tony, discovering it was the second hospital his son had been in since the beating in Alexandria. He'd escaped from the first. "You were in danger," Tony said through damaged lips. Before the sedatives took full effect, Reg heard the halting tale of the two thugs and how they'd left Tony for dead. He told Tony about Andone and the assignment, but not about Reinhard.

The phone jangled again through two pillows jammed over his head. Reg hurled them to the floor and tried melting the insistent demon with a bleary, red-rimmed look of warning. "Reg, lad, if you're there, pick up the phone!" implored Bascomb.

Danson went for the handset like an enraged Rottweiler. "Listen, Bascomb, and listen good! I am a lot of things—a naturalist, an explorer, a tenor in somewhat good standing with the church choir director—but I am not, repeat *not,* some gun-toting espionage agent. I love God, country, family, and being in one piece so you can just strike me from the payroll as of right now! Why don't you take out an ad in *Soldier of Fortune* magazine? Bet you'd find some real sweethearts just itching to go for a ride with an assassin!"

It was late morning. Gray autumn daylight pried at the closed venetian blinds. Reg stood between the bed and the wall, shivering in thin boxer shorts. At eye level was a framed photo of Tony at age five, clad in red swim trunks and cowboy chaps, shooting the cameraman with a water pistol. *Bang! Bang! You're wet!*

"I'm sorry, Reg," said Bascomb in his booming baritone. He did sound regretful. "This thing has gotten ugly fast. I've thought about pulling you off but I think much more is at stake here than a few religious treasures—"

Danson almost threw the phone across the room. *"Religious treasures?!* Is that what you think I'm in this for? To save somebody's blessed idol? To help the Catholic church keep iron control of people's superstitions? To—"

"Have you had your coffee yet this morning?" interrupted Bascomb. "You seem a bit ragged. I find you far more reasonable on a good quart of java." Reg snickered humorlessly. Before he could resume his tirade, Bascomb continued. "Of course, I wouldn't deliberately place you in harm's way for a few museum pieces. The Shroud is a true enigma and warrants further study, but the face cloth, the Coat—anybody's guess. And what if they are authentic? We are not saved by Christ's wardrobe.

"What demands our attention, Reggie"—Bascomb always used that grating endearment when he wanted something—"is the fact that people are dying over these relics in a sudden cruel blitzkrieg of holy sites. I fear something larger has been set in motion. The fury, the strange calling card . . . It demands a person of spiritual sensitivity to unravel the facts. Call it a gut hunch, but I feel this extends far beyond the Catholic church."

Reg jammed the receiver under his armpit and fought for calm. He looked imploringly at Tony's picture. He almost asked to borrow the squirt gun.

With a sigh and a quick prayer, he spoke. "You want me to risk life and limb because you've got indigestion? I'd be off this project in a blink if they hadn't hurt Tony."

"Tony?! Is he all right? What happened?" Reg was touched by the genuine concern in Bascomb's voice.

"Two guys beat him senseless trying to find out my whereabouts. They dumped him in the Potomac River and he nearly drowned. He'll recover; he's in the hospital here. Whoever or whatever this Kaspar is, going for my son was a stupid move. They figured to warn me off. But instead, I'm going to be like a bad case of varicose veins. All the wishing in the world won't make me disappear!"

"I don't like the sound of this, Reginald." Bascomb resorted to the formal when changing course. "I want you off this thing now. When they start going for your family . . . You lost your dear wife in that tragic accident at Loch Ness. I won't have the innocent dependents of my employees hunted down by renegades. You're reassigned. Go back to the extinct animal preservation project. Take a month off first. You're right, I have been too demanding of you. Lay low and they'll see that you've lost interest—"

"Oh, but I haven't lost interest!" Reg whacked the blinds with the back of the receiver and dust flew. Where was the number of the cleaning lady? He was living like a slob. He had to regain order. His head felt clearer now. The blood was pumping.

"My interest level is way up! A brush with death will do that to you." He was pacing. There was so much to be done. He shouldn't be on the phone. Call waiting beeped in his ear. "Can you hold, Richard?"

He switched callers. "Mr. Danson? This is Melody Crain from KING-5 News. Can you confirm reports that—" Click. "Bascomb, you still there? Perhaps you'd be kind enough to alert the media that I am off limits right now. Hold a news conference. Sic Andone on them. Tell them whatever you think will work. Meanwhile, I've got a lot of work to do."

"Reg." The way Bascomb said it was cold water in the face. "You don't sound quite together. You can't go storming off like papa bear in defense of your cub. You might do something rash. We can't lose sight of who we both work for. Are you praying on this one? Let's leave the guns and shootouts to the police. God can use them, too, and they're trained in this sort of thing."

Reg cleared his throat. It was too late to back off now. "You're right, Mr. Bascomb. I apologize for sounding off like that. I need to talk with God and ask him to go ahead of me and give me wisdom. But he's a God of action and like you said, this is big. Bigger than our misgivings. But not bigger than the Lord. Call off the reporters. Please. I'll check in when I have a sharper picture of things."

No sooner had he hung up than the phone rang again. It vibrated in his hand like a rattlesnake, and Reg took its head off. "Forget it, Bascomb! I've resigned. I've—"

"You've a bad case of foul mood." It was Leo. "Ya sound like you're bein' audited by the IRS. How was Roma?"

"Sorry, Leo," mumbled Reg, chastened. "I'm a bit off my feed. Let's just say the milk of life has turned a bit sour."

"So make buttermilk pancakes! The good Sister Mary Finley, my fourth grade teacher at Immaculate Conception, had a sure cure for the sours." Leo paused like he always did when about to tell one of his awful jokes. Reg knew better than to say a thing. "'Twas the Litany of St. Fidgeta. Last part went something like, 'From demonic possession, scabby knees, blue mold, furry food, the desire to itch where we shouldn't when we shouldn't, and the fear of the Communists crawling in over the window sill during the night and taking Mother Superior hostage, sweet Fidgeta, deliver us!'"

Reg laughed despite his anxiety. "That would be St. Francis Fidgeta of Tormento in southern Italy, the patroness of unruly children?" Leo was good medicine.

"Saints be praised!" Leo shouted. "Have you, yourself, received a visitation from the holy woman?"

Reg grew sober. This was no time for banter. Quickly, he filled Leo in on the events of the past three days, sparing nothing. When he got to the attempts on his and Tony's lives, Leo practically crawled through the phone.

"In the name of the Father, I *told* ya! But no, you had to mess with the hatemongers! Mr. Invincible Danson! Well, near as I know, there's no saint assigned to look after explorers with fat heads and fatter egos. You get yourself killed by them and people will wonder why it didn't happen sooner!"

Reg squirmed under the lashing until Leo dropped his voice. "Sorry, mate. No one holier than a reformed sea dog like meself. I just don't have time in my busy schedule for funerals, is all. Uh, because I know ya, though, and the fact ya won't let loose of this one 'til every last louse is accounted for, I got someone here who says she needs to see ya right away. Ya know 'er. She's one o' them Nazi females eggin' the poor guy to jump the other night. She's sittin' here in my cafe all shaved up one side and white as a sheet. I ain't had a customer in here since she sat down!"

"Leo, Leo." Reg squinted at the clock. "You don't even open for lunch for another half hour."

"Same difference, Mr. Knows-How-to-Tell-Time. Hank from the bakery who delivers the donuts dumped the trays inside the front door and left without takin' the empties. Phil, my mail carrier, slaps a stack of 'Dear Occupants' on the counter and hightails it without his coffee. He can't cross the street without three cups o' Leo's nitro, but one look at her and he was doin' the sayonara shuffle right out o' here!"

Reg thought a moment, then said, "Tell her to meet me at the statue in Pioneer Square in twenty minutes. And Leo, thanks."

Leo's rough breathing from too many years sucking cigarettes crackled over the line. "I just hope I'm doin' the right thing. She won't talk except to ask for you. 'I want to see the savior of the black guy.' She's said that maybe ten times already."

Just before he hung up, Reg stopped him. "Come on over tonight and give me a hand with the research. I've got to figure out if and where the Kaspar crowd will strike next. It's going to take some digging, several pots of your deadliest, and an angel on every shoulder. What do you say?"

Leo snorted. "I say no self-respecting angel'd come within a wingspan of either of us!"

She wasn't coming. He was a fool not to have gone straight to Leo's even if it was bad for business. Instinct told him it would take something important for her to break ranks with the skinheads and ask to see him. He remembered the soft, little girl face beneath the bizarre hairdo.

He remembered how she'd watched him intently until the police had taken her away. She wasn't like the others, screaming epithets and resisting arrest. Maybe she wanted to warn him.

Maybe she wanted to kill him.

Reg shooed the thought away, but it nagged at the edge of his consciousness, a distant angry wasp.

Wind whipped the square. He turned up the collar of his jacket, and the transients snuggled tighter against the steam grates. Car tires squealed around the corner and a horse clopped tiredly past, pulling a carriage of young lovers. Even the statue of a muscular man hammering his sword into a plowshare looked cold and in need of a coat.

She hurried into view, same oversized flak jacket, same black jackboots, same orange hair half there, half gone. The metal swastikas in her ear clanked together like parts of an evil wind chime.

She saw him and stopped. They stood looking at one another, not saying anything. Finally, she jerked her head toward the bus shelter and walked there. He joined her at the end of the bench. They sat for a time without speaking.

When she did talk, it was without turning her head, as if to do so would validate their acquaintance. "Why did you stop the black from jumping?"

She wanted to appear cool, detached, but the trembling question said otherwise.

Danson matched her reserve and did not turn to reply. "It was the right thing to do. He needed help, not hate."

"Did you know that less than 15 percent of the world's population is white and that in sixty years, it will be less than 5 percent?" Her voice was eerily flat, drained of emotion as she recited the party line.

"Even if that were true, why is it significant?" Reg asked.

"Like the ZOG, the black goons will eventually squeeze out the pure whites and your grandchildren will have no place to call their own."

"The ZOG?" The conversation was getting more surreal by the second.

"The Zionist Occupational Government in Washington, D.C. Only the blind cannot see that our nation is controlled by international Jewish bankers who create wars for profit. They are breeding at an unprecedented rate. But not for long." Her words had changed from flat monotone and ended high. Fear?

"May I know your name?" He looked at her when he asked. The kindness in the words made her turn, hesitantly, to stare at him with liquid gray eyes. Her face! The cruel scratching of the capital letters "WWRR" on her left cheek marred its loveliness like a burning brand. What did this young lost girl have to do with murderers and thieves?

"I—I prefer no names."

"You know mine. It was all over the newspapers."

"How do I know you won't try to press charges or something?"

"Why would you go to all the trouble of finding me? And what about your standing with your friends? I don't imagine they'd like knowing we talked."

The gray eyes flashed naked fear. He'd struck a nerve.

But truth be known, he was frightened too. "Did you come to harm me?"

She shook her head and looked quickly down at her lap where slender fingers with chewed nails twined nervously around one of the jacket drawstrings. If she'd come to kill him, there were multiple pockets in the green fatigues in which to hide a gun or knife. But if that were her plan, why would she agree to come to so public a place? He relaxed.

"My name's Connie," she said quietly, lower lip quivering. "I've never known anyone who would risk physical harm to save another person. We think it's a sign of weakness. We believe in taming the mud races by whatever means necessary and partitioning them into their own segregated territories. The Aryan nations are warrior peoples." The eerie flatness took over Connie's speech like the automated voice on a vending machine.

But when she looked at him again, two big tears fell from the liquid eyes. "What you did, though, didn't seem weak to me. A weak person would have fled the other way or joined the mob. It took real courage to defy all of us and grab that man the way you did. Aren't you scared of us?"

A panhandler made a beeline for the two sitting on the bus bench. After gaining a good look at Connie, he thought better of it and crossed the street to a more promising pair of senior citizens.

It broke the tension. Reg and Connie giggled. "Happens to me all the time," she said, wiping her eyes. "One of the advantages of being a walking freak show."

"Why do you choose to look that way?" asked Reg, gently.

Switch to monotone. "It manifests our anger. Anger that we are legally denied a white state. Anger that the descendants of Satan, the Jews, have usurped our rights as the true Chosen People. Anger that Hitler was not given a fair hearing in the international court of public opinion because of lies about him perpetrated by inferior people. Anger because we cannot enjoy the same freedom of assembly that you enjoy. If more than two of us appear together, we are harassed by the police state . . ." Connie's face crumpled. Thin shoulders convulsed. She cried out to the sooty ceiling of the damp little shelter. "Anger because my parents can't stand to look at me. Anger because they will not hear what I have to say. Anger because they cannot bear to touch me." The sobs ended in a shriek of pain. "Anger because my flag-waving father's last words to me were, 'You disgust me. I wish we'd aborted you when we'd had the chance!'"

She drew her legs and arms into a fetal position on the bench and lay her head on Danson's knee. *She must be about Tony's age . . .*

People stared at the strange tableau at the bus stop. Only a large black woman with snow-white hair, with two huge shopping bags and three freshly scrubbed grandkids in tow, dared share the rest of the bench. She settled with a weary huff and ordered the little ones to their seats with a look. Two boys in bow ties and a girl in pink pinafore, they stared wide-eyed at the sobbing woman and the uncomfortable man.

"Here, honey," said the grandmother, extracting a package of tissues from one of the bags and handing it to Reg. "Feeling a little distressed myself. Must of been something I ate!"

"Bless you," Reg said, handing several tissues to Connie. She wadded them to her bosom and that seemed to provide some comfort. The sobbing subsided. Reg helped her sit up. "Care to walk?"

She smiled fleetingly and nodded. Then, eyeing the grandmother and her charges, she looked down at the tissues in her hand. Reg thought she might hand them back. "Thanks," she said.

The children scrambled to occupy the space left by the departing couple, glad for the extra few feet of freedom from their grandmother's scrutiny. "Laws, child, think nothing of it," the big woman called after them. "Lord knows, many's the time a good cry was the only thing keepin' this ol' girl from the booby hatch. Blessed be the name of the Lord!"

Back out in the cold wind, they walked close and Reg could smell the days of street living on the girl. "Been gone long? From home, I mean."

"Six months." A pigeon with purplish brown feathers kept comic pace with the couple, and Connie made kissing sounds at it.

"Did you come looking for the cause or did the cause come looking for you?"

"Bit of both. My family lived on some acreage by a pond but couldn't enjoy it. My mom got cancer and Dad would drag her—and me—off to every faith healer that came along hoping for a miracle. But he couldn't please her. Every time she'd come back just as sick as she went, she'd blame him for not having enough faith! So he'd drain the savings one more time, pack us in the van, and haul us off to some new mineral spring or mud treatment advertised in the auto club magazine. I finally said I was finished with it and if their faith was so important to them, why didn't they just stay home and talk to God about it? Daddy was livid, but to me racing all over creation in search of some magic potion or the latest charismatic counterfeit denied the power of God.

"I love my mother and wish I could take her pain, but I saw enough of their religion to turn me off God for good."

The purple-brown pigeon was joined by a mottled white and black one, making it a foursome. Connie laughed musically at their feathered companions, and Reg decided there really was a country girl inside the strange costume.

He stopped and faced her. "What you saw that night at the bridge over the freeway was God's doing. I was shaking like a leaf, but a man named Terrence needed hope. He needed to know that circumstances are a lousy gauge of reality. The reality is that Jesus Christ went way out on a limb for anyone courageous enough to believe in the Son of God. No loss of job, no low self-esteem, no names like 'nigger' or 'goon' can change that inescapable fact."

"I know what comes next," said Connie. "'Not even your mother's cancer or a father disowning you can change the fact that Jesus loves you, Connie.' Am I right?"

"Bingo!" said Reg with a grin. "Look, back there you said you'd never seen anyone risk their own safety to help another human being. Well, Jesus did it a long time ago. He let himself be crucified because if he hadn't, every one of us would jump to our death—or might as well. Life wouldn't mean a thing. You said you wished you could take your mother's pain. Jesus did that for you and me."

"Save it," said Connie, resuming the walk. "I've got a graduate degree in faith healing, remember? I know heaven's not real because the Bible says it'll be populated with people of every tongue and nation. Whoever wrote that needs to wake up and smell the coffee. Look around you. The only real equality is separation of the races. Then each race can live in peace with their own kind."

Reg stopped and took her hands in his. "Peace is not made with friends. Peace is made with enemies."

The pale, dead look slid once again over her features. "Thus saith Jesus Christ, right?"

"Actually, that statement came from the Israeli statesman Yitzhak Rabin," said Reg, letting go of her hands, not wanting to look at death again. "But it was a paraphrase of Christ's teaching."

"Jew pig!" she spat, crossing her arms and looking at him with contempt.

"That's a pretty barbaric response to truth," said Danson, feeling sick.

"Yes, we are barbarians! We want to be barbarians! It is an honorable title. We shall rejuvenate the world." Connie's lips twisted defiantly.

"Adolf Hitler?" Reg said.

"Bingo!" Connie replied with a sneer. "Adolph Hitler who had the blessing of the stridently nationalistic German Protestants. Many belonged to both the German Christian movement *and* the Nazi Party. They had the good sense to call for the elimination of the Old Testament as Jew propaganda. They published a revised version of the New Testament, free of any mention of Jews and Judaism. Christ's genealogy? Gone! The line that says, 'Salvation comes from the Jews' was altered to read, 'The Jews are our misfortune.' Now there was a Bible I could believe in!"

Reg was stunned. "That was no Bible at all."

"What do you mean?"

"Jesus was a Jew. Take away his Jewishness and you cancel out the promise of God. Nullify the promise and you do away with God himself. Without God, we are lost."

Connie dropped to her knees and studied the pigeons. For several minutes neither she nor Reg said anything. Then she sighed and stood. "*Der Fuehrer* believed that Christ preached an effeminate creed of pity-ethics. Hitler preached a strong, heroic belief in God in nature, God in the Aryan people, in their destiny, in their blood. He believed in free men who feel and know that God is in themselves!"

Reg couldn't keep the disgust from his voice. "Then how come the God in Hitler took a pistol and shot himself to death in a Berlin bunker?"

The slap landed hard against Danson's right cheek. Connie balled her fists in defense of the German leader, shaking and crying. "Kaspar is alive," she sobbed. "Listen to what Kaspar says. 'When I have a member of the mud race in my sights, then I am God. I can choose to kill it or let it live. When I choose to kill it, I am acting as a just God, ridding the earth of one more defective, defending the purity of the masterful white race. For that I do not apologize. One does not apologize for crushing a cockroach. Hitler did not apologize!' "

Reg fought to control his tone, to keep from giving away his excitement at hearing the cryptic name and his revulsion that it was a living person. "Does Kaspar admire Hitler?"

Connie straightened defiantly. "Kaspar worships Hitler."

"Does Kaspar believe in Hitler's philosophies?"

"Explicitly."

"That the terminally ill, the weak, and the old are also defective?"

"Certainly."

Reg stood and grabbed Connie's shoulders. He forced her to look at him. "Then Kaspar would kill your mother."

She tore loose from him in a swirl of clanking swastikas and facial brand. "You're good at twisting words. You positively reek of piety. But we're not talking about the physically ill. Your tolerance for the races is the view of a feeble minority. No less than that great original Protestant, Martin Luther, was a German. He didn't coddle the masses. He called the Jews a 'plague and a pestilence.' He wrote a pamphlet advising the princes of Germany to burn down Jewish homes and synagogues, to forbid rabbis to teach upon pain of death, and to confiscate all Jewish assets. The Nazis simply took Luther's advice!"

"Now who's twisting words?" Reg was sweating despite the cool afternoon. How far did he dare push Connie before he'd scare her off? He had to find out who—and where—Kaspar was. "The German Reich made Luther in their own image to suit their ends. He may have had his racial prejudices, but he never dreamed of the horrors of World War II. Who is this Kaspar that you should follow him?"

The passion drained from her face like water from a pitcher. Down came the mask of the unbreakable soldier. "You will hear much of Kaspar when Kaspar chooses to reveal his plans to rule the earth. Kaspar has *Kultur,* the mystical spirit unique to pure-blooded Germans. It is a destiny more powerful than any other. The great Germanic poet Heinrich Heine wrote of the day when revolutionary forces would be unleashed that would 'break forth and fill the world with terror and astonishment.' The world wars gave a taste, but only a taste. What will soon come will be the full battle-madness of the Teutonic Knights, when the unchaining of the 'demonic energies of German pantheism' overpowers the earth!"

"Soon?" asked Danson, as evenly as possible.

A ghastly transformation ripped away the mask. In its place was a debased leer, brutish and remorseless. She stepped forward. They were toe to toe. She whipped her head to the right and pulled at her cheek with a torn and dirty nail. "Beware the World Wide Race Revolution!" The crude black letters seemed to bubble from the stretched skin.

She ran, scattering pigeons and nearly knocking down a wizened old man salvaging through a trash can.

"Connie!" he called after her. "Wait!"

She slowed a moment and looked back over her shoulder. "Arm yourself, Reg Danson. The demons are coming!"

And she was gone.

CHAPTER 6

He stood before the mirror, a strong, young Aryan. By force of will he slowed the rapid pulse until the breaths came again in easy, smooth inhalations. Each exhalation was equally calm and even.

Control.

He peeled the sweat-soaked shirt from the lean, chiseled torso and cursed the nail marks on his neck and chest. The Jew had been a fighter, he had to give him that.

Goebbels stirred. The German shepherd looked to his master but knew better than to rise. When his master stood before the mirror, no beast dared disturb.

The young Aryan's *die Freuden,* his joy, was complete. *She* would not be pleased, of course. She was never pleased. But it had been necessary. The stage was being boldly set and soon the brave players would strut for all the world to see.

He flexed before the mirror and remained tensed until the thick veins in his wide neck bulged purple. But the red streaks down the powerful arms and the dark splatters on his denim trousers did not belong to the man in the mirror.

They belonged to the Jew.

He'd quickly abandoned the knife and finished the job by strangulation. The dead man had joined the movement out of self-preservation, yet his duplicity bought his ruin. Imagine trying to pass oneself off as Germanic when one was one-quarter Jew! The image in the mirror smiled sardonically.

With both hands, he slapped the white skin stretched so powerfully over muscle and sinew. Harder and harder the loud, smacking blows fell until the skin glowed and Goebbels whined in apprehension.

"Nein, Goebbels, *nein!"* he calmed the dog. He turned and knelt before the animal. The slippery pink tongue lapped at the reddish streaks that marred the arms of the master. *"Vorsicht bissiger Hund,"* he whispered affectionately. "Beware of the dog!" He patted the shepherd's head and scratched behind its ears.

Suddenly, the Aryan stood erect, snapping to rigid attention, *"Eins!"* he shouted the one count. Goebbels went stiff, lips curling back to reveal bone white teeth.

"Zwei!" Two. A fierce growl rose in the canine's throat. Ears flat against the skull, eyes slant, body rigid.

"Drei!" On three, the animal rose menacingly to its feet, snarling, flecks of spittle flying from its lips and gums.

"Vier!" Four. Barking in conditioned rage, the animal lunged at an unseen enemy, snapping, tearing flesh and grinding limbs.

"Zwanzig!" The dog instantly sat, stoic as a statue. Only the rippling of its coat and a string of saliva dangling from its muzzle betrayed the residual madness. The command to desist, the number twenty, was so far out of sequence that even if the master were incapacitated and unable to speak, victims were unlikely to guess the right number in time to stop the beast from killing them. And the dog obeyed only those voices it had been trained to obey—the master's . . . and hers. It was the one small concession he had allowed her.

"Gut, gut!" murmured the Aryan approvingly without touching the shepherd. Too much contact and the dog would be useless for control.

Control. *Der Fuehrer* had it. When the war was lost, Hitler discovered S.S. Chief Heinrich Himmler trying to make peace with the Allies. Instead of panic, Hitler employed great restraint. He did not wish to be captured by the Russians and put on display in Moscow. He would rather die the only way open to a man truly in control of his own destiny. Suicide.

But the glass ampules of cyanide kept for that purpose had been supplied by the traitor Himmler. Hitler was brilliant. Logic told him that the cyanide was more likely to be a knockout drug that would allow the great German leader to be sold, bound and gagged, to the Russians. Only one way to be certain. Give some to the dog.

Instead of testing the suspect cyanide on some stray cur as a weaker man might do, Hitler had the contents of one ampule fed to Blondi, his prize German shepherd female. She was the most trusting and he loved her most.

It proved to be cyanide after all. In his sorrow, Hitler had Blondi's five pups shot to death. Before long, in a bunker in Berlin, Hitler shot himself and followed his beloved Blondi and her offspring to their graves.

Control. Never prize emotion above expediency. Remain above all earthly attachments. Know when the game is up.

He smiled at Goebbels, clucking endearments, making petting motions but never, never touching. The animal squirmed, craving human contact. He spoke low and the dog's front feet danced in anticipation. "'A new age of magic interpretation of the world is coming,'" he said, quoting *der Fuehrer.* He reached for a plate of *Streuselkuchen* tea cakes and took a bite. The dog yipped faintly, and the master waved the pastry enticingly out of reach. "Denial! Denial!" he chanted, smacking his lips, enjoying the dog's discomfort. "You will be a much better dog through denial!"

And so would the world. He had denied the world one of its most inexplicable treasures. The first few thefts had just been practice, proving so deceptively easy that he hadn't even hesitated to plot the most shocking burglary yet. There'd been too much bloodshed to declare the most recent a clean larceny, but the troops had performed well under pressure. They were ready now for the final movement, an act so breathtakingly brazen the civilized inhabitants of the earth would yet be reeling in disbelief when it came time to administer the Final Solution.

He raised his hands before the mirror and admired the light glinting off the four gold rings on the right hand. He would not mar the perfect beauty of his skin as he expected his people to do. Naturally not. He was above them. The mantle of Teutonic conquest had fallen to him. He alone possessed sufficient intelligence and cunning to birth order out of chaos. The races had too long been allowed to run their course. His power to change all that and to flush inferior blood from superior veins was enormous.

He made a fist of his right hand. Each ring sparked fire. Each bore a capital letter representing the code name for the Final Solution. WWRR. World Wide Race Revolution. The Aryan liked it. WWRR had been suggested by a leader of the movement in the United States. Pity. The man would have to be killed eventually. No one was allowed to have better ideas than the master.

Enough Aryan brothers and sisters and their sympathizers across the earth were in place that once he gave the signal they would launch a cleansing of unprecedented proportions. By mass, simultaneous arson, looting, vandalism, desecration, rape, and murder against nonwhites and their benefactors, the world would come to its collective senses and listen to his plan of permanent segregation.

And it would succeed. He'd done meticulous groundwork to unify the world's most virulent racial reconstructionists. Neo-Nazis, Klansmen, skinheads, and Aryan armies everywhere had been carefully cultivated, shown how there was far greater strength through numbers and cooperative union. Naturally, and rightly, their chief commanders had demanded proof of his ability to marshal world attention and negotiation. He'd shown his deadly and precision strike force by plundering the very seat of spirituality and seizing the precious icons of the church. That served two other very useful purposes. It produced life-threatening cracks in the foundations of religious faith to which millions were anchored, and that left them emotionally and psychologically vulnerable to him. In private matters such as that occasioned by the now-dead Jew, you take a man's life and get him out of the way. But to subdue the masses, you take their faith and make them ever your slaves.

The other very useful purpose served by snatching the icons was that it provided him with powerful talismans from which he knew occult energy flowed.

Sometimes he wore the Coat, wrapping himself in the cloak that had clothed the Christian God. Other times, he wiped the perspiration from his brow with the cloth imprinted with the Messiah's face. Hitler believed in the supernatural power of the relics and so would he. Soon, he would clasp hands with *der Fuehrer,* hefting the very thing Hitler had so coveted and so quickly lost. His was now the obligation. He would succeed where Hitler had failed. Within hours, he would have it.

He removed the bloodstained trousers, then padded in his underwear over to the antique Louis XIV royal bed. On it lay the only thing on earth before which he had trembled. Certainly no living man or woman could affect him this way. His hands shook now; his mouth was dusty dry.

The Christ Shroud was indelibly stained with the haunting image of a man. Not just any man. A man savagely beaten but undefeated. Head wounded, wrists pierced, knees bruised and cut. Whip marks by the score. But a man lying in expectant repose as if waiting for—what?—the precise moment fixed in time when he would emerge from the tomb?

Fourteen feet long, three-and-a-half feet wide, the linen cloth was light and silky to the touch, ivory with age. The young Aryan reached out a shaky hand and lifted the corner of the cloth near the heart. The spear wound was clearly apparent, one and three quarters of an inch long by half an inch wide. The blood flow indicated the thrust had been made after the victim was dead, trickling down instead of bursting forth from a straining, living victim. . . . *When they came to Jesus and saw that He was already dead . . . one of the soldiers pierced His side with a spear . . .*

He slipped beneath the cloth and felt a thrilling surge as it settled gently onto bare skin. Eyes wide, he stared upward through the burial shroud, the room's light filtering in upon him and turning his skin deathly pale.

The next and last robbery—no! he did not steal, he appropriated—would provide the crowning touch to the collection. With it he would signal the waiting troops to let the global mayhem begin.

He suddenly felt clammy and cold. He pulled the Shroud closer about him. He shut his eyes and drifted in and out of drowsiness. From somewhere came the grating of stone upon stone . . . *rolled a large stone against the door of the tomb, and departed . . .*

The strange ululations of an emergency siren sounded, growing steadily closer. Goebbels snapped his head back and gave a primal howl.

The eyes beneath the Shroud flew open. For one awful moment, the master didn't know where he was and fought the clinging cloth. Punching and clawing for an opening, he tumbled off the bed, the centuries-old winding cloth twisted about flailing legs and arms. He yelled in terror, restrained and helpless for the first time in his life. The siren neared. Goebbels' howls turned unearthly.

The arms came free. The man tore loose and rolled clear of the cloth. What had seemed a thing possessed now lay a discarded pile in a corner of the room, just so much dirty laundry. Perhaps he would have it dyed a different color.

The vehicle roared past, siren blasting, sending Goebbels into a fresh fit. With lightning speed, the master jumped to his feet, grabbed for the dresser, and hurled plate and tea cakes at the distressed animal. They caught the dog in a glancing blow to the throat, and the plate shattered on the wooden parquet floor. The cakes skittered beneath the bed and dresser. The passing siren barely covered the dog's yelp of pain.

"Esel! Donkey!" he screamed. Then he laughed, enjoying the mingled sounds of the now receding siren and the injured dog. Goebbels lay on the cool floor, choking and panting spasmodically.

The young Aryan smiled admiringly at the flawless physique in the mirror, winking and humming away the momentary panic. A silly nightmare in the daylight, that was all. The mind played mean tricks. A prank by the subconscious and he'd been caught. No harm done. He ordered the shaking of his limbs to cease, and it did.

Silently he counted to five before the siren died. It had been especially daring of him to perform the execution so near. But the sheer logic, the audacity, the delicious irony!

He was clever but so was she, make no mistake. No matter. He'd arranged his very own stroke of daring. The police were about to have their hands very full indeed. And how delicious that it had been his phone call that had summoned them!

Let her top that.

The intersection at Alexanderstrasse and Wiesenstrasse was crawling with police. They were the only ones moving. The man lying broken on the pavement at the northwest corner of the quiet side street near Nuremberg's Richard Wagner Opera House would never move again. An ever-widening pool of blood welled from beneath the victim, staining the sidewalk a dark red.

Identification said the man was Siegfried Henke, but it was doubtful his mother would recognize him.

"They're getting bolder and bolder," said one investigator, watching the crime lab photographer record the scene.

"Looks like this one tried to play their game," said a second investigator, slipping a piece of paper into an evidence bag. The paper had been clenched in the victim's teeth, declaring in scrawled block letters that the dead man was a "Jew Spy."

Partners, the two veteran police investigators worked all hate crimes. What had once been a small department with little to do had in twenty years become second only to burglary in terms of workload.

They drew the obligatory chalk line around the beaten and strangled body, then allowed its removal to the city morgue.

The chalk silhouette Siegfried Henke left behind was painfully recognizable to everyone at the scene. His broken and battered body had been arranged by his killer or killers in the shape of a human swastika.

Equally recognizable was the white calling card protruding from the left shoe.

Kaspar.

CHAPTER 7

"It's a fact," groused Leo Slugitt wearily. "Doctors'll tell ya that guys like me who work more with our brains than our muscle need more sleep than the other kind."

The remark gained no sympathy, so he tried another tack. "Retired people in the U.S. outnumber all the people in Canada!" Nothing. "I should be retired!" Still nothing.

Leo shrugged and poured himself a fifth—or was it a sixth or a seventh—cup of coffee. Almost immediately the thick brew lubricated his stiffened joints and cleared his muddled senses. He replenished Reg's and Tony's cups and tried to make sense of the stacks of library books, microfilm copies, and document files spilling from the kitchen table and counters. They were borrowed from the Seattle Metro Library and the archives of the Catholic Archdiocese. The archivist was Patty Liske, a no-nonsense brunette who staunchly repeated church policy that no materials leave the premises. The invoking of Monsignor Andone's name, however, and the promise of unlimited free lunches at Leo's two blocks away, had quickly turned the tide. It was the first time Slugitt had ever plied someone with the promise of navy bean soup and sourdough bread. He grinned resignedly. It seemed much more respectable than enticements of fast cars and condos in Hawaii—and more nourishing.

Tony dumped another stack of reference works on the counter, spilling copies of *The Pilgrim Shrines of Europe, Churches and Castles of Medieval France,* and *The Encyclopedia of Relics and Miracles.* "Anybody for some raspberry yogurt?" he inquired, opening the freezer.

Leo winced. "Tutti-frutti's for womenfolk. Got any coffee mocha delight?"

Tony laughed, then winced himself. He'd heal with time. Being on a hunt for answers at home with his dad and Leo was the best medicine. Reg hadn't liked the phone call from the hospital at first, but the frazzled nurses convinced him. They'd tried everything short of physical restraint to keep Tony immobile that day. Nothing doing. Reg finally relented. Tony was badly banged up, but Reg worried less about his son's safety when Tony was right there, scooping dessert in plain sight. The ravenous nineteen-year-old was back to eating anything not nailed down. A very good sign.

Reg, a pencil stuck over one ear, chewed on a pen cap and pored over dictionaries of saints and lists of shrines, churches, monasteries, and convents. On ruled notebook paper he added names and brief descriptions of existing relics ripe for the stealing. Headings included "crucifixes," "apparel," "Passion," "Mary," "bones," and "buildings." Under the last heading he had written:

> HOLY HOUSE OF LORETO, ITALY: Home of Christ's mother in Nazareth transported to Italy in its entirety. Walls made of reddish stone sixteen inches thick. Contains cross bearing inscription "Jesus Nazarenus Rex Judaeorum."
>
> THE PORTIUNCULA OF ST. FRANCIS OF ASSISI: Place of worship and death for St. Francis. Now encased in the Basilica of Santa Maria degli Angeli. Countless pilgrims visit each year.

Under "miscellaneous" were other entries:

BLOOD: Liquefaction "miracles" claimed for the preserved blood of various saints and holy persons. Blood gathered in flasks at time of martyrdom or retained in the blood-soaked clothing stripped from their bodies. St. Januarius, circa fourth century, most famous. His coagulated blood is said to mysteriously liquify eighteen times a year. Liquefaction takes place when vials of the blood are brought into close proximity to a silver bust containing the saint's head.

MANNA: Denotes the colorless, odorless, tasteless oil said to flow from the relics of some saints. Phenomenon first recorded at tomb of St. Andrew the Apostle in Patras, Greece. Said to be so abundant at times, it dripped from the sepulcher and ran halfway down the aisle of the church.

And so it went for sheet after sheet. Weeping, bleeding, and oozing relics and statues. Miraculous healings in the presence of the remains of the holy dead. And no shortage of holy artifacts said to possess supernatural power. The Virgin Mary's green waist belt, an oaken chair used by Simon Peter, the Holy Grail cup used at the Last Supper, the Holy Stairs from the palace of Pontius Pilate.

With a growing sense of futility, the three men worked through the night, finding and cataloging the names, identities, and locations of the most venerated religious objects. The possibilities were endless. Predicting where Kaspar would strike next was like trying to guess the location of the next auto accident. It could literally happen anywhere.

By three A.M., Tony was sprawled on the couch snoring beneath a copy of *A Visit to the Relic Chapels of the Discalced Carmelite*

Nuns. Giddy with fatigue, Leo wrote the title on a piece of well-doodled paper as *A Visit to the Relish Capital of the Declassified Caramel Nannies.* His snorted hoot of laughter startled Reg from his unintended slumber without bothering Tony in the least.

"Look at the time!" Leo exclaimed. "What we need's a fresh java jingle. I'll pour!" He jumped to the task, slapping Reg on the shoulder in passing. Filling the pot with fresh water, he called out, "Didja hear the one about my granddaddy? He was in and out of jail so often they changed his name to Slammer Slugitt. Drink? Oo-whee, could that man stow the whiskey! When he died, he was cremated and burned for three days straight!"

Reg went out on the porch and breathed deeply of the fresh air. The sky was clear, and the gossamer tails of shooting stars painted the night in silver streaks. *Lord, where do I go? What's Kaspar up to right now? What's he after and why? Help me, please. Help me help Connie and anyone else in danger from these madmen. I need your wisdom and I need it bad*

Reg went back inside and took a cold shower, letting the needles of spray sting him awake. He vigorously toweled off. He had to think fast. He had to think with the cold, calculating logic of a lunatic.

Something soft but persistent kept nagging. Some piece of the puzzle that hadn't yet come clear was hiding behind the swing set in the backyard of his mind. *Come out and play. Come out from behind there and let me get a good look at you,* Reg coaxed.

He pulled on sweatpants and a robe and paced the house. He was oblivious to Leo's java and Tony's snoring, but not the racing of the clock. *Come out little friend. Come join the fun.*

Something didn't fit. Like the children's game of like and unlike, there was a similarity in the research, the facts, the relationships between what had already been stolen and what remained for the picking—with the exception of one item. The face cloth, the cloak, the burial shroud were all fabric, all were believed to have come in contact with the Savior's body. It stood to reason, then, that the hunter's next quarry would fit the pattern of the other three: an item of cloth that had touched Christ in some dramatic, private way associated with his Passion.

But all the best possibilities left were not garments or fabric. The crown of thorns had been the object of veneration in Jerusalem for centuries and eventually was carried to Constantinople in the eleventh century. It was used as collateral in a loan made to the Latin emperor by the Venetians. King Louis of France paid off the loan to show support for the weaker Latin king and took possession of the relic. It must have made quite the sight when Louis, barefoot and plainly dressed, humbly went out to meet the entourage bearing the crown to France.

The crown was kept in the Cathedral of Notre Dame in Paris and made but one public appearance a year every Good Friday. It was reduced to a mere circlet, each of its thorns over time having been distributed as relics to a few favored friends of the court.

The true cross would make a stunning addition to any plunderer's collection if it weren't so plagued with legend. The genuine article was said to have been lost, buried, and found more than once, its exact whereabouts and identity revealed via visions, physical healings, and bodily resurrections. King Constantine took a small sliver for himself, set it in a column at the entrance to Constantinople, and declared the city forever unconquerable. A major section of the cross was supposedly brought to Rome by St. Helena and placed in the Holy Cross in the Jerusalem Basilica because it was built on a bed of earth actually carried from Jerusalem. Faithful pilgrims broke through the pavement over the holy ground and hauled away the dirt for worship.

No, those relics were outside the pattern. As were the Scourging Post, the Holy Nails, even the inscription known in the church as The Title. "This is Jesus the King of the Jews" was a sign attached in derision to Christ's cross by the Roman soldiers attending his execution. To protect it from zealous pilgrims, early bishops used to invite the faithful forward to have the inscription touched to their foreheads and eyes.

Wait! There's something else, something I'm forgetting . . . The shy little visitor behind the swing set started to come out . . .

The ring sounded like a gong in the predawn hour. Tony sprang from the couch, knocking the book of discalced nuns to the floor, his fists raised in combat. The infernal phone.

The bashful thought crawled beneath the backyard slide of Reg's mind.

Reg looked at Leo. Leo looked at Tony. Tony, hair messy and eyes still swollen nearly shut, looked terrible. Telephone calls at three A.M. were never good news. Still, Reg's mother had drilled into him that anyone desperate enough to call between midnight and breakfast needed an answer. He reached for the phone.

"Mr. Danson?" The voice was small, feminine, concerned. A mother's voice.

"Yes, this is Reg Danson. Who is this?"

"I'm so very sorry to be calling at this hour. It's getting close to breakfast time here."

"Where's 'here'?" Reg asked warily.

"Savannah, Georgia. My name is Grace Matthews. Perhaps you've read of me in the Catholic press?"

"No ma'am. I don't read the Catholic press." He looked over at the table spilling papers and clippings from various sources including the Catholic press and amended himself. "As a general rule."

"Well, I live on The Farm here on The Holy Hill just north of town. It's been a busy weekend. We get an awful lot of pilgrims this time of year—up until Christmas, really. They come for The Visitations, you know. The Blessed Mother speaks through me, though why she would is a divine mystery all its own.

"Anyway, here I am going on, but the oddest thing happened. Five hours I've prayed about it. The last carload of folks, they was from Fayetteville or maybe Philadelphia, pulled out the drive when this glowing light lit the front porch and I was physically prevented from entering the house. Normally, I get my Visitations on the thirteenth of the month to coincide with the Marian apparitions at Fatima in Portugal, but at five minutes past midnight it was the fourteenth and here was The Glow.

"Now Horace, that's my husband, has to get up early to meet the sewage haulers who come to collect the Port-O-Jons after a busy weekend. We had probably ten thousand people this time, more if the weather hadn't been so threatening. I don't know when I'll get the beans put up or the beets pickled. But here was The Glow—"

"Excuse me, Mrs. Matthews," interrupted Reg. "I don't mean to be rude, ma'am, but unless you have a point to make, I will have to say good-bye."

Grace Matthews sounded genuinely apologetic. "Goodness, yes, hear me go on! I know you must have your hands full trying to make sense of all that's happened to you. Big story in the *Savannah Herald* of how you came so close to death after traipsing halfway 'round the world after ferocious creatures and all. I've been lighting candles on your behalf, make sure of that. When Satan gets his talons into you, it takes a load of candles to loosen his grip.

"Why I called was because the Blessed Mother had a private message for you. She gave me the courage to call. Here it is: '. . . Glory in tribulations, knowing that tribulation produces perseverance; and perseverance, character; and character, hope.' That would be St. Paul's epistle to the Romans, chapter five, verses three and four—"

"Thank you, Mrs. Matthews. I appreciate the encouragement from God's Word, and I assure you I will stick to the task. Good night, now—"

"Wait!" the woman shouted. "Please. There's more. The Blessed Mother began to sing, in German, *Salve Caput Cruentatum,* 'Sacred Head Now Wounded.' She said I should sing it to you and she kept singing the same two lines over and over." The woman began to sing

in a sweet soprano. "*'Ich will hier dir stehen, verachte mich doch nicht; von dir will ich nicht gehen, wenn dir den Herzen bricht.'* What Thou, my Lord, has suffered was all for sinner's gain; mine, mine was the transgression, but Thine the deadly pain."

She did not go on, and Danson realized that she was weeping softly. "Mrs. Matthews, are you all right?"

"Oh, yes, Mr. Danson. I-I never hear that hymn that it doesn't touch me to the core. And when I looked at the Virgin's face, she was crying crimson tears, but smiling, Mr. Danson, smiling with a beatific beauty I cannot describe. Look into and beyond the petal of a rose and you will begin to know the beauty."

"I love that hymn, too," Reg said quietly, despondently. He'd looked under the play slide in his mind and the little friend of an idea who'd come to visit was nowhere to be found.

"It's attributed to Bernard of Clairvaux, you know. Bach did the arranging, of course."

He started again to say a polite good-bye when she beat him to it.

"I have to go now," she said as if he had called her at an unearthly hour. "A network newsmagazine is sending their anchor at seven this morning for ham, eggs, and a twelve-minute segment on how the sun dances in the sky when Mary comes. Horace has to put up a higher fence to protect the children from the curious, and I've got to track down that shipment of 'Blessed Mother' T-shirts from Boston. I don't make any money on this, Mr. Danson. And I didn't call collect. I wouldn't be skeptical if I were you. Good night now."

He took the coffee from Leo this time and was surprised at the slight tremor in his hands. He didn't believe any of it. God wouldn't choose to guide his people through circus sideshows and hocus-pocus. Jesus was the living and revealed Word, and in him all knowledge was complete. The purveyors of religious trinkets and bogus blessings were of the same ilk as those who looted the church for their own gain. Both preyed on the gullible and if someone got hurt in the process, too bad.

Grace Matthews sounded harmless enough. But so had Willie the chauffeur. Satan was known to masquerade as an angel of light. Might he also assume the costume of a reggae cab driver or a motherly diviner?

Reg rubbed his eyes and told the others of the bizarre conversation. They shook their heads and tried to joke the call away. But it hung there in the air, a disturbing oddity, unsettling them all. The coffee went cold. Tony fell back asleep on the couch, and tough old Leo, incongruously wrapped in an orange and green afghan made by Reg's mother, crashed on the living room floor.

Reg couldn't sleep. Urgency gnawed at his innards. Something big was about to happen, an explosion that he was powerless to contain. He knelt and prayed and reread the book of Romans, but his agitation only grew.

The Nazis . . . Kaspar spelled Germanically . . . Heil Hitler . . . the next logical relic for a madman bent on . . . World Wide Race Revolution? . . . Something intimately associated with Christ's Passion . . . pain . . .

Reg swiftly pawed through the piles of reference material. Occasionally a book would thump to the floor, but Tony and Leo remained oblivious. At last, from deep within the chaos, he extracted a book by Hermann Rauschning titled *The Voice of Destruction.* Published in 1940, it told in chilling detail of conversations with Adolf Hitler in a brave but futile attempt to warn the world of the "apocalyptic riders of world annihilation."

He tore through the table of contents and grimly turned to chapter sixteen, "Magic, Black and White."

"My Fuehrer, don't touch black magic," Hitler was warned by a woman in the 1930s. "As yet both white and black are open to you. But once you have embarked upon black magic it will dominate your destiny. It will hold you captive. Don't choose the quick and easy successes. There lies before you a realm of pure spirits. Do not allow yourself to be led away from your true path by earthbound spirits, which will rob you of creative power."

Yet dark and destructive forces appealed to the fanatic in Hitler. Occult power fit nicely with his views of racial purity and the manufacture of a super Aryan race. The author Hermann Rauschning labeled Hitler "the master-enchanter and the high priest of the religious mysteries of Nazidom."

He quoted Hitler declaring an end to the Age of Reason, predicting "a tremendous revolution in moral ideas and in men's spiritual orientation." And these quotes also appeared in Rauschning's book:

"The Ten Commandments have lost their validity."

"Conscience is a Jewish invention. It is a blemish, like circumcision."

"There is no such thing as truth."

Some of the highest ranking Nazis were fervent participants in the occult. Heinrich Himmler, commander of the S.S., and Rudolf Hess, the deputy fuehrer, believed in mystic rites and astrological alignments. Himmler established the Nazi "Occult Bureau" and officially exercised telepathic mind control, even convening a council of twelve top S.S. men in 1938 for the purpose of forcing the chief of the German army to confess to homosexuality. How would they force the confession? By combining their mind power to break his resistance. Not long after their failure to do so, the charges against the army chief were proven false.

But Hitler's belief in his own grand destiny was tied to the power and fate of Frankish kings like Charlemagne and Frederick I. The warrior kings were young Adolf's heroes, and he firmly believed that he was their successor. He believed in a kind of mystic invincibility built on the backs of a selfless, dedicated people who believed in the discipline and order of the state over individual attainment. Hitler longed to lock arms with the rulers of the first and second reichs.

How could he? Psychologically, by spreading his own doctrines of conquest and racial superiority. And mystically, by possessing something of theirs, something sacred, that held magical power. The Ark of the Covenant and the Holy Grail fascinated him not for the good and holy God but for the mystery and awesome supernatural power he was convinced was intrinsic to their existence. The man who owned them owned the power. Whether that charisma was used for evil or for good was entirely up to the one in control of the power.

Reg rubbed his eyes and looked for the hundredth time at the lists of possible relics people counted sacred. He let drop those dealing with the saints. They were too far removed from raw divine power. He discarded those dealing exclusively with people or events surrounding the sacred such as Lazarus, the three wise men, and Mary, Christ's mother. Though they had touched the Savior, been intimately involved in his life to a lesser or greater degree, they were absent now and any of their reputed possessions would not appeal to someone with visions of becoming a modern-day Hitler.

He eliminated those items having to do with Christ's birth. Kaspar was not interested in the trappings of an infant. He hungered for the power of the Lion of Judah. A man without regard for authority or human life would settle for nothing less than something directly involved in the powers of death, resurrection, and ascension.

Reg returned to the porch, the nagging but unnamed something scraping his thinking raw. He removed the robe, stepped to the sidewalk, and jogged in the direction of Elliot Bay. The sky grew lighter and the patches of grass blurring past glistened, damp with morning dew. The cool air bit his bare arms and chest, forcing him to concentrate.

The phone call had come at the worst possible time. He'd just about pieced together the puzzle, and now the missing piece was lost again. He picked up the pace past the Pacific Science Center and plunged over the hill to the waterfront. If he could just run fast and far enough, it would come to him. It had to.

The Spaghetti Factory, Pier One Imports, and the Victoria Clipper cruise terminal stood solid and braced for the day's onslaught of tourists. And from inside Danson's head came the music.

O sacred head, now wounded, with grief and shame weighed down, now scornfully surrounded with thorns, thine only crown . . . No! It can't be the crown of thorns. It is a pale remnant of what it was when worn by the Savior, plus it is a symbol of shame and defeat, not worthy of a sick mind prowling for . . . for what?

He pounded past the aquarium and Ivar's Fish Bar with its famous billboard exhortation to "Keep Clam!" He wished he could, but if he didn't find that puzzle piece soon, Kaspar would get away with another atrocity.

Mine, mine was the transgression, but thine the deadly pain . . .

Deadly pain. Reg slowed, turned around, and headed back. He stopped at the railing between him and the cobalt blue waters of the bay. Goose bumps forced him fully alert. He hopped onto the railing and sat with his legs aimed at the sloshing waters twenty feet below. The air smelled of seaweed and salt. "See the Wonders of the Deep! Tour the Seattle Aquarium Today!"

Pain. Pain. Think like a psychopath, Danson. How hard can it be? The face cloth wiped beads of sweat from the Savior's fevered brow as he struggled beneath the weight of his own cross. The cloak Christ wore was torn to pieces while he hung in agony. The shroud wrapped the dead Christ, sealing his murder but just as surely signaling his mastery over death. Pain, death, life. A fourth something . . . the missing piece. What, and where did it fit?

"Wait a minute," he said to the seagull balanced on a barnacle-encrusted piling jutting from the bottom of the bay. "Wait just one minute!" But the bird faced into the wind and spread its wings. It lifted from the piling and swooped down on a drift of foam before wafting skyward. Its shrill cry was answered by the bass blast of a commuter ferry's horn.

Reg smacked the railing in excitement. "That's it!" The Frankish kings had carried it into war, wielding it against their foes. To hold it aloft was to be invincible. A weapon of war. It had to be!

It was kept in a place called something like the hall or the throne room of the Teutonic Knights somewhere in Europe. Austria, maybe.

"That's it!" he yelled, laughing, slapping his thighs. "I know where the rogue Kaspar will strike next!"

The wire slipped swiftly over his head, down past his shoulders, and encircled his arms. With a powerful yank, the wire cinched fast, pinning his arms to his sides. A black hood fell over his head and knotted tightly around his neck. A foot in the back shoved him into space.

Reg Danson hit the water like a corpse thrown from a bridge.

The diver from Elco Marine Salvage and Repair maneuvered the underwater acetylene torch into place and welded shut the breech at the northeast corner of the shark viewing tank. Corrosive seawater took its toll on metal, but he suspected structural fatigue. The aquarium spent a fortune in maintenance but hundreds of thousands of tourists each year paid for a look into the remorseless eyes of a great white. "The Kingdom Beneath the Sea" exhibit was the most popular and the most labor-intensive.

It didn't help matters that the animals soon grew bored with their limited surroundings and took to playing with the equipment. The sea otters had banged stones against the plate glass of their tank until the thing gave way one night and flooded the main gallery with hundreds of gallons of seawater and five very adventuresome otters. Alarms alerted the caretakers who'd finally cornered the whiskered miscreants in the prep room where they'd gone to help themselves to the herring bins.

The sharks, wearied of the confines of the viewing tank, had passed the time by ramming the perimeter. Fortunately, daily inspections caught the small breech before any mass exodus to the open sea.

Out of the corner of one eye the diver saw something hit the surface of the water twenty yards away, close to shore, and sink in a heavy swirl of bubbles. *Darn fool litterbugs.* They were always throwing garbage off the dock. Cheaper than city disposal. He'd bet he'd fished out a dozen Dumpsters worth of trash in his career. At least they'd bundled it for him so he didn't have to round up stray Dixie Cups, or worse, a bunch of disposable diapers.

He turned his back on the trash. It could wait. He had to get finished. A group of important Japanese dignitaries was arriving for a special early morning reception hosted by Boeing Aerospace officials at the viewing tank. He had to have all the gear out of the way before then or the boss would feed *him* to the sharks.

But something about the way the thing hit the water nagged at him. A bag of garbage would smack the surface and float there. This thing was heavy and sinking fast.

And it moved.

He turned around and faced it. Its legs scissored weakly before settling into the sea bottom silt.

The man dropped the torch and kicked strongly toward the bundle. Whoever it was had been alive when he entered the water. The diver from Elco Marine Salvage and Repair was grimly determined that the person would still be alive when he left.

CHAPTER 8

"Kaspar, you cannot hide! You are an international outlaw and you will be tried for your crimes against humanity!"

Reg Danson looked directly into the cameras. The blazing eyes did not flicker; the handsome face—relayed by powerful communications satellites and captured by equally powerful earth receivers—was unyielding. No compromise. Kaspar had a date with justice, and justice would not be denied.

"You waste your time trying to get at me," Danson continued tightly. He wore the same sweatpants heavy with seawater. Leo Slugitt convinced him to pull on a Notre Dame sweatshirt before generating a media storm. Good thing. The storm was gale force.

A thick nest of microphones threatened to topple the makeshift podium at the top of the Danson porch. Electronic cables snaked over the grass from the stairs to the curb and on across the street, umbilical network links to the "scene."

Reporters, neighbors, camera crews, and curious commuters shared the sidewalk, the street, and the hoods and roofs of vehicles. Each wanted a good look at the man declaring war on the terrorist known only as "Kaspar."

Next to Danson stood the salvage diver who pulled Reg from the water. He looked decidedly uncomfortable in the glare of media attention. He was just glad he hadn't had to fish out a dead body.

"Go ahead and drown me if you can," said Danson, voice rising in barely containable anger. "Thanks to this good man—" Reg placed a hand on the diver's shoulder—"you've failed again. But I've seen your work. I know your patterns. And I know what you're after! *This* time, you can't have it! International intelligence agencies have been notified of your next target. You will be met with open arms and given the coward's welcome you so richly deserve!"

"Easy, Reg lad, go easy," Leo mumbled to himself. Perched atop the porch railing, he shifted apprehensively and scanned the crowd—for what? A gun? He wished Reg Danson weren't so vocal, so confrontational. He had no guarantees of international assistance; that was just wishful thinking. The explorer was way out of his league and allowing the enemy a clear view of a very short fuse. Better they should be in a church basement praying with the saints.

Inside the house, Tony Danson tried his jaw, gingerly working it side to side. It felt better, the swelling reduced. If the crowd cheered his dad's remarks, he wanted to be the loudest. Reg Danson didn't back down from any threat. Kaspar had met his match.

"Surrender now and you will be treated with all fairness under the law." For Reg, there were no reporters, no international viewing audience. It was as if he were talking to one man and one man only. Kaspar, as faceless as he was for the moment. *Come out, you devil. Let me get a good look at you.*

"European authorities are standing by, fully mobilized for your surrender at a location of your choosing. Show yourself now and you will not be harmed. Continue a fugitive and you will be taken dead or alive. Stop the killing, stop the thefts, or you *will* be hunted down!" In millions of homes and shops and churches around the world, the face of Reg Danson, unwavering, filled the television screens of the innocent and the guilty.

One large screen covered half the wall above the antique Louis XIV royal bed in Nuremberg. Reg Danson's head loomed six feet tall. A cruel smile curled the lips of the strong young Aryan watching from the bed, wrapped in the burial shroud of a once strong young Jew.

". . . you *will* be hunted down!"

The man on the bed politely tapped the palm of his left hand with the fingers of his right. He locked eyes with the American. *"Zugabe!"* he mocked. "Encore!"

The head of the German shepherd came up at the sound of the master's voice.

With a sudden sweep of an arm, the man pointed at the image of Reg Danson and shouted, *"Vier!"*

The dog launched at the screen, a blur of seething fury. Its demented snarls obliterated the reporters' follow-up questions. Snapping, splintering the wood frame of the television screen, the shepherd devoted itself to killing the image behind the glass. Its nails clawed for a hold on the smooth surface. It smashed its muzzle against the screen repeatedly until streaks of blood from its nostrils mingled with the smears of saliva distorting the American's face.

"Zwanzig!" ordered the Aryan with a snarl of his own. The dog dropped to the floor and sat still, fur matted with the beast's own blood.

The young man placed the sound on mute. He lay there snuggled in the Shroud, excited by the dog's rage. He must get dressed. There was much to do. He would soon be holding a press conference of his own that would make the American's look like a commercial interruption.

He watched Reg Danson silently respond to questions and make a further fool of himself. He studied the sober, handsome features with all the clinical scrutiny of a cosmetic surgeon planning exactly where to make the incisions that would forever alter that face.

There were so many ways to silence a man. As Viennese mourners were fond of saying, he would make *eine schoene Leiche*— a beautiful corpse.

The man on the bed looked over at the quivering animal and smiled.

It was all a matter of *control.*

Austrian Airlines Flight 2303 nonstop from New York to Vienna's Schwechat Airport would put him in the two-thousand-year-old capital in eight hours, about mid-morning. Reg punched the pillow again and curled up against the window. The teriyaki chicken was beginning to settle. Maybe, if the kid in 10C stopped popping her bubble gum, he could catch up on some badly needed sleep.

To get here, he practically had to request police protection— from Tony and Leo. No way was he going off alone, they said. Was he crazy? He barely had time to change socks between the attempts on his life. They'd finally calmed down long enough to pray with him. When they'd finished, they embraced and he reminded them that danger was his business.

"Is Kaspar any more dangerous than an avalanche on Mount Ararat or a poison arrow in the Congo?" he naively asked.

"Yes!" they shouted in unison.

Another hour of arguing went by before he'd stood and firmly insisted that he was leaving. "Sometimes we have to board the ship and trust the winds to God. The apostle Paul made hay with his shipwreck, you know. But I can't endanger the both of you, and time is running out. The best thing you can do for me is to stay here on your knees and remind the Lord that he specializes in lost causes. He's my shepherd and I'll not want! If Bascomb calls, tell him I'm staying at the Rathaus on Lange Gasse."

There was nothing more to say, and they'd stood painfully silent for a few minutes, not wanting to part. Finally, Leo went into the kitchen and brought back a bon voyage gift for Reg—a Thermos of Doomsday swill.

It was hardest leaving Tony. He feared for his son and hated not being there when he was hurting. They hugged. "Mom would want you to go," Tony whispered in his father's ear. "If I wasn't so banged up, I'd be by your side, you know that. Jesus'll keep us in touch." How Reg loved that kid.

Leo promised to stay with Tony, maybe put him on light duty around the restaurant. "Ain't so fancy as that hoity-toity tavern of yours out in Virginia," he kidded. "Make one o' them hysterical speeches to my customers and they'll tell ya to sit down and quit blockin' the stage!"

"His*torical,*" corrected Tony good-naturedly, and they'd all had a laugh.

Flight 2303 droned on through the night, destination: the birthplace of Adolf Hitler. The gum popper slumbered. Reg heaved a grateful sigh and settled down for a much needed nap.

He had to sleep if he was going to stop Kaspar. The alerted Austrian authorities agreed to increase security at the Treasury of the Order of Teutonic Knights. But they'd refused to close the museum entirely on the strength of only Danson's hunch. Vienna was a sightseer's paradise. It teemed with visitors wanting to soak up the grandeur and the glory. It was scandalous to suggest closing any part of its seventy museums and collections. Hitler had had his way with Austria. It would be the height of cowardice to allow Kaspar, the faceless terrorist, to have his.

Within hours, the Austrian authorities would deeply regret their decision.

CHAPTER 9

The fires of the sun licked the edges of gun-gray clouds piled like bunched muscles above the spires and lanes of old Vienna.

She was the ornate ballroom of landlocked Austria. Cream cakes and soft violins, boy singers and prancing Lipizzan stallions, beer gardens and caviar cuisine. The glory days of the Habsburg dynasty were everywhere resplendent in grand architecture from the Imperial Palace to the Vienna State Opera House. The city of the River Danube had been home to a who's who of musical genius including Beethoven, Haydn, Mozart, Schubert, and Strauss. In the early nineteenth century, the glittering Viennese waltz defamed the empire by placing dancing couples in a near-embrace. It was, predictably, an enormous success.

Vienna had its dark reminders, too, for here it was that in the early 1900s a brooding small-time artist named Adolf Hitler sought admission to the Vienna Academy. But his talent went largely ignored, and he lived hand-to-mouth, a few nights in the Refuge for the Roofless in the district of Meidling, a few more in the Home for Men on the Meldemannstrasse. A man who craved the last laugh, Hitler found it in 1938 when he returned with his Nazis to take control of Austria. He made straight for the Imperial Hotel with its old world opulence as if placing the world on notice that he was as good or better than the best.

But on this tart fall day Vienna was free. The sun carved the clouds and made them disappear. It warmed the beech and oak and silver birch of the Vienna Woods and stirred the shopkeepers along the five kilometers of the Mariahilferstrasse, Vienna's longest shopping street.

The sun rose over the enormous gondola cars on the twenty-story giant ferris wheel at Prater Amusement Park and the tables seating 300,000 at scores of *Heurigen,* outdoor food and beverage gardens peppering the city.

It rose over the Treasure Chamber of the Crown Jewels and the regalia of the Holy Roman Empire. It rose over the Spanish Riding School and the mosaic of the Habsburg coat of arms on the roof of St. Stephen's Cathedral.

It rose, too, on an eclectic collection of museums. One was welcome to visit the most popular museums, like Mozart's house or Berggasse 19, the well-known address of Dr. Sigmund Freud. But for those visitors whose tastes ran more to the unusual, Vienna did not disappoint.

Sports buffs had their Museum of Football. Smokers had their Museum of the Tobacco Monopoly. Others visited the three thousand timepieces in the Clock Museum. For the whimsical, there were collections of circuses and clowns, dolls and toys, horseshoes and hairdressing. For the ghoulish, there were displays of dogs' skulls and undertakers' tools. The Museum of the Institute of Forensic Medicine, or *Kriminalmuseum,* housed a morbid collection of specimens illustrating death by drinking, drowning, burning, and various forms of mayhem. Its "weapons of murder" were viewed by appointment only.

At number seven Singerstrasse at the rear of St. Stephen's Cathedral was the conglomerate of massive cloisters and administration buildings of the House of the Teutonic Order built in the seventeenth century. Both Brahms and Mozart lived and wrote music there for a time. Within its walls was housed the Treasury of the Order of Teutonic Knights. In rows of glass cases were the clocks, furniture, ceremonial vessels, astronomical instruments, and Oriental weaponry of the chivalrous order of knights formed at the time of the Crusades. Two original manuscripts of marches written by Beethoven and dedicated to the German Order were a prized part of the collection.

And on a faded red velvet cushion was one of the most mysterious and legendary artifacts of all.

Rudolf Schratt was uneasy this morning. He always was whenever he was given Treasury duty. The forty-four-year-old imperial security officer had in twenty years guarded some of the most priceless art and artifacts in all Vienna. He had preserved paintings by Rubens and Van Dyck. He had charge of six hundred years of elaborate pieces and vestments of the Catholic church presented as gifts to the Habsburg family. He had personally escorted the incomparable bejeweled crown of the Holy Roman Empire.

It had been some time since he'd pulled duty in the Teutonic Treasury. His father, an imperial security officer before him, had been guarding the legendary hall that terrible day when Hitler and his lackeys had stormed the Hofburg Museum and torn its prize centerpiece from the hands of Maximilian Schratt. His father, shamed and broken by the brazen theft, did not live to see the relic restored to Vienna by the Allies eight years later.

Now it was Rudolf's turn to stop a madman from stealing it. He was a pragmatist not given to visions and hallucinations. But now as he looked in at the ancient object, it gleamed wetly. He knew it was probably just the way the light fell on the ancient burnish and not that it was smeared with blood.

He scoffed at himself. Schratt the Superstitious.

He no more believed the relic was in danger of robbery on this day than his father had more than half a century before. Standard precautions of the imperial guard dictated that whenever the international police community issued a terrorist warning, security be enhanced. It was a very long shot that anyone would invade the Treasury in this day and age. Hitler had taken over the country to do it. Hitler was one of a kind. He probably wasn't even human.

Besides, Schratt would like to see anyone find their way to the toilet today, let alone the glass case in the center of Viewing Hall Number Three. A huge tour group was just now arriving by charter buses for a private showing of the collection. They were graduate students of history, members of the private honorary society called Club of the Centuries, a very scholarly bunch from some of the finest universities in Europe. Their project of the month was medieval mysticism as practiced by the Knights. Proudly, he would stand at attention and answer any questions they might have about the holy object.

And try to ignore what looked like blood.

They streamed from six buses, 253 university men and women, polite and orderly for all their youthful exuberance. Find a way to harness the combined brain power among them and Europe's aches would come to an abrupt end. In sweaters and slacks and chic dresses imported from Paris and Milan, they chattered and shadowboxed like any group of spirited young people. But you could detect the intelligent reserve that kept them well short of obnoxious. This was not the German rugger team or the bar girls of Berlin. These were persons of breeding, future heads of state and power brokers of the European Common Market. Very important persons in need of impressing.

They filed into the ornate home of the Treasury of the Order of the Teutonic Knights and passed through the metal detectors almost without incident. But one young man managed to trigger the alarm. His metal belt buckle was a large and ornate reproduction of a turn-of-the-century horse-drawn taxi. Once it was removed, he passed through the detector without difficulty. He sheepishly retrieved the belt and threaded it back through the loops in his trousers. Everyone had a good laugh, but he took it in amiable stride.

When the call came requesting the tour, the museum's curators couldn't say yes fast enough. No, no, references would not be necessary. One hardly needed papers of introduction from the Club of the Centuries! Certainly, a private tour could be arranged. The Treasury administrators would be happy to invoice the Club bank account in Frankfurt at a discreet interval following completion of the tour.

Erwin Dienst, head of security for the Treasury, spoke into the handset pinned to the left shoulder of his uniform. Instantly his voice was heard by all thirty-two guards and tour guides—twenty-four men and eight women, an unusually high ratio of just under one staff person for every eight students. "The guests have arrived," he said. "Five minutes for general assembly, then break the 253 students into seven groups of twenty-five and three groups of twenty-six according to the group numbers on their name tags. Maria Metternich gets the Seeing Eye. Any questions?" There were none. Blind persons with Seeing Eye dogs were not unusual tour guests.

He continued to address the tour leaders. "You have each been given a map showing the exact routes to be followed through the exhibits, route numbers corresponding to group numbers. Under no circumstances are there to be any deviations from these routes. You need to perform periodic head counts and name tag checks to be certain you have the exact students you have been assigned. Please go to the toilet en masse and regroup before resuming the tour. I seriously doubt we will have the slightest hint of trouble with these fine students, but should any one of us decide to get creative in our leadership, it will be grounds for immediate dismissal. Any questions?" Again, there were none.

The students in calm and orderly fashion formed ten groups under numbered signs held aloft by the tour guides.

Maria Metternich smiled appreciatively. Her crop of twenty-six students contained four or five promising young men. She liked how they carried themselves, their smooth good looks and their focused intensity. She was not above a little extra swing in her hips if it might catch the eye of one of them. She might even go back to school if one should earn her admiration.

Especially the blind one. He had a gymnast's build and looked very appealing in his dark glasses. She wondered if the dog went with him everywhere.

"We welcome you to the Treasury of the Order of Teutonic Knights," droned the head guide in her introductory remarks. "We admire your diligent scholarship and abiding interest in these men of daring and conviction. We will do everything within our power to help you understand the importance of the knights and the remarkable era of their service to God and country. While it is imperative that you stay with your assigned tour squadrons at all times, please feel free to ask questions of your guides at any time."

Squadrons? Maria stifled a laugh. She'd like to take her squadron of five boys off on a private tour of their own. Perhaps later that evening they could slip into the Volksgarten for some dancing and a few drinks. She could tell them some things about Vienna they'd never find in a brochure.

"Welcome to tour group number nine. My name is Maria Metternich. We are proud to show you the treasures, implements, and artifacts of a noble order of Christian knights. Their quest for adventure and the folk myths surrounding them have aroused succeeding generations of Europeans to view their destiny with a fierce pride and singleness of purpose unparalleled in human history." She didn't know if she believed everything she was telling them, but to keep the job, she never strayed too far from the tour guide manual.

Maria couldn't help but note the striking difference between these focused, bright-eyed youth and the tough Nazi skinheads who made sport of beating up women and old Jews. Such incidents were on the rise—it was sometimes frightening to walk the streets of Vienna at night—but as long as there were moral, intelligent graduate students like these, one needn't despair. *So long as they aren't too moral,* she amended herself.

She felt wet flesh on the back of her hand and pulled back. The guide dog and its handsome master stood at her side, both grinning. "I hope he didn't startle you. He gets away with more than most Seeing Eyes. My animal likes to take the direct approach when making friends."

My animal? Maria was fascinated by the odd wording. *Is he military?*

"Your voice pleases me," he said, following Maria's lead over to the displays in the central hall. "Your eyes are at about my chest level. What color are they?" She was startled that he had caught her staring appreciatively at his impressive physique. Her step quickened.

"Don't be embarrassed. I could guess from the location of your voice how tall you are. A blind man's trick, nothing more."

"How did you know I was embarrassed?" she asked. She looked at the dark glasses and wished she could see his eyes.

"You said nothing and walked faster."

She glanced sharply at him and was met with a disarming smile. Oh, she definitely had to get to know this one better!

"Brown. My eyes," she said, turning to face her entourage, her back to a wall of suits of armor. The other tour groups formed in front of numerous other displays, the guides beginning their carefully rehearsed orations of past splendors. Together, their strange antiphonal chorus echoed in the dim and somber exhibit halls that radiated like spokes from the central display area. "The Teutonic Knights—also known as the Knights Templar or the Order of the Germans of the Hospital of St. Mary—were one of several military-religious orders founded in the twelfth century during the Crusades." She felt the dog's hot breath on her hand and stepped back, accidentally knocking into an extended metal-plated arm. It clanked, the image of a man to which it was attached tottering slightly from the impact.

"Forgive me!" apologized Maria, who instantly blushed upon realizing she had sought the forgiveness of an empty suit of armor. Her students laughed sympathetically. All but the blind one. He extended a hand, found her arm, and gave it a reassuring squeeze. "Don't give it another thought. Happens to me all the time."

Everyone had a good laugh then, and she marvelled at a man so poised despite his disability. To be that confident!

"Thank you," she said. She tried to make it sound as if she were thanking them all. It didn't.

Flustered, she cleared her throat and continued. "The Order was formed in 1190 during the Third Crusade to nurse the casualties of battle. Within eight years the foundation became an order of men, noble in spirit, fierce defenders of the Christian faith. These champions of the Cross laid claim to considerable real estate, and souls, in the Holy Land, Greece, southern Italy, and Germany. When Crusader zeal began to flag in the early thirteenth century, the knights turned their energies to converting the heathen masses of eastern Europe."

Erwin Dienst relaxed. The extra security was a needless expense as long as the Treasury was full of polite intellects like these. He did wish there were fewer of them. His tactical police training liked clear lines of sight and unobstructed exits. The old St. Stephen's complex, like so many other structures of antiquity, was constructed more for artistic value than for practical access or egress. The buildings were meant to be architectural statements of eternal grandeur for the transaction of business, government, and matters of the church, not the oft-visited repositories of earth's past.

Dienst ran a calloused hand through rapidly silvering hair.

He'd been up too late the night before quaffing at the *beisel,* the corner pub. No matter. His aged grandmother could handle today's assignment, replenish the wood pile, and strip and wax the floors at the same time.

Still, he wished it weren't quite so crowded. Everywhere he looked, students were within close reach of his personnel. Dienst preferred professional distance. Why were so many lagging behind their guides?

He watched group nine gather in the central exhibit area. He was getting to be such an old crank. He supposed that great minds like these soon bored of the canned history lesson. They'd rather be making history than reviewing it.

For that matter, they might rather be out doing a little quaffing of their own.

"... The Order was governed by a grand master, selected for life, who resided first in Venice, then in ..."

Maria felt his closeness and wondered if it was another quirk of blindness to invade the space of one's leader. Normally, it would have made her uncomfortable. But not with him. Not with that bearing, that body, that cologne.

"Membership in the Order was shared between . . . between, uh, I'm sorry," Maria said to her group. She flushed again, forgetting her lines. "Excuse me, I seem to have lost my train of thought for a moment ... I-I, uh—"

"I'm sure you were about to tell us how the grand master owed allegiance to the Holy Roman emperor and was assisted by five grand lords." He flashed a radiant smile and she was in love.

"Yes, yes, that's right," she said stupidly, as if he were the guide and she the student. How did he know the exact place in her spiel? Had he heard it before? She chided herself for losing composure, catching the knowing glances and sly smiles of the others. Hurrying, she pulled away from the blind man. "Membership in the Order was shared between knights and priests. They wore a uniform of a white coat with a black cross." She stopped in front of a display case containing two such uniforms.

But he wasn't listening. He was turned, facing the low, illuminated case guarded by Rudolf Schratt. Against the stream he moved, then stood still as if . . . as if *looking* at the artifact inside the case. He craned his neck to *see* . . .

Schratt tensed instinctively, stepping down from the stool he used to ease the arthritis in his legs. The dog saw the gun in the hip holster and growled menacingly. Its back stiffened, ears cocked forward, eyes locked on the weapon.

"Leicht! Easy!" the young man muttered, only now he didn't seem so young to Maria. Something about his tone made her shiver. The dog's growl turned to a nervous whimper, earning it a sharp cuff above the eye. The yelp of pain sounded like nails on a chalkboard in the hollow recesses of the hall. Others turned to look.

She suddenly wanted to be close to Schratt.

Schratt sincerely wished the Treasury had fewer alcoves and better lighting. His hand felt the heft of the revolver at his hip without touching it.

"New dog," said the blind man apologetically, flashing the enchanted smile. "I'm sorry to discipline him in front of you." He looked slightly past her as a blind person might, not certain now exactly where she stood. He seemed ill at ease, vulnerable. She gave a school girl laugh, half relieved at so simple an explanation for his odd behavior. New dog. Of course.

Austrian Airlines Flight 2303 nonstop from New York City landed flawlessly, and Reg Danson felt the familiar thrill he always felt when the jet engines reversed themselves and rapidly brought so huge a craft to a thunderous stop on the ground. He involuntarily held his breath, letting it out only when all reasonable doubt had been removed that they would not cartwheel tail over cockpit. Now, as always, his landing ritual ended by turning to the passenger nearest him and saying, "Piece of cake!"

The delays were interminable. Murphy's Law said his luggage would be last off and it was. *Der Zollbeamten,* the customs officers, were especially leisurely—and thorough—with their inspection. He almost blurted out that he didn't have time for this, that he was here to catch an international terrorist, but thought better of it. *"Nichts zu verzollen,"* he said meekly. "Nothing to declare."

He was dog-tired again, running on adrenaline. It was 9:00 A.M. Vienna time, midnight Seattle time. He'd check into his hotel later. Kaspar could strike at any moment.

"Wo kann ich ein Taxi bekommen?" he asked a uniformed porter. The man explained that in Vienna it was necessary to phone for a cab. Thirty minutes later, it arrived. Fortunately, the taxi driver informed him, the heavy traffic hour was past and it would take only another thirty minutes to reach downtown. Reg sighed heavily and watched the Viennese landscape. It crept by. His stomach was still upset. *Be anxious for nothing.* He couldn't help it. He had to make it in time. *Lord, calm me, please. Put the teriyaki chicken out of its misery and give the cab wings! "Fahren Sie mich zum Schatzkammer des Deutschen ordens! Hast!"* he said. "Take me to the Treasury of the Order of Teutonic Knights. Hurry!"

She raised her dark, thin eyebrows and said to group nine, "Any questions?"

"Yes," said the blind man without hesitation. "Weren't the knights specially favored by the Holy Roman Emperor Frederick II?"

"Why, yes," replied Maria, too much delight in her voice. "The emperor made them overlords of Prussia. They consolidated their holdings by inviting German peasants and nobles to settle there."

By their agreeable smiles and nods of support, clearly this young man had already made his mark with friends from the Club of the Centuries. Although they must have had inquiries of their own, they deferred, waiting for his next question.

A sightless leader of men, she thought, allowing herself to indulge in pure romance.

"Yes. Their strength in growing numbers enabled them to advance into modern day Estonia and Latvia." The pride with which he said it made those humble strides of conquest seem hugely important.

"But any further advances against the Orthodox Christians of Russia by the knights was repulsed by the superior forces of Alexander Nevsky at Lake Peipus in 1242. That confined the sovereignty of the Order to the Baltic coastlands." She spoke to the group but it was really a private conversation with him. No man had come close to besting her until now. It shocked her that she liked it.

The pleasure was short-lived.

He struggled between anger and control. He wanted to squash the wench, but it was not in the plan.

"Eins!" he said, lifting one finger, the impatient tutor. The dog came swiftly to attention and bared its teeth. "The knights swore vows of poverty, chastity, and obedience to a higher calling, that of the grand and illustrious order of men who counted the individual as nothing!

"Zwei!" A second finger joined the first. The dog went rigid, face horribly feral like a wolf's, emitting a growl that made the hair on Maria's neck stiffen. "The knights nearly exterminated the heathen Baltic savages and began repopulating the area with superior German stock!

"Drei!" Three fingers now commanded the attention of group nine, and the animal's wild snarls turned the hall into an echo chamber of the damned. Unsure, hesitant, Schratt slowly withdrew the revolver from its holster. The tour guides faltered in their recitations,

confused by the commotion. "Out of that chauvinism, out of that contempt for inferior peoples, out of that unrestrained knighthood rose the magnificent Third Reich!" He ripped the dark glasses from his eyes and stared into the core of Maria's soul. His arm swept upward in her direction.

"Vier!"

The dog lunged at the pretty leader of group nine and knocked her screaming to the floor. In unison, thirty-one students sprang behind the guards and other tour guides, circling the necks of their startled hostages with thin strands of guitar string that had been concealed in shoes and waistbands. Schratt's revolver clattered to the floor, useless. He strained against the string, face purpling, fighting for breath. The other guards did not come close to drawing their weapons.

"Zwanzig!" The order to cease. The German shepherd sat back on its haunches, the canine grin fixed in place as if satisfied with the morning's work. Maria, face and arms lacerated, cried and squirmed backward from the beast until stopped by the display case with the white coats and black crosses. The man ran forward, grabbed her bleeding face with a firm hand, and bent close. He smiled at her. "In the future you will find that flirting does not come so easily."

Then he straightened and strode confidently toward the low glass case that had been Schratt's personal charge. The guard groaned.

The young Aryan gazed down upon the prize, arms outspread like a conductor about to order a percussion crescendo. A grin of reverent delight spread over his face. *"Wunderbar!* Wonderful!" he exclaimed. *"Wunderbar!"*

The Holy Lance of Longinus, the Spear of God, lay before him.

Taller than a man, the wooden handle had certainly been replaced, perhaps several times, since the Crucifixion. The spear blade itself was just over thirty centimeters long, about one foot. Made of iron, it tapered with beautiful symmetry to a slender, leaf-shaped point. The spearhead, once broken, was securely rejoined by an expertly crafted silver sheath with gold wiring to secure the whole. Two gold crosses were inlaid into the base near the haft. A single square-headed nail was bound in place by the wires inside a notch of the blade.

The man leapt nimbly atop the display case and swept the hall with a look of utter triumph. Every eye was upon him.

With a shout of victory, the Aryan stomped the glass at his feet, shattering the lid of the display case. He reached down and grasped the spear that had pierced the side of Jesus the Christ.

A security alarm clanged frantically but did not penetrate the roaring in his head. A jolt of pure exhilaration coursed the length of the arm and flowed into the fingers that held the holy wood. He felt clairvoyant, invincible. His hand joined the hands of glorious Roman, Saxon, and Germanic warriors before him who had grasped this very weapon in battle. No fewer than forty-seven great leaders had possessed its power down through the ages:

Gaius Cassius Longinus, the Roman soldier who used it to pierce the side of the Messiah in fulfillment of prophecy.

Charles I, the Frankish king who appropriated the spear's powers and carried it through forty-seven victorious battles.

Heinrich the Fowler, founder of the royal house of the Saxons, who used it to drive the Poles eastward.

Frederick Barbarossa, who, spear in hand, conquered Italy and drove the pope into exile.

And, most glorious of all, the charismatic Adolf Hitler who with the spear in his possession nearly seized all of Europe.

Roaring defiantly, the Aryan rose to his full height and thrust the spear toward the ancient ceiling. Two hundred fifty-two voices roared their approval, making the hall ring with the bloodthirsty expectancy of a Roman coliseum. Only Maria, and those with piano wire binding their necks, said nothing.

"W! W! R! R!" Eyes blazing, the Aryan began the chant and was instantly joined by the crowd, each letter branding itself into the hearts of the terrified guards and tour staff. The German shepherd licked its muzzle, front feet dancing in excitement, almost swaying to the hypnotic chorus.

"W! W! R! R!" The Aryan jumped to the floor, still holding the spear aloft. He ran from person to person, locked eyes with each, and whipped their frenzy with his chant of destruction.

He laughed maniacally in the faces of the hostages and taunted their helplessness. Then he turned on the crying Maria, fastening on her frightened eyes with a baleful expression. He grasped the spear in both hands and lunged at her. She screamed and he stopped on one knee, the tip of the spear inches from her torn face. He burst into laughter, as if they were playing and she'd just lost at spin the spear.

He sneered at her whimpering and jumped again to his feet. He shouted for all to hear, "Lie face down!" and the innocent did so, terrified they would be shot. "Hands behind heads and do not move or you will not move ever again!"

"Come, my supreme ones!" their commander shouted, trotting for the exits, the dog at his side. "Come let us rid the earth of the Jew virus, the black stink, and the yellow scourge. They are a syphilis on the earth and we have the cure!"

They ran from the hall into the light of a bright Viennese day. Sirens sounded in the distance. The Aryan stopped and turned, the spear his baton, the troops his eager orchestra. "Go home and await my signal. Keep your eyes on the spear! When it is thrown, begin the purge!"

They vanished like phantoms down a hundred different avenues and alleyways. Within seconds they mingled with oblivious tourists ogling the spires and the columns of the city of dreams.

Only one remained behind in the shadows of St. Stephen's to watch the frantic arrival of the *polizei* with their loud, abrupt, screeching of tires and brandishing of useless weapons. The officers quickly "captured" the six bewildered and unwitting charter bus drivers who stumbled from the buses at gunpoint.

He held the spear at his side and felt its rigid power press against him. He faded back from the pandemonium, marveling again at his almost bloodless coup. *But for that stupid woman.* The police, the Vatican officials, the news commentators were all fools. They were about to learn a lot from him about the neat, quiet execution of a crime. It would be the last quiet one they would know for a very long time.

Control meant getting his way by means least expected. They thought they knew him when really they knew him not at all.

Except for the American.

CHAPTER

10

Reg was out of the taxi before it came to a halt at the police barrier in the shadow of St. Stephen's forty-five-story South Tower. He ducked around the barrier and ran for the steps of the Treasury past the abandoned tour buses and their bewildered drivers.

Too late.

After identifying himself to the commanding officer and learning there were more than two hundred suspects, Reg dashed into the museum. It wasn't difficult to find where the theft had occurred. Men and women in security and tour guide uniforms stood in a knot to the side of the shattered display case. They rubbed their necks, all striped an ugly red, glad to be free of the guitar string by which they had believed they would die just thirty minutes before. Some told the story in a gush of German, waving their arms excitedly. Others spoke quietly to the police of the common horror they had all just experienced. Still others wept, unable to form any words at all.

Reg stood before the ruined cabinet where the Holy Lance had lain. He put his hands behind his head and groaned. The Vatican should have chosen someone street smart. His timing was lousy. Every time he'd played the board game Espionage with Tony, he'd lost. When they needed a sleuth, why did they turn to the tenor section of the North Seattle Community Church?

A flash of white caught his eye, and he stepped forward for a closer look. A card lay atop the gleaming beads of glass at the center of the case, stiff, pristine, jarringly familiar. No one had to tell him what was written on it.

He sniffed the air, as if testing for Kaspar's scent. He looked for signs of death amidst the destruction, but beyond the broken display case, all else seemed untouched. Of the victims, only one was bleeding. He approached her.

"Ma'am?" he inquired gently. Maria Metternich flinched, not looking, head bowed. Her lovely arms and face bore deep gashes that seeped blood. She held a cloth to her forehead, awaiting further medical attention. "I'm so sorry to bother you, ma'am, but I'm Reg Danson, a—a kind of private investigator of the series of thefts of religious relics that have been in the news. I believe this is another of those. Could you tell me who did this to you?"

She looked at him then, and he felt deeply ashamed that anyone could deliberately injure an innocent person in the name of a quest for power. Something in her eyes told him that she had suffered much more than physical disfigurement this day. "A Greek god did this to me," she said bitterly. "A man who first cast a spell over me, then ordered his animal to attack me."

"Did he have a name tag or give any clue to his identity?" He felt stupid asking the question, but he needed to put a face on Kaspar.

"A man who pretends to be blind, attacks you with his Seeing Eye dog, and steals a valuable museum piece does not bother with introductions!" She saw how uncomfortable Danson was and sighed raggedly. "I'm sorry. This is not your fault. He was a fair-haired man about your height, twenty-three, twenty-four years of age, German by his accent, very well proportioned and muscular." She related as many other details as she could, including the chilling chant of "W! W! R! R!" World Wide Race Revolution.

The police commander waved Danson away from the injured woman. He turned to go.

"Thank you for the information," said Reg. He smiled reassuringly. "You should get hazardous duty pay."

She laughed sadly. "Yes. Museums just aren't safe places for a woman anymore, are they?"

He touched her lightly on the shoulder. "God bless you and bring you complete healing."

"Nothing a few cosmetics can't hide," she said gamely, brushing at a strand of wayward hair. "Best of luck with your investigation. If you find this man, please tell him that dog's breath needs attention!"

He nodded and waved. She had spunk.

"One other thing," she called after him. "He told his followers to rid the earth of Jews, blacks, and Orientals. Then he told them to wait at home for his signal. It would be when the spear is thrown, he said, and somehow they would all know. It was then he said they should begin the purge. Do you know what that means?"

"I'm not sure," he said evasively. In his heart, he was afraid he did know.

Dejected, Danson called for a taxi to the Rathaus Hotel, a moderately priced lodging. He needed time to think and pray about what to do next.

The day was beginning to warm, and Danson asked to be let out several blocks from the hotel. A brisk walk ought to sharpen the senses. He sent his bags on ahead.

En route he discovered the home of Ignaz Kuranda, a Jew and ironically the founder of the German National Party. Political Zionism had also gotten its start in Vienna. Jews had taken a prominent role in the Austro-Hungarian army and in the technical and industrial development of the Austrian nation. Prior to the outbreak of World War II, four Austrians were awarded the Nobel prize for medicine and physiology. Three of the recipients were Jews.

But the war drastically altered the respected status of the Austrian Jews. The Jewish population of Vienna numbered 180,000 in 1938. In the ensuing years of persecution, expulsion, and extermination, that number was reduced to the current level of no more than ten thousand.

Reg reached the hotel and went immediately to the front desk. He declared his name and the clerk handed him an urgent message from Richard Bascomb:

> Reg, lad, hope all's well. God's ways are most mysterious. Have received offer of help to locate quarry. Lady Katherine von Feuerbach is a devout Catholic who heads the Jewish Repatriation League at Leipziger Strasse No. 7, Nuremberg. Thank her for me. Richard.

It was a slender strand of hope and Reg grabbed for it like a sinking sailor. Tired as he was, he asked the clerk to send his bags up to the room, then headed for a bank of phones. He called the airport and booked an afternoon flight to Nuremberg. He would speak with Lady Katherine—he smiled at the Old World elegance of the title—and hopefully be back in Vienna before bedtime. He phoned another taxi and stopped at a news kiosk to purchase a copy of the daily English language paper. Too soon for news of the museum robbery, but he wanted to get the flavor of the city.

"Hate Crimes Not Isolated Problem" shouted a headline three columns wide. He'd had quite enough of hate, but he read on:

> BERLIN—American FBI Director Leonard Beehles, arriving in a country long thought to have an acute problem with hate groups, said Tuesday that hate-crime murders are at least as common in the United States as in Germany.

The article went on to cite alarming statistics for the previous year of more than 7,600 U.S. incidents of hate-motivated intimidation, vandalism, and assaults. Twenty of those incidents involved murder. But even those statistics were low, volunteered by law enforcement agencies covering only 56 percent of the nation's population.

> Germany has garnered world attention for hate violence by neo-Nazis, skinheads, and other groups, mostly directed at foreign workers during high unemployment brought on by combining the prosperous West with the underdeveloped East.

And directed at researchers of earth's mysteries who stick their noses in where they are ill-equipped to do any good. "But isn't one of the greatest mysteries of all why some people live their lives hating other people for nothing more than a difference of color, creed, or origin?" Reg asked the question of a pigeon that seemed to bob its head yes. It reminded Reg of Connie and their bizarre walk in the park.

This taste of the city was decidedly bitter.

The flight to Nuremberg took little more than an hour, and from the airport it was just five kilometers to Leipziger Strasse No. 7.

Headquarters for the Jewish Repatriation League was a huge stately residence of brick and dark, almost burnt wood. It rambled off to the rear, doglegging unexpectedly in several directions, a sprawl of a nineteenth-century residence. Three stories high, it possessed a clock tower with ornate filigree and windows of curved framing resembling giant keyholes. The front doors were double with leaded glass etchings of scrolls and bearded patriarchs. The door plate bid welcome: "As for me and my house, we will serve the Lord" read the declaration from the Old Testament book of Joshua.

From within drifted the sweet, bright strains of a harp, gracefully swelling and diminishing like waves on the shore.

When he stepped across the threshold, Reg felt an involuntary shiver of apprehension and a tingle of delight. The apprehension came from the cold, austere interior of the residence, which appeared cavernous and as unending as the exterior. He walked across an enormous entry to an even more enormous parlor filled with dark furniture, old tapestries, and dimly lighted paintings framed in curlicues of faded gold. Dark carvings of real land creatures locked in frozen hisses and roars covered tea table and desk. Imaginary sea serpents entwined brass lamp stands and the feet and arms of plush antique sofas and chairs in dusky velvet blues and tans.

The tingle of delight came from the highly polished harp in the middle of a black and tan carpet—and the equally arresting woman who was one with the instrument. She graced her place in the room like an ivory cameo, white lace and a strand of gray pearls at her throat. A shimmering satin gown of cinnamon brown delicately draped her slender figure. Auburn-colored hair cascaded to her shoulders in whirls and twists of fascinating variety. Her head held proud, more than a hint of aristocracy in the confident set of the chin, the high cheek bones, and the soft sparks in eyes of blue-gray.

But the single most alluring attribute about the woman were her hands. Small and exquisitely feminine, a flash of sapphire on one, the glint of topaz on the other. Pink rose-lacquered nails tipped the long, narrow fingers that flew among the strings as if harvesting the notes from a field ripe with music. Now her arms windmilled across the nylon strings, sending ripples of sound splashing against the walls and ceiling. Now her arms held close to her body, slender and steady, the sure fingers picking the petals of melody and tucking them away in the palms of her hands.

Abruptly, she switched to an oddly discordant piece, fingers skipping out of control from high notes to low, and back again. It was as unsettling as the previous piece had been tender and caressing. He must have frowned, for she looked at him and stopped mid-note.

"Music needn't always be pleasant or entertaining," she said, all alto, and it felt like a scolding. "Music is communication of the most intimate sort, whether harmonious or argumentative. I call this piece 'Interruptions.' Like life, it is unpredictable and fragmentary. Don't you find it so?"

Her accent was full of smooth places and gracious inflections, but the tone was direct, as was her gaze. He followed suit. "If you mean life, it is most certainly surprising. If you mean that piece, I think I would play it only in private."

She gave a bare smile and switched back to the softer piece. "I thought I was playing it in private."

She bent to her work, stroking the glossy walnut harp with a nurturing touch that yielded the fruit of music gorgeous and moving. Without even knowing he had, Reg Danson sank to the sofa in front of the harpist, forgetting the mission that brought him.

Following a particularly fragile waterfall of tone, the lovely fingers hovered in place, slowly drawing the fullness of two notes from the nylon strings that contained them. She watched the tension drain from the handsome face before her, the eyes closed.

"'I play the notes as they are written, but it is God who makes the music.' J. S. Bach."

"Yes," answered Reg, strangely captivated by the music—or by the fingers that produced it. "I suspect he was on to something."

Soon, an uneasy and more insistent impression took hold of Danson. His eyes strayed into the darker recesses of the room to a massive six-foot black and white portrait of a man in a military-style jacket with two rows of brass buttons, a short man with little hair; brooding, close-set eyes; and a wild, unruly handlebar mustache.

"Alois Hitler," she said, following his gaze, fingers treading softly on the harp strings. "The abusive drunkard who made Adolf's life a living hell. I keep him around to remind me of the consequences of too much wine."

Suddenly she strayed into a sweet entanglement of strings, plucking them individually and softly, producing a repetitive rhythm, hypnotic and forlorn. "Maid of gentle birth, your father was a knight, he fathered you from a mother who was a noble farmer's daughter." The words were spoken like narrative, deftly woven among the rise and fall of the notes. "The more I look at you, the fairer you seem to me, and your joy I would share . . ."

Her eyes met his, and he felt uncomfortably warm. "The love poetry of medieval troubadours," she said. She stopped playing and placed the small hands carefully in her lap. "I believe I am descended from one of them. *Troubadour* means composer, inventor. My music is my invention."

Reg shifted awkwardly and leaned forward, hands upon his knees. The soft German accent was cultured and beguiling. She sat framed like a painting herself in the glistening black walnut of the harp that stood between them. She looked sad somehow and vulnerable, as if the delicate vertical strings were the bars of a tiny cell high in some ancient castle to which she had been forever banished.

He blinked to clear the image and steel himself. This was no gothic novel, and he had urgent business. "I'm Reg Danson and—"

"I hoped you were," she interrupted. "I am Lady Katherine von Feuerbach. You may call me Lady Katherine. It is an honorary title bestowed upon me by the grateful Jews of the Rhineland. I have resettled more than five thousand of them on farms of their own in Israel. Welcome to *Tore der Hoffnung,* the Gates of Hope." She reached for a silver bell beside the chair and rang.

A large maid dressed in somber black appeared from the shadows with a tray and set it lightly upon the low ebony tea table. She stepped back, and when she did, she stared above Danson's head, stiffened, and crossed herself. Then she melted back into the shadows and disappeared.

Reg turned. He was at the foot of another enormous painting, a dark and ghastly rendering of Christ upon the cross. Prominent was a flow of blood from the right side of the chest, staining the loincloth of the otherwise unclothed figure, and spilling down onto the straining thighs of the Crucified One.

"It is a bad but valuable rendering of Caravaggio's 'The Deposition,'" said his hostess, staring at the painting, head oddly tilted as if trying to peer into the face hidden by the crown of thorns digging the bowed head raw. "The artist is Adolf Hitler. He was a passable watercolorist but a lout at human anatomy. Do you find it shocking that he painted the Crucifixion?"

Now she was looking at him in that same odd way as if he needed to be checked for signs of life. "No. Yes," he stammered. "I mean, I find both paintings a startling contrast to a room in which a woman of your grace and beauty is the captivating center."

It was her turn to be ruffled. Reg smiled, enjoying his suave recovery. Maybe there was a touch of James Bond in his character after all. *Now put the lady at ease.* "I'd love some tea," he said.

She talked while she poured. "These paintings are my constant reminder of the horrors the Hitler epidemic visited upon the poor and defenseless. They are my goads to action."

Reg made no attempt to hide his fascination with her hands. She poured the steamy amber liquid left-handed from an elegant silver tea service into two fine china cups. When he took a cup from her, their fingers touched. The sapphire ring and the pink nails electrified the gloomy room.

"My grandfather's first wife, Eleanor Stein, was killed in the camps by Nazi overlords. An entire people looted, raped, and murdered for *Lebensraum,* living space, Hitler's promise of a land that was Jew-free and for Aryans only. I believe in *Lebensraum* and have been doing everything within my power to secure it before it is too late."

Reg set his cup down with a clatter. "I don't understand. I thought you defended Jews."

She did not pour herself any tea. Instead, she walked over to the harp and gently brushed the carefully fashioned contours of the instrument. "Millions of dollars from benefactors around the world flow into the Jewish Repatriation League. Our mandate is to bring an end to the diaspora, the brutal exodus and attempted genocide that has hounded and dispersed Jews to the four winds. They must return to Palestine, for that is the land God gave them. When people are forced by economics or slavery or brutality to leave their God-given lands, you create a world of hate that spirals out of control. We see it today worse than ever."

Her beautiful blue-gray eyes flashed defiantly. "Yes, I believe in *Lebensraum.* As a devout Catholic on my father's side, what other choice do I have? Allow the continued slaughter of one color over another? It is a fallen world, Herr Danson, and I must do what I can to end the madness whether it fits every definition of freedom and democracy or not!"

She braced for rebuttal. It did not come. Instead, he sipped his tea thoughtfully. The only sounds were the ticking of an enormous clock somewhere in the dark shadows and an occasional car passing on the street. At last he cleared his throat. "Call me Reg," he said.

She laughed softly and shook her head. The satin and cinnamon of her loveliness softened even the grim specter of Alois Hitler. Perhaps she was the best medicine for the sickness of bigotry.

"Der Fuehrer was fascinated with the *Heilige Lanze,* the Holy Lance. See how he exaggerates the wound between the fourth and fifth ribs made by the spear thrust to prove that Christ was already dead and not in need of having his legs broken as was the custom of the day. But the resulting flow of blood proved that the sacred heart of Jesus still beat at the time of the stabbing. Mingled with the pleural fluid from the lungs, it proved the account of Saint John and the ancient prophecy of the Old Testament."

She went to the foot of the painting and again gave the odd impression of a person trying to catch the eye of the dying Savior.

"'But one of the soldiers pierced His side with a spear, and immediately blood and water came out,'" she recited the words from the nineteenth chapter of John's Gospel. "'And he who has seen has testified, and his testimony is true; and he knows that he is telling the truth, so that you may believe. For these things were done that the Scripture should be fulfilled, "Not one of His bones shall be broken."'"

She was weeping softly and Reg went to her. "Lady Katherine," he said gently, "you must tell me what you know so that with God's help I can prevent more suffering of innocents." She bowed her head to her breast and her shoulders shook. He reached out and held her soft arms, the feel of satin stirring dormant sorrow for the wife he'd lost a few short years before. Lady Katherine yielded to his touch, and he fought to keep from kissing the smooth, downy neck. He leaned close, breathing her delicate perfume, feeling the warm brush of auburn coils against his cheek.

Eyes closed, she felt him so near her, a strong arm moving to encircle her small waist.

Quietly, he asked, "Who is Kaspar?"

She tensed and opened her eyes. He was holding a white calling card in front of her. It was emblazoned with a gold lightning bolt connecting "Kaspar" to "WWRR."

Brusquely, she left him. The harp between them, she was safe again in her cell. "The historical revisionists would have us believe that the Holocaust is an enormous lie perpetrated by the very ones whose loved ones died in it by the hundreds of thousands. Perhaps this Kaspar is actually doing us a favor by forcing us to deal with the issue of racial differences so that another Holocaust never occurs. If oil and water do not mix, do not try. Separate them. If white and black and Jew do not mix, do not try. Separate them. Hitler called it *Entjudung* or de-Jewing. Germany should be de-Jewed. Palestine should not. It should be de-Arabed."

"That is a very dangerous philosophy," Reg said, his anger rising. "Are we to de-Africanize America by bombing black churches? Do we de-Asianize California by burning down the home of a Japanese-American city councilman? Do we allow the Nation of Islam to de-white South Africa by giving the white citizens twenty-four hours to get out of town? That's an insane scenario!"

"What we have now is insane," said Lady Katherine evenly. "White supremacists and black power brokers the world over are not going to allow things to continue the way they are. I'm afraid you may be a hundred years too late to stop the violence now. Man's heart is exceedingly dark, Reg Danson, and perhaps we should consider cutting our losses and agreeing to the lesser of two evils—repatriation of the races."

Reg stared at her. Except for her exquisite beauty, sophistication, and station in life, she could be a lawyer for Connie and her skinhead siblings. "The only real equality is separation of the races," Connie had said. But at what terrible price?

Lady Katherine studied the troubled face of her visitor and broke into merry laughter. It was a sound so pure, so clean, so passionate with life that Danson, despite himself, joined in. It was inexplicably joyous to hear her abandoned amusement. The keeper of the Gates of Hope was never more captivating.

"Forgive me, Reg, for my poor manners." She gasped for breath and dabbed her eyes with a pale blue hanky extracted from the sleeve of the gown. "My mother would sentence me to hard kitchen labor for such shabby behavior. You are my guest, you've been through so much, and here I treat you no better than a commoner. We can debate another time how to ultimately achieve what we both want—brotherhood and harmony. Of course I want to help you find this terrorist before he harms another soul. My contacts among the German Jews have been tracking his movements.

"Don't look so surprised. You'd be amazed at the efficiency of a civilian underground when the authorities have trouble finding their very shoes in the dark. The Jews were not obliterated from Germany thanks to a network of Jewish *and* Gentile informants.

"They will soon bring us news. We must be patient and wait. There is nothing more we can do. You are, of course, to be my guest. It will be nice to have someone of your presence in the house. It has been such a long time since my Frederich died in the auto accident. I know you hoped I had more immediate news, but it can't be more than a day or two at most before we hear."

Her invitation both annoyed and exhilarated him. He couldn't just park himself like some casual lodger at a bed and breakfast. Kaspar had made attempts on his life and Tony's and succeeded at killing others. Kaspar was a threat to global stability.

Katherine von Feuerbach smiled teasingly, then hid behind a finely sculpted hand. It would be easy to leave the entire matter in those alluringly capable hands.

She widened her eyes questioningly and laughed again. He laughed, too, shrugged, and at last nodded his agreement. Just one day. What could it hurt? Kaspar would take that long to savor his latest theft. She plucked out a merry melody on the harp to seal the contract between them. Reg stepped lively to the reel, and it was difficult to tell the glad music from her bubbling laughter.

Only one nagging question tried to poke its crabby way into the festivities. *Where are the staff, the people who handle the millions in contributions that pay for repatriating Katherine's Jews?*

But such a question didn't stand a ghost of a chance at a party where everyone was all smiles.

Except for Alois Hitler. His face was as dark as ever. There was not a shred of a smile on the face of Adolf's father.

CHAPTER

11

Whoever possesses this Holy Lance and understands the powers it serves, holds in his hand the destiny of the world for good or evil.

— Runic Prophecy

For good or evil . . . for good or evil . . . for good or evil. The young Aryan felt the vitality flow from the shaft of the spear. Mentally, he recited the ancient runic prophecy first deciphered by German Colonel Maximilian Hartmann. Energy coursed up the strong, naked arms until it seemed to stream into his very heart. He kissed the handle along its length, knowing that at some point his lips touched the sacred places where *der Fuehrer* himself had grasped the spear.

His lips were on fire.

"Adolf Hitler, you are our great Leader," he prayed, intoning the desecrated Lord's Prayer once sanctioned for German school children. "Thy name makes the enemy tremble. Thy Third Reich comes, thy will alone is law upon earth. Let us hear daily thy voice and order us by thy leadership, for we will obey to the end even with our lives. We praise thee! *Heil Hitler!*"

He stretched prone, barefoot, shirtless, brown military trousers stained with sweat. Outstretched arms kept the Lance elevated. His words were muffled, spoken into the cement floor. *"Heil Hitler! Heil Hitler! Ein Volk, ein Reich, ein Fuehrer!* Hail Hitler! Hail Hitler! One folk, one empire, one leader!"

From behind came the swell of one hundred male voices in unison. *"Heil Hitler! Heil Hitler! Ein Volk, ein Reich, ein Fuehrer!"* Each man was similarly barefoot, shirtless, head shaved, dressed in brown military trousers. They stood at the ready in rows of ten, their legs spread, hands clasped behind their backs, their eyes riveted on the wall. They were his personal crack corps and he their supreme centurion. They hated him and feared him and obeyed him without question. He had done everything he said he would do and soon they would rule with him in the Fourth Reich. To a man, their parents were divorced or separated, and they had been either physically or sexually abused as children. Most were unemployed, few had completed high school, and all consumed a steady diet of violence and destruction in music, television, and films. These neo-Nazis were graduates of the street gangs that once served as their families. They were storm troopers of the *Volksgemeinschaft,* the pure racial community. They were handpicked to carry out the bloodletting in Germany that would lead to the sorting out of the races.

Many thousands more like them were strategically stationed in the more civilized, and therefore more racially confused, nations on earth. They stood by in Austria, Australia, Canada, France, Hungary, Japan, Poland, and Switzerland. In New Zealand, they were the National Alliance. In England, the Justice Federation. In the United States, the groups numbered in the hundreds with names like Confederated Forces of the Knights of the Ku Klux Klan, the Iron Fist, the Aryan Separatist Youth Party, and the New Dawn Skinheads for the Advancement of White People.

And now all that remained was to await the signal. Explosives and weapons stockpiles were ready. Millions of rounds of ammunition, handguns, knives, and sophisticated semi-automatic and fully automatic assault rifles awaited the hands that would use them to cleanse the earth. Lax inventory controls at military installations meant thousands of machine guns and grenades were now controlled by the racial separatists. Warehouses full of military weaponry from the old Soviet Union had been appropriated for the right price.

It had taken three years of lobbying, courting, and cajoling the diverse leadership of the world's hatemongers to arrive at this moment in history, when for the first time, cooperation among them was virtually assured. The promise of domination was as intoxicating an incentive as any.

He rose and turned to face the superbly conditioned troops. They glistened in the heat of the close quarters. He held the spear aloft, and every eye locked on it. He spoke. "As Jesus freed men from sin and hell . . ."

One hundred voices repeated the phrase.

". . . so Hitler freed the German people from destruction!"

Again, the strong voices shouted the words from the Hitler-approved parallel drawn between him and the Messiah.

"Jesus and Hitler were persecuted . . ."

"Jesus and Hitler were persecuted . . ."

". . . but while Jesus was crucified, Hitler was raised to the Chancellorship!"

". . . but while Jesus was crucified, Hitler was raised to the Chancellorship!"

He brought the Lance down to his belly, then without warning lunged at the near row of warriors.

Just one blinked. A punishable weakness. The offender, no more than eighteen or nineteen years of age, trembled beneath the scathing rake of the young Aryan master's eyes. Then the master smiled and the soldier relaxed, so glad to serve a long-suffering master. He would do better next time.

With lightning swiftness, the butt of the lance struck the offender a savage blow to the head. He dropped to the floor unconscious. A seeping purple knot rose over the left ear, but no one dared go to the fallen man's aid. He had wavered, and he had paid. The knot would serve to remind him of his good fortune—not to have been killed outright.

"What two words are not permitted in your vocabulary?" shouted the master.

"Unmoeglich und niemals!" came the shouted reply. "Impossible and never!"

Reg Danson paused appreciatively, a forkful of pickled pot roast halfway to his mouth.

"Your *sauerbraten* is to your liking?" Lady Katherine was breathtaking in a taffeta gown the color of golden wheat. A pair of stunning gold earrings in the form of half moons captured the flicker of the candles. *How many women still dress for dinner?* he wondered appreciatively. *How many look as radiant when they do?*

The harp stood by, its curves irresistible, asking to be touched. Reg caressed its high-polished smoothness. It felt glassy and cool.

The beer was an acquired taste, but it was so inextricably a part of the German culture, he didn't wish to offend. He sipped it tentatively.

"A man who sips his brew is a rare find," she said, playfully arching her eyebrows.

He chuckled. "German beer has more body than most American stews. What am I drinking?"

"That is Hamburger beer from Hamburg, created by Professor Peter Oldenburg of the Beerology faculty at the university. We Germans take our beer seriously!"

He grinned. "Ah, lady, you could tell me the moon is made of strudel and I'd believe you!"

She toyed with the fork, tapping it against the tip of her tongue. "Don't be silly," she said. "Everyone knows that moon is made of *Eisbein.*"

"Eisbein?"

"Pig knuckles," she replied, laughing in that fresh, musical way of hers. He joined in.

They dipped bread into a communal deep dish of rich roast gravy. The dish was a *tryblioi,* a large ceramic reproduction of the bowl used at Hebrew meals. "It's like the household pottery found at Masada," she explained. "Jesus alludes to one in Matthew 26." Perhaps they imagined it, but it seemed they ate a quantity of bread that evening, their fingers touching often in the warm sop.

"I hear music and you need to hear it too!" she said suddenly, springing gaily from the table. In one flowing motion she straddled the harp and leaned into a loud, frivolous piece that thumped and clattered across the strings like a drunken sailor.

He slapped time on the table and hooted her antics. "Where did that thing come from?" he heckled.

She paused, breathing hard. "From the beer hall in Munich," she growled in a mannish way and resumed the noisy ditty. Frau Heppler entered with the sparkling *Lebkuchen* and frowned at the goings on. She stiffly planted a mountain of baked decadence in front of Danson and an only slightly smaller piece at Lady Katherine's place. The Frau looked sternly at Reg as if dinner were reduced to a bacchanal and it was all his fault. He looked suitably cowed, and Frau Heppler took her leave rather more huffily even than she had come.

They somehow found room for the mouth-melting dessert, wasting not a crumb. Either Lady Katherine was a jogger or she seldom indulged in *Lebkuchen.* Reg was stuffed.

"You don't eat this way every day?" he said, pushing back from the table at last.

"Oh my no," she said, the little golden moons in her ears reflecting the candle flame. "Some days we eliminate the meat and bread altogether!"

It was good to laugh again after running so long against an unseen adversary. Reg was completely intrigued by this woman. His defenses were down, and what's more, he didn't care.

"Should you be in need of a bromo, I have just the thing," she said mischievously. "What do you suppose is the number one non-prescription balm in Germany today?"

"Aspirin?"

"How American! No, garlic is the German cure for the common ailments and is by far the most frequently taken in pill form. It's said to prolong life, aid digestion, and soothe the nervous system."

"In that case, I'll take a large helping!" Reg sighed heavily.

"This nasty business is getting to you, isn't it?" She looked at him with concern, and he wondered if garlic lowered an elevated heart rate.

Lady Katherine sucked the tines of her fork and studied his lean good looks. The threads of silver in the soft brown hair, the tanned face, the determined jaw, the amber brown eyes that so easily switched from merriment to concern and back. He wore a soft blue wool shirt that perfectly draped the hardened adventurer's body. A man comfortable to be with but a man not likely to remain by the fire long. She tapped the fork against her chin and smiled sympathetically. He smiled self-consciously, unsettled by the close female scrutiny. Any woman wishing to detain Reg Danson had better not plan on many long, candlelight meals. From what she'd read of him, he was pure wanderlust, and the light in those eyes was the light of jungle campfires and high mountain dawns.

Reg returned her look earnestly, searching for clues in the soft hues of her beauty. She seemed so incongruous to the dark, hulking interior of the Gates of Hope. Night was falling now, and the candle flames seemed ill-equipped to fend it off.

"When the Berlin Wall fell and crimes of hate rose, I determined with God's help to do what I could to restore Germany's honor. Through my husband's contacts in government—he was aide to a vice chancellor—I founded the League and immediately resettled fifty Russian Jews, highly educated doctors and engineers, in Haifa, Israel. We were able to find them factory jobs and apartments to rent for their families. Now we're helping the Falasha Jews of Ethiopia."

"Factory jobs?" interjected Reg. "I thought you said the Russians were professionals?"

"Yes, but because of the influx of so many Jewish immigrants to Israel, unemployment runs high. There is an excess of twelve thousand medical doctors and ten thousand engineers. The economy is strained, but the homeless are few and no one goes hungry."

Now her beauty was marred by sadness. Yet when her voice came again, there was steel in it. "Then the hate began. Molotov cocktails through my windows. Swastikas painted on my doors. Those things I could stand. But then came the day I opened the door to a small boy, no more than five or six years, who called me a Jew whore and spit on my shoes. He carried a small wooden toy top in his grubby little fist and could barely pronounce the words of venom he'd been fed. The little trained dog ran back to his cowardly masters and I almost gave up.

"But then came the outpouring from London, Rome, New York, Tel Aviv. Cash, checks, stocks, deeds of property in support of the return to Israel. I couldn't ransom people fast enough." She rose and stepped to a nearby bookcase where she extracted a large three-ring binder and opened it in front of him. He saw the smiling photos of wrinkled elderly, babies in arms, young couples smiling in gratitude. The photos were signed "Shalom!" and "Thank you, Angel von Feuerbach."

"My family!" she said proudly.

"It must be very satisfying work," Danson said, watching her sit down. "And at times trying."

She merely nodded, returning the fork to pursed lips.

"Tell me, Katherine. You're Catholic. How could Kaspar kill so many in order to gain some ancient cloth, a bit of sacred iron? Are they so important to his cause?"

She stared into the flame, her focus far removed from that room. "We would do well not to underestimate the value of the sacred objects," she said at last, wresting her attention from those far thoughts. "No less than Thomas Aquinas called the bodily fragments of saints the 'limbs of God' for those were what remained of the children and friends of the Creator. They walked the earth in his name, acted in his name, spoke in his name. Their holiness was an example to all and worthy of love and remembrance.

"Those things touching Christ were all the more venerable. The spearhead itself, dipped in the very blood of Jesus, was no mere 'bit of sacred iron.' In fulfillment of ancient prophecy, it brought one chapter of all creation to a close, and opened quite another . . ."

"A talisman!" Reg barged in. "That's all it is. The spear didn't make history, Jesus Christ did! God willed his own Son's death, and Jesus complied. The power and the majesty are in the redemption purchased by the Savior's blood, not in the crown of thorns or in the cross of wood or in some Roman spear. Relics like those only blind people to the true glory of salvation that comes not by material objects but by the might of the Lord!"

She dropped her fork with a clatter. "A pretty speech, Herr Danson, and about as ignorant a one as I've heard! A contempt for the grand and sacred traditions of the church is the last thing I expected from you."

Reg looked into the dish where they'd been so happily dipping bread not long before. "I'm sorry. I do try to ride my high horse more than I should. But the excesses of the church are well documented. For decades armed deacons had to stand guard at the true cross in Jerusalem to insure that pilgrims only kissed it and did not chew splinters off for future blessing. Forged relics, stolen fingers, tomb dust—terrible fraud and abuse. It was the kind of foolishness bishops came to call 'detestable presumption.'"

Katherine stood. She was trembling. "And that is exactly the kind of contempt for the sacred things and the power behind them that drove Adolf Hitler from the church. He was raised Catholic, was an altar boy, but by the time he was eleven he was already beginning to renounce the faith. He believed that once-muscular religion had been reduced to an effeminate club of grovelers and do-gooders, that Christ himself gave up on the cross and essentially committed suicide."

Reg threw his napkin on the table. "Blame the church for Hitler's insanity? The gospel according to Adolf Hitler!"

She stormed over as if to slap him, then checked herself. Her words bit like shrapnel. "By the time he was a young man, Hitler was well read in Eastern mysticism, godless philosophers, the occult masters, and the fanciful legends of *Herrenvolk,* the Master Race. He thought he was the reincarnation of Caesar. Whatever kind of magic it took to reach his proud destiny as the Aryan Messiah, he would seize it and make it his own. The Holy Lance was to become his Reich's Lance. It was the same spear said to have been raised in the hand of Joshua at the command to shout down the walls of Jericho; the same spear forged by the ancient prophet Phineas to symbolize the magical, supernatural powers inherent in the blood of God's chosen people. It was that blood power that Hitler wanted to appropriate for the German people.

"I weep for the German people that he was able to gain their allegiance when the church could not. Hitler was a monster for whom there were no restraints. Because of a bungled assassination attempt, he had his own officers executed and their death filmed. He watched that film over and over again, and every time he laughed in delight." She whimpered softly. "Somehow someone has got to stop the madness."

Reg shuddered in revulsion, whether from thoughts of Hitler's excesses or the strangeness of the house, he wasn't sure. He felt if he was to venture now from this woman or her harp, he would never find his way back again. "Surely Hitler had one redeeming quality," he mumbled.

"Yes." She stared past him into the darkness. "There was one."

"What was it?" he asked.

"That he was not born a twin."

CHAPTER 12

Monsignor Claudio Andone, the pope's under-secretary for foreign relations, hurried inside the Vatican Embassy. He'd never liked Vienna and he didn't like it now. Perhaps it was all the pastries. He loathed pastries. And waltzes. And all the ornate ostentation dripping like syrup from every crenellated rooftop and concert hall. Opulence belonged in the church.

He also didn't like being summoned overnight by the papal nuncio, Andone the Summoner of Vatican City! Protocol demanded at least a week's notice, but who followed protocol anymore? Civility was a dying art.

The nuncio was a relative newcomer to these circles. Small wonder he erred. There would have to be an official reckoning when this business was done. The man begged correction. This being ripped from one's important duties by every underling in vestments had to stop. The church was getting sloppy. Andone wouldn't have come at all save for the fact the papal seal was affixed to the request. How had a novice performed that trick?

He smoothed the sleeves of a blue Italian tailored suit and corrected the tilt of the red handkerchief in the breast pocket.

He needn't go to pieces.

He paused before the door marked "Green Parlor" and straightened to his full five feet two inches. Where are the personnel? This leaving everything wide open to vandals is a disgrace. He arranged his features in a suitably irritated scowl, then entered.

To his surprise, he was alone in the room with one individual who stood by the back wall. Andone assumed he was to at least have the courtesy of being introduced.

Sloppy.

The man did not acknowledge Andone's presence. He was pale, stocky, and dressed in tan trousers, tan shirt with a gold pin in the lapel, and black boots with a mirror shine. He wore dark glasses and had not a hair on his polished skull. Arms straight at his sides, he held himself in the manner of the military.

"Sit!" Something menacing in the man's tone left no room for negotiation.

Seething, Andone sat. "Where is the nuncio?" he inquired sharply. "I have traveled from Rome without proper prepar—"

"Silence!" shouted the stocky man without moving. Andone started to rise at such impertinence, then thought better of it. The Holy Father would hear of this outrage.

"Listen carefully for my time is valuable. You're here for one reason and one reason only. You have hired the American Reg Danson to find your precious relics for you. Let me assure you that if you do not order him off the investigation tonight, you will hasten the day of your death."

Andone shot up from the divan like a Roman candle. "I don't know who you are or how you got in here, but let me assure you that our business is now concluded for the evening. As a member of the international diplomatic community, I do not engage in conversation with any unofficial delegation, if that's what you are, nor do I allow myself to be threatened by a person or persons unnamed. Be warned that this will be taken as an affront and explored fully with the constituted authorities. Now if you will excuse me, I need to speak with the Vatican ambassador."

A meaty hand slammed into the monsignor's throat, lifting him off his feet. Andone grabbed for the pin in the man's lapel and was hurled to the floor. The bald man leaped on top of the neat little man, jabbed a thick thumb against Andone's eyeball, and drove one knee into the thin chest. The breastbone threatened to crack and bright multicolored explosions of pain burst inside Andone's eye.

"You're not going anywhere, you pompous peon. Either you call Danson off tonight or we burn the Shroud and melt the spear. And history shall record that one Claudio Andone destroyed Christendom's two most priceless possessions!"

He strode from the room without a backward glance. How could Andone bargain the precious artifacts of Christ? They must not be desecrated or denigrated. Millions looked to them for inspiration and grounding in the faith. They'd been stolen on his watch and now they would be—

He felt something small and hard in his hand. It was a small gold pin in the shape of a lightning bolt. Insignia of the Nazi S.S., the dreaded secret police groomed by Hitler for torture and killing. The insignia of Kaspar! *Unthinkable!* The vermin had to be brought to justice just as Hitler and his kind were hunted down and made to pay for their crimes against humanity.

There was no turning back.

Andone ran from the room, calling on St. Augustine, St. Jerome, St. Ignatius, and the rest to lead a heavenly force against the evil assailing the church.

He ran into the dark streets outside the embassy, tripping over his leather Italian loafers, calling after the receding figure of the bald man. "In the name of God, I will *not* do what you demand! Reg Danson will find you and drain your pool of scum once and for all! You cannot win against the power *behind* the spear!"

The man did not break stride nor look back. He turned a

corner and disappeared. Andone stood in the street cold, alone, unsure, the pain in his chest sharp and insistent. Something was cracked. A car honked and swerved to miss him, but he did not care. He stood there for three or four minutes, peering at the corner where he last saw the bald man.

At last Claudio Andone turned and started walking. He had no particular destination, only knew that if he went anywhere near a telephone, he would call whoever it took to stop Reg Danson. Was it the relics or his reputation he cared for the most? *Keep moving.* Stop, and his mind would answer the question.

Lost in thought, the Vatican's under-secretary for foreign relations did not hear the rushing of tires, the motor's sudden acceleration. He was hit in the right side and hurled over a parked vehicle outside the Savoy *Konditorei.* The windows of the pastry shop were brightly lit and frosted to look like winter ice. Delights of spun sugar and rich cakes awaited the traditional mound of *Schlagobers,* a fluffy, freshly whipped cream. The kind of place Andone, alive, would never have been caught dead.

The pastry patrons abandoned their warm refreshment and found the body on the sidewalk, bright red handkerchief still smartly in place. The police were called and a news reporter who happened to be inside having a chocolate confection wrote the story up on paper towels from the men's room. Two hours later, the body, the police, and the patrons all left. The lights went off and the owner locked up.

Routine hit-and-run, if it hadn't been a Vatican official. International diplomacy was a sticky business under ideal conditions. Who knew what the poor old man had been up to? Time alone would tell.

The police had been thorough. But it would take the coroner to make something of the bruise over the breastbone with its hairline fracture and the burst blood vessels in the eye, apparently unrelated to the automobile mishap.

But all in all a tidy first day of police procedure. In fact, only one other small item had they overlooked. Near the storm grate opposite the pastry shop rested a small lapel pin in the form of a golden lightning bolt.

CHAPTER 13

Tony Danson thought the ringing of the phone was the big old alley cat on the back fence of his dream about Kathleen Snow, the dazzling serving girl at Gadsby's Tavern. They were walking the top of the fence like aerial artists when she slipped and fell and he had to rescue her from . . . from gorillas dressed like clowns riding motorcycles with sidecars. Each sidecar contained one of the Three Stooges.

Man, I've got to give up either pepperoni pizza with anchovies or late night classic comedies.

Try as he might, he could not rewind to that part of the dream where she fell and he leapt to her side without a single thought for his own personal safety. He hated it when dreams wouldn't hold still at the best parts but insisted rather on careening off into bizarre territory where nothing at all made any sense.

Except for the ringing of the phone. As sleep fled to another room, it was obvious that the sound was the one real part of the dream. He'd have to analyze the alley cat symbolism later—and find the phone number for Gadsby's. Miss Snow must surely be frantic for word of her gentleman friend.

Getting up, Tony frowned. The room stank of anchovies.

"All right, all right, I'm coming!" Tony was sleeping in his dad's bed so he didn't have far to go, but there was a family size pizza box between him and the alley cat. He sailed the box like a Frisbee into the bathroom and pounced on the jangling cat.

"Hello, this is the Danson residence."

It was a bad connection, static and fuzz, rendering the caller faint and distant. "Tony . . . come quickly. Need you now . . . first flight out . . . meet . . . Rathaus . . . Vienna . . ." The line went dead.

Heart racing, Tony said a quick prayer and pawed through the debris on the nightstand searching for the paper with his dad's Vienna phone number. It was the last one, securely stuck to the nightstand by a ring of spilled cola. "You'd be proud of me, Mom," he said to her photo on the nightstand. "Right by the phone where you told me always to keep the most important numbers."

He dialed the international number. After what seemed an eternity of overseas switchings and clickings, Tony heard, "Rathaus, Vienna." The connection was still poor.

"Yes, uh, *bitte, konnen Sie—*"

"Excuse me, sir, but English is spoken here. May I help you?"

"Oh, yes, can you tell me please if you have a Reg Danson from America registered?"

The hotel clerk replied, "A Mr. Danson from Seattle, Washington?"

"Yes! That's him! He is with you, then?"

"Yes, he is fully registered. He asked assistance in making an overseas telephone call just now to his home in America."

Tony felt sheepish asking, but in light of recent events, better safe than beaten. "How can you be certain it was him? This is his son."

"He showed his passport when registering in order to bill the room to the Vatican Embassy. I happened also to see a photo of his deceased wife—your mother?—and commented to him on her loveliness. I comment on the same to you. Obviously the woman was the pride of his life!"

Tony felt a yank of recognition. *It has to be Dad. He loves showing off photos of Mom and me.*

"He said you might call back to verify. He said to tell you to come. Urgent! He was somewhat agitated and most adamant."

"Please tell him I am on my way."

"Will there be anything else?"

"Yeah, tell him—tell him to take good care of himself."

Tony called the airline, then plowed through his father's drawers looking for clean socks and underwear. He'd managed a pair of boxers and one sock when he saw the note from Leo stuck to the mirror with gum. "Hey, kid, I've gone to clean up the joint. Make yerself some Cheerios and I'll bring soup for lunch." Tony felt a momentary stab of guilt. He wouldn't be there for lunch. And he didn't want to argue with Leo about it.

Tony finished dressing, scribbled a hasty note of explanation, and stuck it back on the gum. He threw necessities into an overnight bag, closed the front door behind him, and nearly collided with a girl coming up the stairs. She wore army fatigues and black jackboots, hair shaved up one side and streaked orange. Metal swastikas dangled from her right ear, rattling in the breeze. The letters "WWRR" glared from her cheek like an ugly boil.

They eyed each other warily, unsure what to say. She stuffed her hands in the pockets of the flak jacket and gave Tony the once over. "Except for the part of your face that resembles a punching bag, I'd say you were Danson's kid."

"Bingo!" said Tony, anxious to get away.

"You even use the same strong language he does," she said with a sarcastic little smile. "Where you off to in such a hurry?"

"Uh . . . milk. Yeah, we're out of milk. Gotta go get some." He pointed vaguely in the direction of the nearest grocery.

"Do you always pack a bag for a trip to the store?"

He looked at her and grinned despite himself. "Always was a lousy liar."

"That's 'cause Christians don't lie." She looked past him, trying to see inside the house. "Your dad home?"

"No, actually, he's away on business. Who shall I say called?"

Her smile broadened and she laughed. "Boy, you are really bad. Do you get out much?"

She was beginning to get irritating. Besides, Tony guessed who she was and he didn't like it one bit. "You must be the Connie my dad told me about. The Connie who taunts black people. The Connie who worships Kaspar. The Connie who hangs out with the kind of people who use other people as punching bags!"

Connie looked crestfallen and her eyes teared up. "Yeah, that's the part I don't like. When people you know, and care about, get hurt."

"You don't care about me or my dad," Tony said hotly. "In fact, how do I know you're not here to bomb our house or that your good friends aren't lurking in the bushes somewhere ready to finish what they started with me?"

She bit back the first thing that came to mind. Instead, she looked away to the street and beyond. "Do you think this has any chance of becoming a serious relationship?" She looked back at him and smiled bravely.

He couldn't help smiling back. "In another time and place, with a change of clothes and a different hairdo, maybe . . ."

She crossed her arms and traced an imaginary star on the porch with the toe of a badly scuffed boot. "So you don't think my mother dresses me?"

"Uh, hardly. Look, I don't mean to be a jerk, but I really need to be going. I literally have a plane to catch. Later on, if you want to talk, well . . . I'll think on it."

"Your father's a good man," she said, a quiver in her voice. "He took time with me and listened, even though he didn't much like what I had to say. The way he helped that black guy and stood up to us . . . well, if you're anything like him, you're lucky."

She seemed vulnerable, nothing like the costume.

"I don't know if I could ever be like him exactly," Tony said, setting his overnight bag on the railing. "But you're right about him being a good guy. He's the best."

"Is that where you're going, to be with him?"

Startled, he looked sharply at her, trying to fathom any treachery in her eyes. He saw none that he recognized. He sagged against the railing, surprised at how much he wanted—needed—to talk to someone about the sudden phone call. "He insisted I *not* come with him before, that I stay here and recuperate from the beating. You know about that?" He saw from the embarrassed way she studied the toe of her boot that she did. "But just now he called and said come, that he needs me urgently. But he wouldn't—or couldn't—talk with me about it. His voice sounded real faint and kind of funny, not quite like him. And when I called back, he'd just left, but not without repeating the message to the hotel clerk like he was fully expecting me to call back. I'm worried."

"I don't blame you. That's why I came over here. Things have gotten kind of . . . kind of rough with my people, and it's not healthy for a girl to hang out there. I think something big's about to happen. I think the revolution's about to break."

"The worldwide race revolution?" Tony said, only half mocking.

She nodded and looked away from him, her chin buried in the neck of the oversized jacket. "I'm almost sorry I ever heard that term."

"Almost?"

She looked up, chin quivering, eyes full with tears. When she looked at him, the tears spilled over. "Funny thing about conquest," she said, with difficulty. "It sounds real good on paper. It rolls nicely off the tongue. It makes wonderful sense until you've lived with a conqueror and washed his underwear. It's not too many days before you see past the fine, blond slogan-spouting exterior to the cancer underneath. There you find this dark and spongy mass of contradictions." She hesitated, wiping her nose on a sleeve. She slumped to the porch floor and held her head. "You haven't lived until you've been called 'slut' and fetched a lead pipe for the master." Her voice was bitter with defeat. "You can't imagine what a turn-on it is to watch him take that pipe and slash a watermelon to pulp knowing he'll do the same to the head of his next victim. And then to have him turn to you with longing and feel the wet, sour lips—" She broke off, lost in the horror.

Tony thought of the thugs and the automatic, remorseless way they had assaulted him, a man they didn't even know. To think of them doing that, or worse, to Connie made his stomach turn over. Their conquest was not about race. It was about dominance. "I'm sorry, Connie," he said quietly. "These maniacs eat their young. Each is out to gain as much as he can for himself. Red or yellow, black or white—race is just the smoke screen for a giant power grab."

Connie jerked to her feet, eyes ablaze. "Racial purity *is* the highest principle!" she shouted. Then, in a strange, dispassionate monotone: "Mixing of blood was the original sin that caused our loss of place in paradise. Pure racial stock unites. Racial contamination divides. There is no revolution that is not racial. It is *not* about economics, politics, or social upheaval. It is always the struggle of the weak, lower races against the dominant, higher races! Beware the Jew peril! Beware the Negro peril! Beware the—"

He grabbed her arms and shook her. "Stop it, Connie. Stop it! They've brainwashed you to think this way so you won't see the truth. They want to rule the world and to rule it by force. Originality, creativity, independent thought—none of that can be tolerated in their world, don't you see? Your personality, your imagination, your ideas must all be absorbed by the machine they have made. Don't you see that it's already begun? You repeat their garbage at the push of a button. Come on, you're much too intelligent to be their puppet. And much too pretty to go around looking like the creature from the Nazi lagoon!"

She was herself again. "Is that what this is all about? I used the wrong eye shadow?"

He released her and turned away, embarrassed. He hadn't meant to get so riled. Nazi sympathizers weren't his type. "It's not funny. You've got too much to offer to waste your talents sowing prejudice."

"Talents?" she scoffed. "Let's see, I can march in step, make jewelry with an attitude"—she jangled the swastikas in her ear for effect—"and say 'Shut your ugly face' in German. Now if I could just type . . ."

Disheartened, Tony slung the backpack over one shoulder and started down the steps. "Good, Connie. If hate doesn't work, there's always ridicule. I've got a plane to catch."

"Take me with you!"

She stood on the top step, painted and shaved like a trick-or-treater out of season. The army fatigues drooped on the thin frame, a pathetic scarecrow losing its stuffing. And still Tony could see the girl inside. Something his mom had said long ago to an impatient little boy came unbidden now: "Don't judge a book by its cover. Once you get past the first few pages, you may find an enchanting story." *Oh, Mom, you oughtta get a load of this book's cover!*

He kept going and reached the sidewalk. "Can't. Connie the Skinhead's too much of a risk. See ya later."

"Quitter!" she screamed.

Tony stopped.

"Yeah, you!" She was half yelling, half crying. "I'd thought I was a prime candidate for a little of your Christian charity. Wouldn't I make a prize convert? Think of how I'd play at one of those nice, clean-cut youth rallies! 'Come hear the former street queen tell of a life in the sewers of degradation! See how overnight the power of

God transformed one kitten-stomping, Jew-baiting, Hitler babe into a loving, cookie-baking, stand-by-her-man paragon of virtue! Let us pray.'"

She averted her eyes from the hurt in his. "Sorry," she said. "You didn't deserve that. I'm afraid, okay? I think it's likely our first meeting could be our last. I don't want it to be. I think the signal's coming down in the next couple of days, and when it does, you better hope you're stranded on a desert island. So you can't really blame a girl for thinking a trip to Austria with the handsome young son of a world adventurer has a nicer ring to it."

He grinned despite the surreal conversation. "Handsome?"

She grinned back. "Well, yeah, relatively speaking. Compared to guys who don't flush and think charm comes in a six-pack."

"Look, I'd say come but I—I've never traveled with a . . . a . . ."

"Neo-Nazi. Go ahead, say it. *Knee-o friggin' knots-ee.* If it'll make you feel any better, we can take separate planes." She hopped down the stairs and came over to him. She was still grinning hopefully.

Tony shook his head. "No, I mean *female.* I've never gone away with one—a female, that is—other than my mother. It wouldn't be right." He looked disconcerted.

Connie hooted in delight. "This ain't no tryst, Tarzan. Strictly business. I speak the language of the lunatic, and you know all the Boy Scout stuff. Together, maybe we can do your father some good."

Tony still wasn't sure. "You'll have to pack, won't you?"

"Done!"

He looked her over dubiously. "What about a toothbrush?"

"Ta-dah!" She produced a pink-handled one from a side pocket. "You'd be amazed all you can fit into one of Uncle Sammy's dinner jackets. Gotta spare pair of socks in here, some rock-hard mascara, my passport, couple of linty breath mints—wintergreen, I think. Ten minutes in a youth hostel and I'm fresh as a daisy. Promise!"

Tony tried one last objection. "And just how are you paying for your trip over?"

"Same as you. The Tony Danson trust fund. College can wait when adventure calls!"

The taxi pulled to the curb with a squeal of brakes. Tony thought a moment, opened the rear door, and stepped back. "After you, Constance." At that moment, hair and all, she smiled more beautifully than did Miss Snow at Gadsby's Tavern.

The cab driver did a double take at the bizarre, tear-streaked fare in the rearview mirror. They caught his startled look. Tony quickly took Connie's hand. "My dear Scarlett, don't you fear," he said loudly. "We will find the scoundrel who did this to you. But darlin', why do you suppose he shaved but one half of your pretty little head?"

Connie fussed dramatically. "Oh, Rhett, dear Rhett! It was simply awful. The rogue had but one eye so that the hair on the other half was on his blind side!"

Tony turned from anxious to grim. "Driver! The airport, if you please. Justice demands to be served!"

The cabby shook his head. Kids!

At the corner, the taxi turned in front of a weathered, bandy-legged fellow making his cautious way across the street with a kettle of steaming ham and navy bean soup. He halted with a slosh to let the vehicle pass and heard peals of laughter erupt from inside the cab. Leo Slugitt frowned at the sounds of carefree youth. "Devilment!" he muttered crankily.

The soup stopped slopping, and he resumed his mission of mercy. Ham and navy bean soup was just what the doctor ordered for poor, sore Tony Danson.

CHAPTER 14

Reg Danson could not sleep. Something primal in him wanted—demanded—the clank of armor, the battle clamor of orders and threats. He wanted a host of heaven to *crush* Kaspar. He craved the mighty shout that reduced the walls of Jericho to rubble. He needed the noise of the Lord Almighty triumphant!

Not this silence. Not this smothering, stagnant nothing.

Valor did not go to bed. The just did not slumber.

Danson threw back the covers and sat up. The very silence was a threat. Inaction was a poison. He jumped from the thick, downy comfort of the old brass bed, snapped on the table lamp, and padded restlessly over the cool smoothness of the hardwood floor.

He was somewhere deep within the inner recesses of the sprawling estate where Frau Heppler left him. "You will want to remain in your room, Herr Danson," she admonished before closing the door. "It is not advisable to wander at night in a strange house." He badly wanted to ask if she meant *unfamiliar* strange or *peculiar* strange, but he already knew.

Alien strange.

Even the ticking of the grandfather clock did not penetrate

here. Quarantine. It felt like quarantine—no one allowed in, no one out. He was an untouchable, a plague carrier.

Uninhabited. The house felt devoid of human life.

Or was it her he missed?

He sneered at the reflection in the oval dressing mirror, then dropped his eyes. This was absurd. He couldn't even face himself.

He hurried to the door to try the knob. It turned and quickly he shut it again. *I've watched too many B movies where the victim's locked in by an evil keeper.* He went back to the mirror and pointed a finger at the reflection. "You *do* miss her! Two hours with her and she has you eating out of her hand. Are you so gullible?"

He paced and listened to his pulse race. "God, have I done all I can do? Richard Bascomb thinks Lady Katherine's an answer to prayer. I'm acting like she's an answer to prayer all right, but not the kind he means. Did you bring me all the way to Nuremberg to leave it in her hands? Or is there something I've overlooked? You can see Kaspar right now, Lord. You know what he's thinking and plotting. Show him to me!"

The light from the table lamp fell on his Bible and he picked it up. He turned to the story of the fall of Jericho. He was arrested by the words of Joshua, the commander of the people of Israel: "You shall not shout or make any noise with your voice, nor shall a word proceed out of your mouth, until the day I say to you, 'Shout!' Then you shall shout." Reg eyed the reflection in the mirror and saw that his mouth was open. He shut it.

For six days, he read, hundreds of thousands of people marched around the fortified city of Jericho in silence except for the blowing of rams' horns.

It was not until that seventh day that the people, in unison, shouted down those mighty, impenetrable walls in exact obedience to God's orders delivered through Joshua.

Reg Danson would have to learn patience.

But he was uneasy. Lady Katherine was an enigma. One minute

she sounded like Mother Teresa, the next like Attila the Hun. One minute defending Hitler's views on racial segregation, the next castigating his methods. How could she be both a defender of Jews and a proponent of forced ethnicity? And where was her staff? It had to take a great deal of paperwork and shuttle diplomacy to process so many applicants for relocation.

The beautiful, beguiling strains of the harp came to mind. The flying fingers of exquisite workmanship, the attractive, seductive woman . . .

"You fool!" he berated himself, noticing for the first time that the room had no windows. "She takes you in, treats you kindly, promises you all the resources within her power to find the madman, and the highest compliment you can pay is to call her a seductress. Remind me never to invite you to dinner!" Of course she had far more contacts and much more hope of locating Kaspar than he did. She had been cultivating a network of eyes and ears for many years while Reg had been slogging through steaming jungles and climbing treacherous mountains in search of answers to life's more esoteric riddles. What did he know of the dark places where she and those she helped had been—or what it had taken to survive? She of all people knew what made a hatemonger tick.

He was too quick to judge.

Still, sleep would not come. He felt hot. He wrestled the bedclothes into twisted lumps. He punched the mattress in frustration. "When Frau Heppler comes to make the bed tomorrow, what's she going to think?" He sat on the bed with the Bible open before him. The paintings on the bedroom walls were every bit as dim and somber as those in the sitting room, but less grotesque. A joyless Christ carrying a joyless sheep. A dangerously listing ship on a storm-tossed sea. That was another thing that didn't match. A captivating, empathetic woman with a taste for the morose?

He turned to the twenty-sixth chapter of the Gospel of St.

Matthew, idly browsing for the part Katherine said mentioned the communal dish, like the one they had dipped from at dinner.

"When evening had come, He sat down with the twelve. Now as they were eating, He said, 'Assuredly, I say to you, one of you will betray Me.' And they were exceedingly sorrowful, and each of them began to say to Him, 'Lord, is it I?' He answered and said, 'He who dipped his hand with Me in the dish will betray Me.'"

Reg started. He'd forgotten this link to Judas the Betrayer. The passage cross-referenced to the forty-first Psalm. He turned there and read: "Even my own familiar friend in whom I trusted, who ate my bread, has lifted up his heel against me."

Oddly rattled, Reg closed the Bible and sat back, hugging his knees to his chest. "This old house is getting to me," he said aloud, just to hear a voice. He let out a little explosion of air that was meant to be a laugh.

He stretched out on the floor, allowing the cool wood to draw the heat from his bare back and legs. He closed his eyes and tried not to think of the tossing ship or the cruel Father Hitler or the Jesus that did not smile. Flashes from dinner crossed his mind, her soft, perfectly formed hand brushing his brawny, calloused one. He turned over and started doing push-ups to rid his mind of a thought he wouldn't dignify by putting it into words. It was the house. Nothing good lighting and several coats of white paint wouldn't fix.

Or cover up.

He flipped over and started situps, double time, his labored breath another sign of life. Seventy-one . . . eighty-two . . . ninety-six . . . He kept at it until the sweat poured from him and he began seeing red. He lay back and watched the rise and fall of his rib cage. "Another wild night in Nuremberg!" he said, giving his belly a hard slap. It wasn't quite flat, but not bad for a guy staring down the barrel of a fortieth birthday.

Reg flopped face-first onto the bed, trying to find relief. He wondered if he were running a fever. Maybe he should go soak his head in the wash basin. He wondered if Frau Heppler was on hall patrol.

He pulled on a pair of sweatpants, smoothed his hair in the mirror, and was about to brave the hall when he thought better of it. He added a white T-shirt to his ensemble, checked himself once more in the mirror, pronounced it good, and opened the door.

He was instantly struck by the chill. The hall floor felt stone cold on bare feet and he stepped lively, closing the door behind him. The depth of the darkness was disorienting, and before many steps, Danson was not at all certain where he was or if in fact he was headed toward the bathroom. An amusing picture formed in his mind of a confrontation with Frau Heppler the next morning in which he took her to task for forgetting to leave a night-light on for the guest.

Breathing. Someone near, breathing. "Oh, hello, Katherine?" Silence. "Frau Heppler?" Nothing. He put out a hand and felt the rough masonry of the wall. The place was built like a castle. All strength and little warmth. He touched fur.

Startled, Reg reared back and fell to the floor, his face buried in coarse fur. *A coat.* He'd found a coatrack near the side service entrance. Wrong way.

An emptiness stretched to his left. Another hall, dark and fathomless. He'd stick with the one he was in.

Something told him to return to the room. He groped along the wall, his fingers closing at last on a doorknob. It turned, but did not open. A bit farther along, he felt another. The door swung open, but instead of welcoming light, there was more yawning darkness.

"Bloody barn!" he grumped, feeling for a light switch. None. He closed the door. Maybe he had remembered to pack a flashlight.

Where is the bedroom?

He started forward again, rammed a toe against a heating grate, and collided with a hall table. The table tipped over and in trying to stop its fall, Reg pitched forward and slammed forehead-first into the wall.

Instead of awakening the dead, however, there was dead silence. He lay there until his dazed senses cleared. A trickle of blood leaked into one eye. He stripped off the T-shirt and pressed it against the cut. But there was nothing, nothing at all, to apply to the tremor of fear creeping up from the base of his spine.

The ears pricked forward, alert to the distant crash. Muscles in the animal's chest bunched tautly, every nerve at attention. The powerful hindquarters stretched into a long, angular lean forward, the tail held rigid between the hock bones. Part wolf, part canine, it sniffed the cold air for answers.

Man scent, heated, filled the nostrils with stink. Unauthorized man.

The animal moved forward. Bred to a heightened awareness, it was not subject to easy distraction. Attack-trained, it was expertly agitated to distinguish actions, motives, intent. It also knew what was out of place and what things demanded enforcement.

Licking its muzzle, the animal ascended the ramp leading from its chambers to the upper house. It moved deliberately with stealth. The intruder needed to be far enough inside the estate so that retreat could be effectively cut off. In the wilds, rushing the prey too soon meant starvation. Wait patiently and the fight would come all of its own.

Control.

"Katherine!" He called her name for the fifth time. For the fifth time, his call met the same pressing silence. In his mind, he held her still and again experienced the warmth and sheen of her hair, the downy nape of her neck . . . They had said their good nights shortly thereafter, agreeing without saying so that rest and a new day was a wiser course than to remain. "Love is a flame, a devil's thing," he recited, a snippet of long-forgotten English lit come back to haunt him. Things were rapidly taking on the weirdness of a Macbethan tragedy.

He struggled to his feet and waited for the dizziness to subside. Tony could find his way back to bed from the bathroom at age two, so what was Pop Danson's problem? The problem was he hadn't yet found the bathroom. He was lost somewhere in between.

He groped along the hallway, bare toes probing the hardwood path, a man unsure how close he is to the edge of the cliff.

Reg needed a stiff dose of his mother's homespun practicality. He continued along the wall, trying to lead with his hand instead of his foot.

With enormous relief, he at last felt the familiarity of a light switch and flipped it up.

Nothing.

He jiggled the switch. Nothing. The gloom darkened another shade.

Defective? Power failure?

Deliberate.

His brain didn't bother to pose it as a question. He *had* heard someone breathing. That someone knew he was there and cut the power.

"The Lord is my shepherd," Reg began and resolutely moved forward. "I don't know what's up ahead, but you know. Clear me a path."

The wall made an abrupt left. The floor slanted downward and the air cooled another couple of degrees. A faint light showed against the wall at the far end of the passage where it again turned left and down.

Reg froze.

Silhouetted in the light on the wall was the feral form of an animal coming up the passage toward him, growing larger one calculated step at a time.

It was in no hurry. It was . . . *listening.* When Danson stopped, it stopped.

He fought not to yell.

He was being stalked—by a wolf.

The animal started forward of its own accord, creeping low to the floor, the smell of man fear strong in its nostrils.

Danson gauged his chances. Could he outrun it? Where would he run to? *The service entrance near the coatrack!* If he stayed, he would need a blunt object to fight with. He cast about frantically for something, anything. The animal was almost to the corner. *Dear God!*

He ran. Ran for his life, stumbling on the incline, bare feet slipping on the slick hardwood surface. He made it to the top and tore to the right, the sound of thick nails clicking madly behind as four feet fought for a purchase on the flooring.

The creature had rushed its quarry and the man taken flight too early. That instinct added strength to the surging hindquarters.

Reg careened down the hallway, colliding with tables and lamps. He fell, got up, and fell again. The creature turned the corner and gained sure footing on the now level plain. Its night vision bore into the back of the man's head. It snarled in savage anticipation.

Danson crashed into a bookcase, negotiated around it, and pulled it over behind him. *The coatrack! The service door is just beyond it!*

The creature hurdled the dumped books, saw in an instant its quarry's escape hatch, and veered off into the side hall next to the coatrack.

Reg stopped. The sound of the mournful harp floated through the wall beside him. He looked back. The wolf had vanished. *Thank you, my provider,* Reg prayed. He turned back to the service door and yelled.

The canine stood at the door, coil spring muscles tensed for attack. Danson had been outflanked, outwitted by an animal a great deal more familiar with the layout of the Gates of Hope than a visitor.

The beast lunged at the man.

Reg screamed and dove against the nearest door. He felt a stab of pain in the right calf and heard the ripping of cloth, but the door gave.

He crashed through into the sitting room and nearly knocked Lady Katherine from her stool at the harp. She gasped. Her face a mixture of surprised shock and iron will, she snapped, *"Zwanzig!"* and rushed to close the door.

Reg's head was swimming.

"Oh, you've been hurt!" she cried, kneeling beside him. Reg pulled back from her touch and applied the T-shirt from his cut forehead to the tooth marks on his calf. "Yeow!"

Katherine summoned Frau Heppler and the necessary medicine for cleaning and dressing the wound. "I'm afraid your pants leg is shorter by some," she said apologetically when finished.

"Better my pants than my leg!" Reg moaned. He wrapped the fringed sofa cover around his shirtless torso. "Can you explain to me why I wasn't warned about that man-eater and why no one answered my shouts and why there's no electricity in that hallway and what's down beneath this place anyway and—"

Katherine held up a hand and laughed infectiously. "Stop! Your mouth exceeds the speed limit. This is not the autobahn!"

He eyed her sternly and waited.

She sighed, sat on the sofa beside him, and patted the good leg. "You have been treated rather badly since supper," she said, a gleam in her eye. "Frankly, two women alone in this big house need the protection the shepherd affords, especially in the current—ah—cultural climate. And as we just met this evening, I couldn't be entirely certain of your intentions."

She stopped his protestations with another wave of her hand. "You don't know the half of what I've seen and heard, Reg. You could be a very clever decoy sent by the hatemongers to convince me to drop my guard, then in they come and *poof!* They would steal my photos and my records and set the work back many months. All I've worked for would come to a halt."

Lady Katherine arched her eyebrows and waggled a finger at him. "Frau Heppler told you not to go roaming at night."

"She failed to mention that to do so might mean a German shepherd plastered to my backside!"

Lady Katherine looked at Frau Heppler, who immediately withdrew from the room, melting into the unlighted recesses of the house from which she had materialized. "This old house is difficult to heat and light," said Katherine apologetically. "I'm afraid I spend very little on maintenance—the wiring is frightfully old and the fuses have to be specially ordered. I resent a single dollar going for anything but rescuing my dear lambs."

His bandaged leg propped on the tea table, Danson pulled the fringed sofa cover more tightly around his bare shoulders and eyed her green silk dressing gown and carefully maintained appearance. "I saw light coming from somewhere below." Reg fought not to look at her softness, the way the lamplight shimmered on green silk.

Lady Katherine took her seat at the harp. The elegant fingers brushed the strings, delicate as a mother strokes infant cheeks. She crooned to it, a tender lullaby. She wove her reply to him in snippets of melody.

"The Gates of Hope sits atop the underground bombproof vaults of Hitler—la la dee, la la dee—his secret hiding place for the Habsburg regalia including the Holy Lance. La dee, la dee, la la la dee dum de la. On April 16, 1945, the American Seventh Army surrounded the city and its 22,000 S.S. troops, one hundred Panzer tanks, and twenty-two regiments of artillery. Dee dee, la la dee dee da dum. For four terrifying days the American Thunderbird Division pounded away, then broke through to victory. The date was April twentieth—Hitler's fifty-sixth birthday."

She stopped playing and leaned back in the chair, lovely gray-green eyes distant and oddly moist. "Lieutenant William Horn, commander of Company C of the U.S. Army's Third Military Government Regiment, led his men in a search for the Habsburg treasure. A hundred yards from here they discovered that a shell had blown the way through the brickwork to the entrance of a series of underground vaults. Blasting through a set of steel doors, they entered an underground chamber containing the Hitler horde—the fabulous wealth of the Habsburg dynasty. But Lieutenant Horn passed up the glittering, bejeweled fortune to stand before a bed of faded red velvet upon which lay the fabled spear of Longinus the Roman centurion. He reached out a trembling hand and took possession of the Lance in the name of the United States government."

Reg momentarily forgot his injury and limped over to stand by her, eyes aflame with the excitement of discovery. "You mean just now I was on my way down to the treasure room of the Third Reich?"

She looked up at the eager, little-boy enthusiasm wrapped in a sofa cover, and chuckled. "Yes, Commander Magellan," she teased, "if only you hadn't tangled with the local fauna, you might have discovered some very big and very empty rooms!"

He looked annoyed. "I don't see what's so funny. This is where history was made."

She fought to keep a straight face. "Yes, history was made here. I just don't think it was made by a barefoot man dressed in a fringe shawl and torn jogging trousers!"

He laughed with her, wanting to suppress the feeling that something was amiss.

"The German government is restoring the vaults, hoping one day to use this house as a tour center. Apparently, it was used for a brief time during the war as a Nazi communications center and secret entrance to the underground chambers. But the preservation funds keep running out. They've been at the project for years. You do have an overactive imagination." She smiled innocently up at him.

Part of him wanted badly to trust this woman with his life.

Flashes of the terror in the hallway were not easily forced from his mind, but his feelings for her were strong enough for the task. The sofa cover slipped from his shoulders and fell to his lap.

"Play," he said huskily, forcing himself away. He sank into a chair facing the painting of the Crucifixion, wanting at all costs to avoid the disapproving gaze of Alois Hitler. She looked at him curiously before weaving another spell on the strings, a complex syncopated piece interspersed with elaborate trills and sweeping glissandos of sound.

"The music of Paraguay by the Austrian Jesuit Antonio Sepp von Reinegg," she explained during a soft interlude. "Paraguayan harpists can imitate bird calls, drum rolls, the beating of a butterfly's wings"—she demonstrated each with a flourish—"even the sobbing of a young girl." She drew a wrenching sound of heartbreak from the strings, then slid into a moody, desolate refrain that rose and fell in waves of grief.

"Don't." Reg said it without thinking, a reflex reaction to the intense regret being wrung from the harp.

"I can't help it," Katherine said, her cheeks wet with tears. "So many great men of history have rued the day they came in contact with the spear. Charlemagne carried it into forty-seven victorious campaigns. On the forty-eighth, he accidentally dropped it and died. The charismatic Frederick Barbarossa used the spear to bring all of Italy and the church to its knees, but stumbled while wading a stream in Sicily, dropped the Lance, and within minutes was dead. And on the very day that Lieutenant William Horn seized the Lance for America, Adolf Hitler committed suicide in a Berlin bunker."

The notes comprised a funeral dirge. Katherine's shoulders slumped in defeat, the lovely hair obscuring her face behind a veil of regret.

Troubled, Reg went to her, grabbed the gentle hands, and stopped the music. "You needn't weep for Hitler, Lady Katherine."

She looked deep inside him, sorrow vandalizing her beauty. "So much waste," she whispered. "So much potential squandered for personal gain. I weep for the wasted opportunity to lead a people up out of the mire of defeat and give them back their respect. I weep for the wasted opportunity of the church to inspire a people to stop a madman and to fashion a new nation from self-sacrifice. I weep for a world wasted by hatred—"

She sighed heavily. "I don't know what Hitler was. He claimed to be able to see beyond this earthly dimension, and I don't doubt it. A young German freedom fighter in World War I, 'something' told him to leave his trench position just moments before an artillery round blew the position to pieces. Again, in 1939, a bomb shattered the speaker's platform of a beer hall in Munich just minutes after Hitler had departed the area. Six days prior, Swiss astrologer Karl Krafft had predicted peril for the German leader at almost that exact moment. Hitler had taken the prediction to heart. For public consumption, however, *der Fuehrer* had the poor man thoroughly investigated as an accomplice in the bombing."

Reg released her hands and laughed mirthlessly. "I know the end to that one. Later, Hitler's security goons hired Krafft to study the stars and chart the future of the Nazi party!"

Katherine continued to play softly, the sweet strings hard-pressed to counter the Nazi insanity.

"They say there is healing in the harp," she said. "Sometimes music is prescribed for the terminally ill. A harp at their bedside can, at the very least, ease the departure. Some music is so stunning that it almost stops the heart. When the great composer Rachmaninoff heard his third concerto performed by Vladimir Horowitz, he was so moved that he himself refused to ever play it again!"

Reg cast the fringed sofa cover aside. "Enough, Katherine! Nero fiddled while Rome burned. We cannot sit here whiling away the hours while Kaspar prepares for Armageddon. Don't you read the papers? White supremacists at the University of East Germany are using medical cadavers in crush experiments to determine how much pressure human bones can withstand before snapping. It is nothing more than refined torture techniques for subduing the races under Kaspar's tyranny!

"Who are your contacts? I must meet with them now. Whatever it takes, Katherine. Blindfolded, if that's the way they want it. I have to be there when they pinpoint Kaspar. We've got to isolate him and corner the renegade now. We haven't any time left!"

Katherine jumped to her feet, arms folded, face rigid, as dangerous as molten steel. "You really don't know what you're up against, do you? Nuremberg is crawling with hate." She pointed to a silver dollar-sized bare spot in the wallpaper, freshly puttied. "Two nights ago someone shot out my front window, the bullet lodging there. Yesterday, Frau Heppler found Kaspar's calling card pinned to the front door with a knife. Read it!"

She opened a drawer in the tea stand and handed him a copy of the by now too familiar white card, only this one possessed a jagged tear through the lightning bolt. On the back, the German word *"Halt!* Stop!" was handwritten with what looked like *"Hizb ut-Tahrir"* beneath.

He looked at her quizzically. She did not meet his gaze. "Assassins!" she said, hissing the *s*'s. "The *Hizb ut-Tahrir* is the extremist Muslim Liberation Party that systematically targets Jews for extermination—one at a time. The MLP is virulently anti-Christian. They have attempted coups in Iraq, Jordan, Syria, and Tunisia to form a pan-Islamic state under rabid Islamic law. The MLP is so despised that membership carries the death penalty in Iraq.

"If Kaspar has aligned with the MLP, then we dare not leave this place."

"What?!" Reg said angrily. "You got me to come here knowing this? I won't be a prisoner to Kaspar's hatred! We'll call the police and have them scour the city and burn every filthy neo-Nazi nest they find!" He snatched up the bloody T-shirt. He would pay the police commandant a personal visit.

She held out a hand to stop him. "This is the safest place for you right now. And what use are the police? Look how thoroughly they mishandled things in Vienna. One of the greatest ancient relics in existence was taken from beneath their very noses! They are powerless to perform little more than cleanup duty for the flood of hate crimes that pollute this nation. They couldn't protect us from our own shadows. In fact, they could end up *getting* us killed!"

"The government, then. We'll convince the chancellor to place the country under martial law. The army can do a house-to-house search and flush them out."

Katherine looked at him as if he were delirious. "*This* government? This Christian Democratic Party whose only pick for president is the extremist Karl Verheugen? He counts the number of foreigners living in Germany and equates it to the number of jobs 'stolen' from the German people. The Social Democrats are no better. Thanks to their leadership, the country reeks with eighty right-wing extremist groups with a total membership of fifty thousand. Drive the hate underground and they communicate by car phone or modem."

Reg eyed the beautiful mistress of Jewish repatriation. *Something oddly rehearsed about her.* "The German state has prohibited the publication of hate material," he said. "German security forces regularly seize tons of neo-Nazi leaflets, posters, and newspapers shipped from the United States. They have made great strides in helping the American FBI prosecute the printers of that filth. A man is free to print hate in the U.S.A., but he cannot use it to aid or abet a crime of hate."

Katherine waved her hand in dismissal. "The so-called 'Farmbelt Fuehrer' continues to print *The United Order* out of a barn in Nebraska. Its German circulation alone is estimated at twenty-five thousand. The 'Harrisburg Hatemeister' enchants thousands of German neo-Nazis from his hardware store in Pennsylvania by claiming to unmask the Holocaust lie. I tell you, our only hope is to take matters into our own hands and have Kaspar 'disappear' for good."

"You mean, *we* become the assassins?"

She nodded.

He felt cold all over. This time, it wasn't the house. "That's insane, Katherine, and immoral. We can't hope to win by using their tactics. I don't like these monsters any more than you, but that's the beauty of freedom of speech. Hatemongers hang themselves by their own ugly, irrational arguments. Expose them to the light of truth and they slither away. But attempt to exterminate them and you only create martyrs for the cause."

In reply, she walked to the front door, shot closed a shiny new security bolt, and slid a companion safety chain into place.

"I thought you were leaving yourself wide open yesterday when I walked in on you playing the harp," Reg said. Wise as the extra precautions seemed under the circumstances, he felt decidedly uneasy at being locked in. And why had she waited until after midnight to secure the door?

"The dog," she said, turning to lean against the door, hands behind her back. "I let him out to patrol the perimeter. As you know only too well, he has recently returned."

She tried a teasing smile but seemed tense, unsure. "I often leave the door open in the middle of the day. It airs the place out and allows me to express my freedoms by flinging them in the faces of those who would take them away. My 'fiddling,' as you called it, keeps me sane if nothing else. It is also my way of filling the air inside and outside this house with life and acceptance. Call it a woman's foolish romanticism if you wish, but I prefer to think of it as a nonviolent means of fighting back."

She suddenly looked weary of the whole business. "Race accommodation is what got us into this mess. Work with me, Reg Danson, and at the very least we can send all the Jews home to Israel where they will no longer bear the cruelty of rejection. If they are God's chosen ones, God will be especially pleased."

Reg looked as if he were about to feel *her* brow for signs of a fever. "I don't want to rain on your parade, but all is not well in the Promised Land. Surely you're aware that many Israelis consider the African Falashas you help relocate to be the literal black sheep of world Jewry. They are rejected for their skin color, rabbis refuse to marry them, and because of their backward rituals so out of step with the rest of Judaism, one Jerusalem editorial writer dared to characterize them as primitive people who have only recently 'come down from thc trees.' I'm telling you, Katherine, the only hope for peace among the nations is changed hearts, not a change in address."

A flinty hardness now masked the beautiful face. "Take them out of harm's way first, then educate the people on matters of tolerance and compassion," she said. "Had we done that in Europe, there might be very many more Jews alive today. Hitler, rightly or wrongly, forced the issue by capitalizing on the humiliation of defeated Germans in the 1920s and using successful Jewish businessmen as scapegoats. And now here we are again with German unemployment today very near the level of the 1930s Weimar Republic. Kaspar, whatever you think of the methods, is again forcing the issue. Are you willing to wait and see what develops, or can we try for a very different outcome this time?"

The way she said it was almost as if she welcomed Kaspar's rise to power as a way to accomplish her own agenda. "When have the ends ever justified the means?" he asked, shaken by another glimpse into her frightening mix of sympathies. "There's no time for us to stand here debating philosophy. Put me in direct communication with your contacts or I go straight to the authorities."

Lady Katherine wet her lips with her tongue, thinking, examining the American for weakness. The handsome features did not waver.

She spoke low and confidently. "We will be contacted in the morning with Kaspar's exact whereabouts. More than that, I cannot say."

She held out a hand for the blood-soiled T-shirt. "Meanwhile," she smiled, as warm and hospitable as ever, "let's put this to soak."

CHAPTER

15

David Brewster glared at the fax and turned beet red. Sylvia Ricks braced herself. The commandant of the Iron Fist Nationalist Party was going ballistic.

"Again!" he thundered, stopping the work of eight office staff. "Again we have failed! Listen to this communiqué from Munich: 'Recent report published in German press August 22 states results of two studies of the Schwabing Institute of Societal Research. The first, a comprehensive survey of teenage German students finds that one in three of those aged sixteen to nineteen carry knives or pepper gas to school. The second, an equally comprehensive survey of the general German population, found that one in five Germans believes solutions to society's problems are possible only through use of force.'" Brewster's voice had steadily risen until now it was perhaps a mere two decibels away from exceeding the range of human volume.

He balled his fists at his side and torched each person with a blistering look of contempt. "Perhaps that wasn't quite clear. I said it says they said the *only* solution to what's wrong with the world is the *use of force!* Every fifth German, for the love of Mike! And one in three of their kids are out arming themselves for the fight. Why can't *we* come up with statistics like that for the bloody United States of

Socialist America? U.S.S.A., ladies and gentlemen! U.S.S. stinkin' A.! Within forty-eight hours, it is bloody highly likely the signal will be given and there won't be enough assault rifles in existence to mow down all the gutless resisters of change because you and I have not had the discipline to get out there and convince more people that it takes a periodic firestorm to cleanse the land." He crumpled the fax and threw it at Sylvia. "Why?!"

Every eye in the room turned on Sylvia. She chewed her lower lip and tried to look unaffected. She badly wanted to say that the reason they didn't have statistics like that for the American populace was because that was not what the American populace believed. Instead, she reached for a sheaf of papers, stood, and faced David Brewster.

"I beg your indulgence, Herr Commandant. Our field agents have yet to secure those figures. I am happy to report, however, that we have made significant gains elsewhere. Here we have"—and she picked off the top sheet—"The *Wall Street Journal* reports the gap in life expectancy between whites and blacks is rapidly widening. For most of the century, that gap was narrowing. But in the 1980s, white life expectancy continued to increase while black life expectancy began to decrease substantially among black males and to a lesser extent among black women. Black men are now dying eight years sooner on average than comparable white men, an increase of 25 percent sooner. Would you care to hear the reasons why according to the National Center for Health Statistics? Apparently, heart disease among white males dropped much more than in—"

Brewster's blood pressure visibly dropped, and the other workers in the room released their collective breath. He interrupted his secretary gruffly. "I don't care *why,*" he sneered. "And Miss Ricks, if you want to keep your job, this is the last time I will have to remind you that *blacks* are *niggers* in this office. And another thing. Never use the term 'comparable' when speaking of the two races. There *is* no comparison! Is that clear?"

Sylvia Ricks sighed to herself. Outwardly, she said, "Yes, Herr Commandant. I am also happy to report that the Institute for Historical Review (IHR) and other Holocaust refuters are making gains. Increasing numbers of American school children are now aware of the Jew propagandists and their gross misstatements of World War II atrocities. They understand that Russia's Stalin was the real monster and that if anyone baked in anyone's ovens, Joseph Stalin was chief baker!"

Brewster looked pleased at that statement, favoring the secretary with a look of arrogant approval. "Kikes, Miss Ricks, *kike* propagandists," he said, but gently.

She took it as her due.

"Is Dick Weber available for lunch?" he asked.

She shrugged. How was she supposed to keep track of Weber's schedule? The head of the Liberty Lobby, the largest anti-Jew organization in the country, was not her responsibility. One puffed-up tyrant was more than enough for anyone's plate. "I will see if he has an opening."

Brewster paced in short, narrowly defined paths before the fax machine. He hooked fat thumbs in the bulging belt loops that hadn't required a belt in ages. "Get McCalden on the phone over at IHR. Tell him I've got an idea for countering the charges that no one on their staff has academic credentials. We can get 'em a trunkful of credentials overnight express from my connections in the mail-order industry. This time tomorrow *Doctor* McCalden will be turning those Zionists to Jew jelly, slick as can be!"

The commandant lost interest in the noncommittal secretary. He crossed the room to a light table and examined the work of artist Bill Links. The pen-and-ink drawing near completion was a deliberately coarse rendering of a burly black man surrounded by three obviously pregnant black women and thirty or more children. The caption read: "Not to worry. His welfare check's in the mail." Plastering the walls above the table were highly sophisticated posters crudely declaring war on minorities:

"Trash 'em! Smash 'em! Make 'em die!"

"Join the White Aryan Resistance."

"White Revolution—the *Only* Solution!"

"Reap a Righteous Massacre!"

The last showed a grinning death's head in Nazi military uniform standing amidst bursting bombs and a city on fire. The body of a black man lay nearby, a noose tight around his neck.

"Good, Bill, nice touch," Brewster said, waiting for the beaming artist to pause, then clapping him on the shoulder. "See if you can make those women just a little more pregnant, would you?" Wink, wink. "We want this poster to be as realistic as we can make it!" He doubled over in spasms of laughter in which the artist joined.

David Brewster dabbed at his eyes, then blew loudly into a handkerchief. He walked to his office door, entered, and called back into the room he had so noisily exited. "Pete, a moment please."

His second in command, whippet-thin Peter Smyth, glanced at Sylvia Ricks and raised his eyebrows in a question mark. She shook her head. She didn't know what the volatile maestro wanted. Smyth was on his own.

"Petie, my faithful Petie," cooed Brewster, shutting the office door behind Smyth. "Have you seen the latest printouts from the Coalition?"

Smyth barely smiled. He had seen them. Brewster knew he had seen them.

"It would appear we are rolling in sweet clover." The commandant picked the report from the nest of chocolate wrappers and computer output that obliterated any sign of a desk. "There are now 492 bona fide white supremacist orders operating in these fifty United States, counting Klan, neo-Nazi, tax protest, and skinhead. Throw in another fifty, sixty anti-kike Christian Identity factions and you have got one toxic mix. From the Blue-Eyed Patriots of

Portsmouth, New Hampshire, to the Church of Jesus Christ United KKK in Oxnard, California, we are more than we have ever been. Now, you count in another two thousand-plus Aryan orders from Auckland to Stockholm and the world as we know it is in deep manure. The Iron Fist Nationalist Party is still one of the biggest with three thousand members." Smyth knew the figure was closer to fifteen hundred, and a fourth of those old rednecked geezers languished in nursing homes. They always inflated the numbers. But, of course, he said nothing. David Brewster knew he knew.

"Kaspar has given shape and form to the Invisible Empire at last," Brewster droned on. "He has marshaled the forces, formed the Coalition, corralled a bunch of lone rangers into a unified, rabid fighting force, and we are mere hours away from supreme rule!" Brewster wet his lips at the thought of revolution. Given enough firepower, a man could "buy" clout. Given enough bullets, he could send all the rats back to the sewers they crawled from. And those who refused to go would fertilize the gardens of a New Order.

"And what did the mighty Fuehrer say?" Brewster quizzed.

Smyth knew the drill. "'Man owes everything that is of any importance to the principle of struggle and to one race which has carried itself forward successfully!'"

Brewster jumped in excitedly, belly bumping Smyth from the stage. The glorious punch line was always Brewster's to say. Always. "'Take away the Nordic Germans,' the illustrious Fuehrer did conclude, 'and nothing remains but the dance of the apes!'" He laughed outrageously. "The dance of the apes! Imagine it, Petie!" The rude guffaws ripped through the office walls and made the others exchange knowing glances. Sylvia Ricks put on her coat. She needed air.

Brewster beamed at the printouts which went on to chronicle the "achievements" of the Coalition in the past year. Bombings, assaults, arson, and harassments of every sort. In April, a plastic surgeon was shot to death in Wilmette, Illinois, for allegedly making nonwhites look Aryan. That same month a hairdresser in San Francisco was gunned down for bleaching his clients' hair. In May, a Cambodian immigrant was killed for dating a white woman in St. Louis. In July, an elderly Atlantic City black man was beaten to death for asking a white youth for spare change.

Minorities, David Brewster was convinced, carried mutant genes that made them unnaturally uppity.

The commandant fixed Peter Smyth with an accusing eye. "How we coming with the Anti-Defamation League?"

Smyth hated the inquisition. The ADL was big, well-established, and counted friends in very high places. Very high. Yet Brewster expected Smyth to single-handedly discredit the most powerful defender of Jewry. "They're clean, David. It's not like they go around looting and pillaging." No sooner had he spoken the words than he devoutly wished he could take them back.

"Lousy little weasel!" screamed Brewster, his face again beet red. "If I hadn't done such a thorough genealogical background check on you, I'd swear you were more Jew than Rabbi Moses H. Hanukkah himself!" Smyth could smell the beefy leader's agitation. He didn't have to look into the livid, sweaty face just inches from his own to know that the man was on the edge of cardiac arrest.

For a split second, Smyth wondered how far he'd have to push to send the obese man into a full stroke. But as usual, he chose the safer, more passive route. There were just too many loaded weapons within the big man's reach. "Now David, I didn't mean nothing's being done about the ADL. We've just reprinted two hundred thousand copies of Arthur Butz's *The Hoax of the Twentieth Century.* It's a quite reasoned case against the presumed extermination of European Jewry. And Professor Charleş Irving at the prestigious University of Auburn, New York, has just released an excellent treatise clearly demonstrating how the kikes actually used photos of German civilians, killed by the barbarian Allies at the incineration of Dresden, and claimed they were pictures of God's children slain by the Germans in the great Holohoax."

Brewster brightened, allowing much of the blood in his face to return to general circulation. "Holohoax," he said, wrapping his tongue around the word, as delighted as a kid with a new bike. "Holohoax! The man's a genius! I want a bottle of wine sent around to his office by this afternoon. Medium price range. Nothing more than ten years old. Add a note, something modest, something like, 'Professor Irving, a man of your intellect is an asset to his race. We salute you, sir!' Holohoax! Don't that beat all?"

Smyth allowed that it did beat anything he had ever heard and seized the congenial moment to take his hasty leave of David Brewster. Down by the water cooler he whispered the latest to Sylvia Ricks, back from her break. They agreed that if the commandant survived the WWRR, they would seek out a small, uninhabited atoll off the coast of Alaska and go native. For no amount of power did they want to share the New World with Bonkers Brewster.

CHAPTER 16

"I am an Aryan. I serve the forces that guard my Aryan race. I am prepared to give my life in defense of my race." There were two Connies spouting the Aryan Fighting Code—the Connie in the mirror and the Connie applying auburn hair color to the traces of orange left in her new, and now evenly trimmed, hairdo.

Tony Danson, the barber, stood by and blew bright orange hairs from the electric clippers like a Texas gunslinger blowing smoke from the end of his Colt .45. The swastika earrings were in the garbage bin.

"I am an Aryan. I will never surrender my mind to my captors. I will never betray other Aryan people." She made a face at that. She was well on her way to betraying a whole lot of Aryan people. Losing her bravado for a moment, she looked over at Tony, the flicker of panic beneath the wet scalp reminding him of the expression on a kitten having its first bath. "Keep going," he encouraged. "You are doing the right thing."

"I am an Aryan," she continued shakily, taking one last opportunity to expunge her system of the code she had been required to recite six times a day. "If I am incarcerated, I will remember at all times my duty as an Aryan. I will aid other Aryan prisoners, if possible. I will accept no special favors from—from my captors." She looked fearfully at Tony, suddenly seeing him differently.

"Whoa, Scarlett," Tony cautioned. "Don't be looking at me like I'm the enemy. I represent rational thought, remember?"

She bent over the basin and ran her fingers through the hair, evenly distributing the bottled color. Her voice was tinged with scorn. "You represent middle-class, status quo, my-country-right-or-wrong conservatism, mister!"

"Hold on!" he yelped defensively, waving the clippers. "You watch your mouth, Scarlett, or I might have to apply these babies to the nubs you have left and turn you into a billiard ball. I'll have you know that not too long ago I was an anti-nuke, save-the-whales tree-hugger who thought conformity was having breakfast three days in a row. For finals one semester I gutted my girlfriend's teddy bear and wore the carcass on my head for two days. Does that sound so conservative?"

Connie stuck her head beneath the hand dryer and pressed the button. "Girlfriend?" she shouted over the noisy roar.

"Well, you know—yeah, girlfriend. Nice kid from Boston. Her dad's a corporate lawyer—way too establishment for it to have lasted very long." He grinned at the spectacle of the woman now squatting beneath the dryer like a skinny Buddha.

She grinned back. "You better watch it, mister. Remember, you're a guy in a girl's restroom, a very vulnerable position."

He shook his head. "I knew this would happen. I fly away with a girl and before I know it, I'm behaving in a totally bizarre manner."

"Bizarre? This from a man with a dead teddy bear on his head?"

Their shared laughter echoed off the tiles of the public restroom at Vienna's Schwechat Airport. They'd used an "out of order" sign from the janitor's cart that stood at the men's room door, but knew they were on borrowed time.

"Can't you hurry this along?" Tony said, glancing nervously

around. "Any minute now, a crazed custodian is going to come busting through that door." That made them laugh even louder, ending all hope of not attracting attention. "Did you hear me?" he said, failing in one last attempt to quiet her down.

"I am an Aryan," she said. Tony rolled his eyeballs. "As a racial political prisoner of war, I will answer only with my age, name, and address when questioned. I will make no oral or written statements disloyal to my race."

Tony chased her from the restroom just as a frowning janitor retrieved the missing sign. They thanked him, tipped him, and left him staring after them in amused bewilderment.

"What is your last name, anyway?" Tony asked.

"Where to now, my daring Rhett?" Connie replied, ignoring his question.

"To the Rathaus, my dear, and here, why don't you put on this baseball cap, just until your hair's had a chance to recover from its recent fling with the peculiar."

She stared at the bright red St. Louis Cardinals hat emblazoned with white lettering. "Oh, good, we're sure not to attract any attention now."

"You've got a real mouth on you, you know that?" Tony ducked her playful swipe at his jaw. "Fortunately, your aim is as off as your crazy Aryan philosophies."

"Careful, Rhett," she said, "or I'll sic the dogs of war on you!"

"Sorry, Scarlett," he retorted, "we just covered over the scariest part of you." Even as he said it and she made a face, he wondered if it was really true. A cosmetic surgeon could remove the ugly brand "WWRR" from her cheek. But could a person become unbrainwashed this fast? The hug she gave him next drove the doubt away.

"Mmm, nice!" she murmured. "It's been a long time since I've been hugged by someone who cared."

They walked down the concourse toward the passenger loading

area. "What about your parents?" Tony asked, knowing it was probably a risky question. It was.

"They no longer care to hug the daughter from another planet," she said, her voice surprisingly calm. "Can't blame them, I guess."

"Doctors advise eight hugs a day for maintenance, twelve for growth," Tony replied. "They're like vegetables. Nobody ever gets enough." He looked over at her and gave a startled cry. "Oh, no! Somebody do something! It's a dreaded Cardinals fan. Help!"

She chased him to the bottom of the ramp into the main terminal area until they were slowed by the heavy crowd. "What was that all about?" she said and smacked him playfully across the arm.

"Ow! Watch it. Still sore. I thought you knew. The Cardinals, you know, scientific name *cellarous dwellerous.* Cellar dwellers. Bottom feeders. Last place pariahs. The closest they'll ever get to a pennant race this year is if you hand pennants out to each player and make them run around the field!"

He sprinted for the exit, beaten every step of the way by a bright red baseball cap.

Reg Danson held the cool silver handset to his ear and waited anxiously for Tony's reassuring voice to come on the line. Reg's leg ached.

Behind him, Lady Katherine greeted the reluctant dawn on the harp in plain, coaxing notes. But the morning chill persisted. Unwelcome clouds of dismal gray clotted the early skies. The mistress of the Gates of Hope played with eyes closed, mind fixed on a place other than gray Nuremberg.

"Hullo, Danson residence, Leo Slugitt speaking." The old crab bait sounded upset.

"Leo! Reg. How's my patron saint of jazz has-beens?"

"I'd be a whole lot better off if you'd just tell me what in thunder you mean by haulin' your son outta here on short notice. What's so all-fired important? The poor kid needs to lay still and mend, not go off half-cocked to Europe 'cuz you need a glorified go-fer!"

"Whoa, Leo, whoa! What are you saying? Tony's here, in Europe?"

The sickening truth struck them both at once. Tony had been taken—long distance.

Leo found the strength to speak first. "You didn't call and tell Tony to come, it was urgent? He took off while I was gettin' the restaurant open. Left a note—"

"You left him alone in the house after all that's happened?"

Lady Katherine's eyes remained closed. She hummed softly.

Leo fought the same panic that choked Reg's voice. "Last I saw he was sleepin' off a pizza binge in your bed, all peaceful like. I figured I could slip out for just a half hour, get some nice hot soup into him. You know how fast people get well on my soup! I locked the doors."

There was hurt in the old sailor's voice, and remorse. Reg felt shame for accusing his friend of negligence. Leo was a sweetheart who only had the bachelor Dansons' welfare at heart. "Sorry, old man. Didn't mean to take your nose off. Tony's his father's son and just as headstrong. Even if you had been there, he would have convinced you to let him go."

They were talking details to avoid the main issue. Tony was in mortal danger.

"I was fixin' to call you, chew ya out for this. Tony left a note saying he was meetin' you at your hotel. Where're you now?"

"Nuremberg. Long story. Gotta go, Leo. I'll call once I know something for sure."

Reg dialed the Rathaus. Busy. He slammed the phone onto its cradle. Lady Katherine played on.

"Will you stop strumming that thing!" Reg shouted, stomach churning. "Kaspar's got Tony!"

"Daring Treasury Robbery: Kaspar Invades Vienna!" The headline jumped at them like a coiled snake, venom in every word. They were outside the Rathaus, a large, imposing stone structure that looked as if it had been carved from land. Flags of several western European nations flew from metal poles arching over the entryway. Connie took Tony's hand. He was trembling.

"That's why Dad needs me," he said, taking the paper from the newsman at the corner kiosk and devouring the few known facts about the theft of the Holy Lance. "Dad was right!" he exclaimed excitedly, folding the paper and stuffing it under his arm.

He missed entirely the brief story on page seven: "Vatican Envoy Victim of Hit-and-Run."

In the lobby, a knot of sober-faced priests in clerical garb stood talking in subdued tones near the elevator. Two massive ceramic pots on either side of the front desk contained spiky green tendrils of plant life. The name *Rathaus* in raised gilt lettering on dark wood soared above an ornate coat of arms over the check-in area. Connie and Tony stood in line beneath a grand chandelier sparking fire from thousands of crystal facets. Otherwise, the room was low light and deep umber.

Four patrons waited ahead of them, including a pair of newlyweds who loudly and frequently announced their marital status to anyone who in the least appeared not to have heard the news. Tony debated going to the front of the line and declaring an emergency check-in, but thought better of it. There was an air of tension in the lobby and he had no desire to add to it.

"Beats the alley at Sixth and Seneca," said Connie, craning her neck at the old world decor. She blew a bubble with well-chewed gum and fidgeted on one foot and the other. "Wonder why I never took up smoking?"

Tony grinned, shook his head, and looked at the ceiling as if to bore a hole to the upper floors. *Which room you in, Dad? Hang on. We'll be right up.*

The large woman two places ahead of them in line had a complaint about her bill, and no amount of diplomacy on the part of the desk clerk of the busy hotel could convince her she was wrong.

"I wish to see the manager," she huffed.

"Madame, I assure you that I am the highest authority on the premises today," replied the clerk, waving reassuringly to the restless guests next in line.

"That is the most ridiculous thing I've ever heard, leaving an underling in charge!" she said, making certain the last in line heard clearly.

That launched another round of dickering over the bill.

"Faint!" Tony whispered fiercely.

"What?" Connie asked, not sure she had heard correctly.

"Drop to the floor in a swoon, groan a little, and with all eyes on you, I'll dart up to the counter and ask for Dad's room number."

"I will not!" Connie whispered just as fiercely. "I already look like a rooster in this cap. Besides, it's dishonest."

They looked at each other and laughed. "Well, well," Tony said. "Welcome back to the land of right and wrong."

The newlyweds, blissfully unaware of the interminable delay in front of them, kept kissing and cooing their undying loyalty to one another. "Just married, you know," the young man told Tony in clipped British accent. "Honeymooning right here. Vienna's the *crème de romance,* don't you think?" Connie nearly burst a blood vessel over the clumsy attempt at French.

Tony was ready to go door-to-door in search of his father when an elderly, immaculately dressed man in turban and curly white mustache stepped forward and quickly helped the woman understand the essence of the discrepancy. The bill was in fact correct, but she no longer seemed to mind. She thanked the man for explaining the error so graciously. Then she paid, glared once more at the clerk, and left.

The other guests in line breathed sighs of relief. A newly arrived priest offered to take the man to dinner. The peacemaker only laughed politely, bowing slightly to a grateful audience, palms together in a gesture of humility. "I would say what Gandhi said. 'An eye for an eye, and soon the whole world would be blind.'"

The small crowd applauded. The man bowed again and resumed his place in line.

"As easy as that," Connie said. The couple ahead of them were shocked out of another dewy embrace by the insistent ringing of the service bell by the harried clerk. They quickly concluded their business and were off to the elevators arm in arm. Tony hesitated, then turned to the man in the turban. "Sir, please go ahead of us. I believe that we are all in agreement that it is the least that can be done in light of your heroic efforts."

"Heavens yes," said the newly arrived priest. "Never have I seen this many souls snatched from purgatory in one smooth transaction!"

The guests laughed and noisily encouraged the old gentleman to the head of the line. He thanked Tony, nodded kindly to Connie, and soothed the anxious clerk with a gentle smile. They made short work of his bill.

Connie and Tony stepped to the counter. "Well," she said, amused. "A regular cloudburst of object lessons in brotherly love. You sure you didn't stage this just for my benefit?"

"No way, Scarlett," he drawled. "If I'd had my druthers, we'd a shot our way to the front and buried two deep anybody who said different." She hit him with the baseball cap, then returned it to her head backward.

Tony smiled at the clerk and asked for Reg Danson.

"Oh!" the clerk brightened, his bald head shiny with perspiration. "I must have spoken with you yesterday. Unfortunately, your father had to rush away to Nuremberg at a moment's notice. He said to tell you there is a new development in the case, said you would know what he means."

The clerk stopped at the crestfallen look on the young American's face. "No need for alarm. He seemed quite relieved over the new information. Meanwhile, he said to tell you that a Father Franz Erlach, of the Vatican delegation, is in the hotel. The good Father stands prepared to look after you until your father's return, which I gather will be soon. You will be safe in the hands of the church. Everyone should be so blessed. These are perilous times. Even the streets of Vienna take on an increasingly sinister cast. Shall I ring the priest?"

Tony sighed and nodded. "Did my father say where in Nuremberg he's gone?"

"No, I'm afraid not." The clerk dialed a number and gave Tony and Connie a reassuring nod. "But you will soon have a nice reunion. It's so gratifying to play a minor role in bringing you and your father together again!"

Tony's warning look kept Connie from rolling her eyes.

CHAPTER 17

"I am afraid that I am in Vienna on sad business, as are my brother clerics," said the handsome blond priest. "But I do not enjoy sackcloth and mourning, and you, undoubtedly, do not wish to spend a day playing backgammon in a hotel room. I have just the remedy. Prater Amusement Park, playground of the Viennese!" He nodded to the hotel clerk, then led the way to the exit.

Connie pleasantly eyed their host. He was a most unlikely Vatican emissary. Clean white teeth, Samson's build, and a rugged carriage that said Matterhorn, not monastery. And slightly ill at ease in the crisp gray vestments and stiff white collar. She figured him for a novitiate and wondered at the faith that would take one so attractive and vital out of the world to be forever set apart.

"Sad business?" asked Tony as they made their way along crowded Praterstrasse toward the waiting bus that would take them to Prater.

"A Vatican official was killed last evening in a tragic accident," said Erlach, making long strides that forced them to keep up. "I and my brother priests have flown from Rome to help in the investigation and to bring his body home for burial. He was a man of convictions, a priest's priest even though he never wore the cloth. He chose not to marry out of a deep personal respect of the priesthood. He took a private vow of empathy, if you will, and we are greatly diminished by the passing of Claudio Andone."

"Excuse me," Tony interjected. "The name you just used. Andone, was it? I know that name from somewhere."

"It is a somewhat common family name in Italy. The Andones are a vineyard-keeping people. Who is your friend, Mr. Danson?"

"Oh, I'm sorry, this is Connie—uh—what *is* your last name, anyway?"

Connie tugged nervously at the brim of her cap. She had been taught never to divulge real names in casual conversation. "Bird," she said evenly.

Tony looked skeptical but caught the warning look. "Connie Bird," he finished. "You know my father?"

The priest spoke without looking at them. "Monsignor Andone knew your father. On behalf of the Holy Roman Catholic Church, he asked your father to undertake an investigation into the mysterious thefts of priceless religious relics."

"Yeah, sure, now I remember Dad telling me about his trip to Rome and how Claudio Andone put so much faith in my dad's abilities to uncover what no one else seemed able to."

The priest tensed at the words, as if angry that they'd been spoken. The moment passed. Tony wondered if that was somehow privileged information.

They jogged across the boulevard and boarded the long, hinged bus idling at the curb. They settled into the last remaining seats and Father Erlach flashed a disarming smile. Connie rated it bright enough to get a girl to convert and covered the tattoo on her cheek with a hand.

"Your father will be sorry he missed our little outing," said Erlach, the smile fading. "I'm sure that chasing the world's most dangerous terrorist leads to a great deal of fatigue."

CHAPTER

18

The telephone at the front desk of the Rathaus Hotel rang insistently. The clerk hoped it was another convention. He received a commission for every one that he booked.

"Hello? This is Reg Danson calling. I'm the registered guest in Room 221. I've just been informed that my son—"

"Mr. Danson?! Your timing is really quite unfortunate. Your son and his friend left not fifteen minutes ago."

Reg fought for calm. "You say my son was just there? What friend? Was someone with Tony?"

"Why, yes, a young woman, rather slight, pale complexion, short hair and military garb, wearing a red hat."

"Did he say who she was?"

"No, no. There were no introductions. They left soon after in the company of the priest I'd seen them talking with. I believe he suggested they spend their time waiting for you at Prater Amusement Park. It is quite lovely this time of—"

"Priest? What priest?"

The clerk glanced impatiently at the lobby, which was beginning to fill again. Three new guests approached the desk. "Why, Mr.

Danson, the priest you arranged to host your son until your return. You remember we talked—"

"I never spoke with you about any priest!"

"Why, yes you did, just last afternoon. You called from the airport to say that I should expect your son and to let him know that you would be returning soon. The priest is here for the funeral, surely you are aware? A tragic waste. A man devotes his life to the church and then God allows him to be struck and killed by a car."

"Killed? Who was killed?"

"Why, Andone, a Vatican secretary. Claudio Andone, I believe the name was. You must excuse me, Mr. Danson, but I have guests to attend to. We shall retain your room, of course, as long as you have need of it. Should your son return, is there a number—"

"Look. Please." Reg, near shock, prayed, his heart pounding. *Lord, what must I do? Andone dead? Tony and some girl gone off with a bald-faced liar?* "Please, just one other thing. Can you describe the priest my son and the girl left with?"

The clerk sighed resignedly. "Fair-haired, thickly built, well distributed for a priest, if you will."

Danson slammed down the phone. "I must return to Vienna at once," he said, overcome with emotion, fighting for control. "My son's in trouble."

Katherine nodded dreamily, elegant nails fingering unseen notes. Her eyes parted slightly to watch the distraught father dial for a taxi.

Difficult to believe this was once the stronghold of Christianity," said the man who had introduced himself as Father Franz Erlach. Tony and Connie sat across from him in facing seats. The bus snorted and lurched from stop to stop, collecting a noisy mix of tourists and citizenry bent on a day at the carnival. "Europe, I mean. A slow, steady decline toward materialism and hedonism. The church, no longer relevant, is now left to the poor and the old. In Paris, one in ten attend Mass with any regularity, if that. A scandal!"

Tony stared out the window, gloomily anxious to talk with his father. "I've heard it said the majority of Rome never sets foot in a church." He hadn't meant to be offensive, but he said the first thing that came to his troubled mind. Connie gave him an elbow to the ribs.

"Sorry." Tony's apology was monotone, his face anxious. "Didn't mean to be rude."

The priest smiled broadly, leaned forward, and planted strong hands on both the knees poking through the black robe. He and Tony looked at one another. "Ever sought God on a Ferris wheel?" the priest asked.

Tony laughed despite the gnawing anxiety he felt. "Once, when we were stuck at the top and my dad rocked the seat on purpose."

Father Erlach clapped him on the knee and gave Connie a friendly wink. "Well, you haven't been to the mountain until you've ridden the *Reisenrad.* That is German for Big Wheel. Sixty meters or nearly two hundred feet above the earth at the top of the arc. One rotation every twenty minutes. But from the giant gondola car you can look down upon Vienna and all its sparkle and embroidery, like looking down upon the top of a splendid wedding cake. And the world's best *bratwurst* may be purchased from a little stand in the shadow of the Big Wheel!"

Connie made a face. "I'd like to skip lunch, all the same. Big wheels and big *bratwurst* sound deadly in combination."

The priest smiled hugely and she felt a pleasant tingle, despite the muddle of their situation. The robed man exuded an energy, a virile strength she found both alluring and intimidating. And very unpriestlike.

The bus barely crept forward, the driver muttering a stream of German invective at the delay. Shrill horns sounded ahead. The driver added the bus's throaty blast to the fray, and soon they were not moving at all. Tony stood and craned his neck, trying to see past other craned necks and the increasingly animated driver. "Accident," he said. "Looks like a chain collision."

"Perfect," said Connie, not sure if she meant to express exasperation or delight at being delayed with so fascinating a host.

"So, Father Erlach, what do you make of invincible ignorance?" Tony crossed his legs into the seat as if settling in for a long wait. He eyed the priest with the look of one trying to solve a crossword puzzle and stumped by fourteen across, a six-letter word for "unexplained anomaly."

Connie choked. Trapped in a bus with two good-looking theology buffs. A date from the pit.

"Don't worry, Miss Bird," the priest said in sympathetic amusement. "I will dispatch this upstart handily, and you and I will soon be strolling past stalls of candied apples on our way to the stars!"

Tony frowned, but Connie inexplicably blushed. Was this priest flirting with her? "Do you think God will be merciful to those who, because of environment or natural ineptitude, are ignorant of or unable to understand Christianity?"

Connie gave Tony a withering look. "So, how's the weather in Rome this time of year?" she asked Father Erlach, desperately wishing she could lose the baseball cap but even less thrilled with the chopped look it mercifully hid.

Erlach's smile faded a few degrees. He fixed Tony Danson with a probing gaze. "God may be merciful to such people because they are much more to be pitied than condemned."

Tony did not flinch. "And your view on syncretism?"

The priest's jaw hardened. "A super faith comprised of many gods and conflicting religious beliefs is alarming at best, sadly unsatisfying at worst."

Connie looked at the two of them in disbelief. What kind of contest was this? "So, boys, how 'bout those Cardinals?" She meant the baseball franchise, of course, but suddenly realized the ambiguity the word held for a man of the Catholic cloth. She blushed red as her cap.

They ignored her. Father Erlach grasped the pewter crucifix on a silver chain about his neck and jerked it toward Tony. "Moses sought him on a mountain; Saint Augustine in his books; General Washington at Valley Forge; and Albert Schweitzer in the steaming jungles of Africa. *How* he is found is not the issue, but only that he *must* be found!" With that, the priest faced the window, and the stuffiness of the stalled bus intensified.

Connie glared at Tony and nodded her head in Father Erlach's direction. Tony cleared his throat. "Uh, thank you for befriending us and being willing to help. I'm frankly worried sick about my dad. This feels bad. Real bad. I hate sitting here doing nothing."

The priest softened and patted Tony's knee. "Jesus said be anxious for nothing. Your father is fine. God is at work. Let us trust to that. Now tell me more about your father and how his investigation fares."

For another half hour, they talked. As Tony related the circumstances of the search for the elusive Kaspar, the all-night research into the world of religious relics, and the theft of the Lance from the Vienna museum, he found relief in the telling and a caring, comforting listener in Father Erlach. Tony grew bolder and less reticent with each passing minute until, with encouraging looks from Connie, he had poured out the details, including the beating in Alexandria and the murder attempt in Seattle.

Franz Erlach sympathized. "You are a very brave and loving son to risk coming here with a deranged lunatic loose. And you, Miss Bird, what is your story?"

Too late, she flashed a warning at Tony. But the young Danson had surrendered all trust to the priest and rushed ahead. "Connie's story is unbelievable! Twenty-four hours ago she was a neo-Nazi hatemonger. Tell him, Connie, tell him what you know about Kaspar."

Sirens sounded in her head. The long months of indoctrination screamed that she state only her name, age, and address, but now that seemed so silly and melodramatic in a crowded tour bus on the way to the fair, sitting across from a father confessor. The collar, the robe, the agony of the crucified pewter Christ overwhelmed her senses; she could not breathe.

"Come, come, dear girl," said Erlach softly. "You do not have to hide the scars of your past."

Connie started, acutely conscious of the hated tattoo beneath her hand. "I—I acknowledge my terrible sins of hate and revenge!" She burst into tears.

The bus started forward again, creeping past the scene of crumpled fenders and heated exchange. With Tony on one side and Father Erlach on the other, their comforting arms entwined around her shoulders, Connie poured out a wrenching tale of recent life among the skinheads. Head bowed, nose running, eyes streaming tears, she clutched the cloth of the priest in her thin, birdlike hands. *Jesus, forgive me. I have sinned against you. Wash me clean and let me be your child.*

From deep within came a rush of disgust for the one who had enslaved her. "I wish I'd never heard the name Kaspar!" she sobbed, her face pressed against the kindly priest's muscled chest. "He is sent by Satan to kill and destroy!"

Neither Tony nor Connie saw the scalding evil peel the kindness from Father Erlach's features. Fire burned in the shadows of his mind. He felt the solid contours of the weapon hard against his hip.

Reg Danson rushed up to the two police officers waiting for him at the end of the jetway. They hurried through the gate toward the main concourse. Schwechat Airport was alive with the costumes and languages of many nations, all converging on Vienna as if it were the last great unspoiled European city. Like a fine Raphael painting, its glory never seemed to fade.

But for Danson, today everything was drained of life and color. Tony was at the mercy of a demon in human form. Even now, Reg might be too late.

The police sedan raced toward the heart of Vienna, siren wailing. They flew over the Danube Canal past the Church of Our Lady of the Riverbank. They wove in and around an accident, police investigators holding traffic and waving them around. In the distance, the massive ring of steel girders that comprised one of the world's largest and oldest Ferris wheels drew them on toward Prater Amusement Park as if the metal monster were magnetized.

They turned onto the magnificent chestnut-lined avenue that traversed what was once Maximilian II's sixteenth-century imperial game preserve. "The Prater opened to the public in 1766," one of the officers informed Reg. "By the time of the World Exhibition in 1873, it was well on its way to becoming the *Wurstelprater,* or grand fun fair that it is today."

Are we having fun yet? He used to always say that to little Tony and his mother whenever the three of them went to the county fair. The memory made Reg Danson's eyes well with tears.

The enormity of the Ferris wheel was breathtaking. Tony, Connie, and Father Erlach approached the base of the twenty-story structure in awe. Built in 1897, it was one of the last survivors of the species once found in Chicago, London, and Paris. Its fifteen large red-and-white-trimmed enclosed observation cars took almost ten minutes to revolve to a height of 212 feet and another ten minutes to float back to earth. Two hundred feet in diameter, it resembled a stately erector set in the toy box of a giant. At night, it glowed bright with lights and was a landmark for miles in every direction.

"Anything like it in Seattle?" Father Erlach glowed, as if the Vatican were somehow responsible for so imposing a machine.

"The Space Needle looks only half as tall," Tony replied, nearly falling over to see to the top of the Ferris wheel. "I'm not even up there yet and already my butterflies are doing the watusi!"

The priest laughed heartily and Connie smiled bravely. She felt so much better after emptying herself of the awful past.

They watched the barn-red cars of the Ferris wheel slowly ascend and descend, each as big as a one-bedroom bungalow. Connie pointed. "Why's that one all in black?"

They watched curiously as one of the cars descended to the boarding platform, empty of passengers and almost entirely draped in black cloth along the sides below the windows.

"Wait here," Father Erlach instructed. "I'll go check with the operator, buy our tickets, and ask about the odd car."

Tony fumbled in his backpack. "Here, I'll help with the fare."

"Not at all," said Erlach pleasantly as he headed for the ticket booth. "My way of welcoming you to Austria!"

They watched him hurry off. "The priesthood sure isn't what it used to be!" Connie exclaimed appreciatively. "Had I known about him, I would have converted sooner."

Tony said nothing at first.

"What?" she prodded, seeing the funny look on his face.

"I don't know," he said. "It's just a comment Father Erlach made back there on the bus: 'Jesus said to be anxious for nothing.' Remember?"

"Yeah, so?"

"So Jesus never said that. The apostle Paul did. You'd think a priest would know."

Connie wrinkled her nose. "Probably just a slip of the tongue. Even monks make mistakes."

"Yeah, probably." Tony watched the transaction at the ticket window. Suddenly, a side door to the operator's shed opened and another man gestured to the priest to come inside. "Now what's that all about?" Tony said.

They watched Erlach disappear inside, the strange man close behind.

Connie caught her breath.

"What?"

She made to pass it off. "No," Tony insisted. "Tell me."

"The man from inside the building, he . . . well, unless I need bifocals, he looked a lot like a skinhead. Shaved head, tattoos, black boots."

"Could be a biker," Tony replied, trying to see through the window of the operator's shed.

"I don't know. Something about him. Remember, I used to keep house with his relatives. But his looks weren't the strangest part."

"What do you mean?"

"Well, call me crazy, but I'd bet the farm he knows our friend from Rome."

The heady aroma of spun candy and fried onions filled the air. Loud oompah music drifted from a strolling brass band and a calliope piped a repetitive circus medley, like the grating refrain of the neighborhood ice cream truck. Screams of laughter sprayed the crowd at the foot of the parachute swings, and an infant squalled its objection to wet diapers. The door of the Ferris wheel operator's shed opened and Father Erlach emerged, alone.

He made straight for them and gave an enthusiastic wave. "Tickets purchased and mystery solved," he called. "I went in and talked to the proprietor. Lovely man. Sadly, though, the president of the management committee that oversees Prater Park died yesterday at breakfast. Heart attack. It is customary in the carnival world whenever the big boss dies to shroud either the first seat on the Ferris wheel or a horse on the carousel in his memory. Shall we?" The priest stood to one side and motioned up the walk to the loading platform.

Tony looked at Connie and they grinned. The ominous man in

the doorway was nothing more than the usual eccentrically dressed seasonal carnival help. Another person inside, undoubtedly very businesslike and neatly dressed, had been so kind as to explain the impressive sign of respect to the visiting priest. How good of Franz Erlach to ask. Tony bet he could impress Miss Snow of Gadsby's Tavern with that little-known fact of carnival lore.

They walked up the incline to the massive passenger dock and were surprised when the priest led them around the long line of excited tourists to the front. They were even more astonished to see the funeral car waiting with the door open. They looked questioningly at the priest. "I pulled rank. Very superstitious, these roustabouts. Invoked the name of a few favorite Austrian saints and told him I would bless the car in the bargain. This way we don't have to crowd in with twenty other people."

Connie started to protest, feeling a little ghoulish, but the priest held up one hand. "It will make for a much more reflective ride. The view won't be blocked in any direction. Tony?"

Tony felt the pressure of the waiting crowd, those at the front beginning to look annoyed at the unexpected delay. If Father Erlach thought it was appropriate . . . "Sure, Connie, let's go."

They ran the rest of the way past the man in black boots and tattoos they'd seen earlier. Connie did a double take. The man wore an open black leather vest. His bare chest was decorated with a dozen crude swastikas as were his biceps. He would not take his eyes off her. She grabbed Tony's arm. "Tony—"

"Come on, Connie," he said, pushing her ahead of him into the waiting car. "Next stop, women's apparel and sporting goods!"

The black cloth rippled in the breeze. She followed Tony inside and Erlach brought up the rear.

The door closed behind them, aided by an unseen hand. A locking pin rammed home with a loud rasp like the scraping of a coffin lid. Huge gears clanked into action, and the car shuddered awake.

The coffin began to rise.

At a trot, Reg Danson and the two police officers rushed past families and couples in love. Acres of possibilities confronted them. The needles in this haystack could be at the golf club, the jockey club, the harness racing track, the cyclodrome, the football stadium, the public gardens, or among the hundreds of concessions lining the fairgrounds proper.

But the most popular attractions providing the largest crowds to get lost in were in the amusement park itself. Reg would start with the park manager in the office at the base of the Ferris wheel. He would enlist park security officers and comb the place.

Danson hoped and prayed that his son hadn't been taken to the remote hunting grounds surrounding the park. There weren't enough law enforcement officers in all of Vienna to search the ponds and woods where royalty once stalked and killed pheasant, fox, and game hens.

And what in the world was Connie doing with him? Who else could it be? *Oh, God, keep thy servants in perfect peace.*

They cut through the line at the Ferris wheel and knocked hard on the operator shed's door.

The man in the vest roughly halted the line, fastening the security chain, and kicked the door to the car closed. He rammed the locking pin home, then grabbed the control lever and pushed it forward. The gondola left the moorings and followed the funeral car into the sky.

The man frowned and watched the officers and the civilian enter the shed. A nervous twitch in his right cheek started the muscles dancing and the right eyelid fluttering. He could not abide the law. They had too much on him. He'd been told to quit Vienna and never return. If they recognized him . . .

Seventy-five seconds later, the next car glided to a halt at the boarding platform. The attendant released the locking pin and opened the door. People poured from within, including a small boy who promptly vomited a pink geyser of accumulated candies, pickled cabbage, and *bratwurst* onto the loading area. The attendant swore and directed the next set of passengers around the mess to take the place of those who had just vacated. He threw the control lever forward.

Under a barrage of profuse apology from the boy's mother and requests for refunds from the faint of heart, he wrestled a mop and bucket to the scene and began the cleanup.

A firm hand gripped his shoulder. He knew instinctively that he'd been sacrificed by the man in the office. He tried to run but was hurled to his face on the wet floor and handcuffed.

Reg knelt by the man's head. "Have you seen a young man, nineteen, who resembles me and was in the company of a priest and a young woman in a red cap?"

The operator's eyes flashed hatred. "No, but I once saw a three-legged pony and a two-headed dog."

He yelled in pain as the policeman's knee hit the small of his back. "Hello, Vest. We haven't had a good talk in such a long time, have we, Vest? Guess you've been keeping small and with good reason. We have a number of real bold crimes against cripples and elderly people with your signature all over them. Now, shall we have a nice long conversation about those or a short discussion on the boy, the girl, and the priest?"

The operator was little more than a boy himself, but the years had not been kind. Scars of past conflict marred his features, including an ugly gash from the middle of his forehead to behind the left ear. A swastika nose ring glinted in the afternoon light and for a moment, Reg thought the officer would yank it out. Instead, he leaned close to the young man's ear. "I can guarantee thirty years hard time for what you've done," the officer said, his voice cold steel. "Cooperate and it's half that."

The young man struggled with indecision, then motioned to sit up. When he had, his head lifted and the eyes of Danson and the officers followed his gaze to the black-shrouded gondola car.

Before they could stop him, Reg ran and leaped at the next cross girder as it came vertical, then started its upward arc. He threw an arm around the girder and swung his feet up once, twice, three times until they found a toehold. The officer grabbed the control lever and pulled back with a jerk. The behemoth halted its revolution with the screech and clang of protesting metal. The cars swung on the metal arms that held them in the grip of the wheel. Cries of alarm penetrated the gondola walls. One hundred sixty feet above the platform, the funeral car was as silent as death.

On the ascent, Tony and Father Erlach had debated antinomianism. Connie stood by the window watching the ghost train and the dodgem cars shrink in size. All of Vienna unfolded before her like a fairy-tale village of tiny houses and tiny autos.

"Count the steeples, Connie," said the priest. "Jesuit, Dominican, Franciscan—you name it, Vienna's got a steeple for it. Meanwhile, I'll set this vagrant straight on faith versus works for eternal salvation. Now, my good man, faith only renders moral law of no consequence."

"I never said that," Tony huffed good-naturedly. "Saved by faith doesn't annul our responsibility to the Ten Commandments. But neither does striving to keep the Law justify us. Salvation is a gift of grace, unmerited favor. I cannot earn it because my righteousness is as filthy rags."

"Quite right," Franz Erlach agreed. "What the theological watchdogs have been on guard against ever since the second century, though, is the heretical doctrine that says it matters not how we live once God locks in our heavenly reward. From the medieval Latin, *antinomus,* opposed to law."

Tony threw his hands in the air. "I told you, Father Erlach, I'm not opposed to the Law. What I'm opposed to is the idea that you or I can do something so lofty or noble that we can expect divine recompense. That takes the saving out of God's hands and places it in mine, which makes me higher than God!"

"Preposterous!" shouted the priest, eyes alight with mirth. "That's not what I'm saying at all. I'm saying beware the sect mentality that so reduces our roles in God's plan that we become little more than—"

A tremendous jolt threw Connie to the floor and the men back against their seats. The car rocked sickeningly, first skyward, then earthward like an aerobatic stunt plane. Startled cries and shouts filtered up from the car below theirs and rained down from the car above. "Oh, Tony!" Connie cried and grabbed on to his foot for stability. "Don't let this thing do any barrel rolls!"

Quickly, the car settled into a gentle rocking motion, each swing less pronounced than the last. The emergency phone on the wall buzzed insistently. Though it was closer to Tony, the priest reached over him and yanked the receiver off the wall mount. "Yes? Yes, what's happening?" He listened a moment, acutely aware his every reaction however slight was analyzed by the boy and the girl. He kept an even tone, but there was an almost imperceptible alteration in his face, a tensing about the eyes. "I see." He covered the mouthpiece. "Anyone hurt?" he asked them. They shook their heads no. "All fine here," he reported to the caller. "Yes, well, inform us when you know how long it may take. Thank you."

Father Erlach replaced the receiver. "Broken fan belt," he laughed in relief and they joined him. Such a small thing, really.

Tony helped Connie into a seat and Erlach went to a window.

He pressed his face hard against the glass and looked down as if trying to see beneath the observation car. He spoke again, his breath leaving a vapor trail of condensation on the window. "It is so difficult to divorce matters of religion from the heated passion in which they are conceived. But a handful have known success in this area. Stalin, Hitler—"

"Success?" Tony interjected, disbelief making his voice shake. "Chesterton said the madman is the one who has lost everything except his reason. That might make Stalin and Hitler efficient in their madness, but hardly moral or spiritual giants!"

Erlach's words returned in a leaden sheath of controlled anger. "The giants in the land are those superhuman souls able to suspend passion long enough to accomplish the greater good, a good number of Crusaders among them. Hitler would have soon tired in his efforts to fortify the Aryan race if he had operated on emotion alone."

Connie's head snapped up at the word *Aryan.* She jumped up and looked wildly at Tony who pressed a finger to his lips in warning. The priest's darting eyes caught the gesture in the reflection from the glass.

"Yes, do proceed with caution, Connie Bird," he said coldly, twisting to see the steel girders above, below, and to the side. "Aryan traitors are worse than Jew scum and subject to immediate extermination."

Tony started to rise. "Now just a min—"

The man whirled and from his priestly folds produced a Luger pistol. Tony moved toward the emergency telephone, but in three strides the gunman in priest's clothing wrenched it from the wall. His left arm extended like a rod of iron in the Nazi salute. The pupils of his eyes were wide and bottomless, empty of compassion but full of fury. They lashed Connie with ferocious intensity. Tony stepped in front of her.

"I can hold my arm like this for two hours rigid and unbending as could my Fuehrer! You cannot hold your allegiance for two minutes! No wonder. For the Fuehrer, misery was a female. Six of his eight women attempted or committed suicide. Would you like to jump now, my dear, or do you need some assistance?"

The young Aryan leveled the gun at Connie's forehead. Tony

moved to shield her, blood rushing to his head. Connie stiffened and averted her eyes. "I was taught that women have an important role in the New Order," she said.

The gunman grinned evilly. "Absolutely. Aryan women breed more Aryans. Beyond that, they are what the Fuehrer called 'cute, cuddly, naive little things.' Pardon my saying so, but you look to be rather frail stock."

Tony couldn't risk Connie's likely heated reply. He had to divert the gunman's attention from her. "Nothing in two thousand years has destroyed faith in God like the Holocaust. Is that what it means to fortify the Aryan race? And why do you parade as a Catholic priest, Kaspar?"

The barrel of the gun swung slowly to a position between Tony Danson's eyes. Tony forced himself to look at the crucifix. The Aryan tore the necklace off and pressed it into Tony's forehead like a brand. Connie cried out.

"Here, take your dead Christ!" He spat the words in hatred and let the crucifix fall to the floor. The barrel of the gun pressed against an indentation in the skin left by the cross. "Are you so certain I am Kaspar? Nothing is as it seems."

His voice increased in volume, and with the recitation of Nazi ideology, his body seemed to swell and fill the observation car with monstrous pride. "The so-called Holocaust was nothing more than a humanitarian effort to free Jewry of the false notions and myths that some grandfatherly god does their bidding. They had to see that it is the Aryan race that bears all culture and ultimate power. In the Aryan race alone is the true representation of humanity. All modern technology sprang from the Nordics. Anything and everything of any significance can be traced to the one race with the courage to struggle for it. You cannot say that of the dark races, the yellow races, or the red races." His voice turned mocking. "Of course, we must thank the niggers for the tango. And to the chinks we owe an eternal debt of gratitude for inventing fireworks. And where would we be without the half-breeds who taught us that burning buffalo dung makes an excellent cooking fire?" He roared with laughter, the veins in his neck and forehead thick and pulsing with blood.

Tony felt Connie press against his back, the gun deadly against his skull. *Living Jesus, defend us.* "You did not set Jews free. Your so-called humanitarian effort stopped Jews from being Jews. Each time you rid the world of another Jew by death or intimidation, anti-Semitism gains ground."

With each of Tony's words, the gun pressed more sharply into his head until the Aryan struck him across the face with the Luger. "Silence! It is only through raw luck that you are still alive and not fish food!"

Tony couldn't stop. "Raw luck? Don't you mean human error? Those Aryan goons of yours bungled the job!"

The gunman fought the fury that threatened to detonate. He smiled brilliantly and slowly started to squeeze the trigger.

A loud bang sounded on the side window. For a split second, the young Aryan's attention shifted sideways. Tony smashed aside the arm and grabbed for the gun.

Reg Danson saw his son struggle with the assailant in priest's clothing. When he'd poked his head up from below to see the situation inside the car, it was as if an unseen hand had forced his fist against the window. As long as he lived, he would never erase from his memory the sight of the gun at Tony's head. And Connie with him! He had trouble recognizing her in a cap, without the wild hairdo.

And as if that weren't shock enough, Reg saw the position of the gun. It was held in the assailant's right hand.

Kaspar was left-handed.

It had to be a mistake. What had he overlooked?

A bullet shattered a window and ricocheted off steel two feet to

Danson's left. He grabbed for the support girder to which the observation car's pivot rod was attached and scrambled to a spot slightly higher than the roof. The wind gusted and the girders creaked, swaying from the unseen push.

Don't look down.

He gasped, straining to keep a clear head. The noise of struggle from inside the car was maddening. With his heart in his mouth, Reg let go of the girder and pushed off with his feet.

He landed on the gray roof of the observation car with all the stealth of a bag of wet sand. Another bullet ripped through the ceiling inches from his foot. The gunman had him pinpointed.

Reg rolled to the edge of the roof and caught a stomach-lurching glimpse of the ground, a sea of red-and-yellow pennants, and a crowd of the curious growing like a spreading oil spill. He heard the shouts of the police trying to herd the people back from danger.

Rude cackles from the fun house mocked and jeered what Reg was about to do.

He felt over the side and discovered a lip of wood running the length of the eaves about a foot above the top of the windows. He desperately wished the officers were there to hold his ankles. But no way could he delay.

Reg plunged his head over the side, but saw the attacker and Tony locked in battle among the seats at the center of the car. Connie, face streaked with tears, saw Reg. "Do something!" she shrieked. "Help us!"

Reg wanted Tony to maneuver the gunman near the window. "Come on, son, come on Tony, buddy, this way. This way!"

Suddenly, the assailant wrenched free. He saw Connie pleading toward the windows and turned and fired. The window disintegrated. Shards narrowly missed Reg's head. The crowd below scattered back from the rain of glass.

Reg hazarded another look just as Tony leapt on the gunman's back. With ferocious strength, the Aryan flipped Tony to the floor and kicked him hard in the side. He stomped the boy, again and again, trying to cave in his rib cage. "At first I was going to kill you and the girl," said the Aryan, gasping with exertion. "Then I thought taking you hostage would kill your father a few times over. But now, I think my first impulse was best. Too bad. You were good with words!"

He didn't see Connie launch herself from the front row of seats. She caught him off balance, threw a stranglehold around his neck, and drove his back hard against the bank of windows, narrowly missing the open one. The entire car pitched and yawed like a rudderless ship in mountainous seas. Reg held on to the bucking roof for dear life.

The car stabilized, and Reg snatched another look through the window. He saw the Aryan's back. Reg stretched far down over the side and gripped the wooden lip of the eaves in both hands. With a prayer and a pull of the arms, he dropped from the roof.

Feet out, he locked his knees like a human battering ram and crashed through the window at the Aryan's back. Connie let go at the same time and the Nazi hurtled forward to the floor beneath the front row of seats, still holding tightly to the Luger. He twisted to fire behind him.

Reg wasn't there. Using the momentum of his entry, he'd jumped the front seats and come up behind the Aryan. The gunman turned too late and found Reg Danson very much in his face. With a mighty swing, Reg decked him and grabbed the gun.

"Don't move!" Reg ordered. "You okay, Connie? Tony?"

They assured him they were in one piece, though all four of the car's occupants were bleeding from glass cuts. Tony groaned from the added beating, but the relief of coming up alive was a powerful salve. A large welt rose over one eyebrow where the butt of the gun had connected.

"Good thing you lift weights on a regular basis, old pal," Reg said, shaking in relief.

Tony sat up with a wince, gingerly feeling his ribs. "I might as well go into professional wrestling. A Texas Death Match looks pretty good by comparison."

The Aryan hulked in the corner, shadows of darkness rippling along his muscles. Reg did not blink. "Kaspar, if that's who you are, your reign of terror is over!"

With a sudden lurch and the moan of protesting metal, the Ferris wheel resumed its rotation. Startled, Reg involuntarily let the gun's muzzle drop and the Aryan pounced like a waiting spider. The gun fired and a bullet burrowed deep into the inside of the Aryan's thigh. But as if it were no more than the wound from a BB, the man stepped forward, plowed a meaty fist into Reg's stomach, grabbed his gun hand, and shoved him toward the front windows, two of which were gone. Reg was no match for the man's superior strength. With a yell of revenge, the Aryan brought Reg's arm up, then down hard across the unyielding frame of a shattered window sill.

"My arm!" yelled Reg, blinded with pain.

"The gun!" shouted Tony and Connie in unison. The Luger flew from Reg's hand and fell into the canyon of steel girders far below.

The falling gun struck against the Ferris wheel's engine cowling and discharged. Like grass flattened in the wind, the crowd hit the ground. The officer at the controls panicked and applied the brakes. Like marionettes at the mercy of a drunken puppeteer, the four occupants of the funeral car were again hurled aside by the sudden, sickening halt of the Big Wheel. Screams and sobs of panic erupted from the other cars. In the confusion, the Aryan tore off his priestly garb, which concealed khaki street clothes. Wrapping one fist in the cassock, he smashed out the small window in the door, removed the locking pin and kicked open the door to the observation car. One hundred fifty feet above the fairgrounds, he jumped to the girders and felt his way down the cold steel toward the ground.

Reg ran to the window and shouted down. "Hey! Look out! A

terrorist is coming down. He's extremely dangerous, but unarmed. Look to the northeast side of the wheel. Hey!" It suddenly occurred to him that he had no guarantees the gunman was now unarmed. Reg prayed there were no concealed weapons.

Danson's shouts brought a smile to the Aryan's lips despite the numbing pain in his thigh and the seething anger in his heart. No one on the ground would be able to understand the warning delivered from fifteen stories in the sky. He must return to headquarters and prepare a welcome for the Danson party.

Reg Danson could not stand in the door of the observation car and watch the man who had eluded capture at every turn slip from his grasp once more. With a prayer for protection, he hurdled the gap between the car and the supporting girder.

He met steel with a bone-jarring thud and a burst of stars. Blood trickled down his right cheek. He tried to focus on the two-inch rivet that had done the job.

No time to stall. Already the Aryan was disappearing into the maze of steel below. Suddenly, to his left, Reg saw another man working his way from the opposite side of the wheel, thick blond hair whipped by the periodic gusts that tried to separate men from machine.

Reinforcements! Probably from the car above. Reg thanked the Lord and maneuvered for the toeholds and handholds that would lower him to a place of meeting with the burly newcomer.

"Careful, Dad!" Tony called from above. Reg looked up, gave a reassuring wave, and kept moving.

"Hello!" Reg called across the canyon, trying to keep one eye on the fading Aryan and his stomach inside his body. It kept threatening to revolt with every glance below.

The burly man wore jeans and an aviator's jacket. Silently, nimbly, as if he worked steel, he danced across the girders at three times Danson's speed. Perhaps he could catch the Aryan in time.

Now they were just ten feet apart. "Thanks, buddy," Reg said, relieved, hugging the girder. "I think he's just passing the next car down. Think you can catch up to him? I don't believe he has any other weap—"

"You armed?" the young, whisker-faced man demanded, slowing his approach. Norwegian, from the sound.

"Me?!" Reg said, surprised. "What's that got to do with anything?"

Without warning, a hammy fist exploded against Danson's chin, and day became the darkest of nights.

Shouts to the left tore the Aryan from his thoughts. He was passing the next car below and people were hanging out the doorway yelling down. The rest were packed against the windows pointing at him and watching his every move.

"Look out!" they shouted in several European and Asian accents. Some shouted it into their emergency phone in a frightened babble of languages. "The criminal is coming down! Very dangerous man. Watch out!"

"Shut up! Shut up!" he yelled at them. They were *Untermenschen.* Subhumans. But the more he yelled, the louder they called in the Big Wheel version of the jungle telegraph.

The occupants of the next car down likewise relayed the news. They shouted and pointed at the culprit. The Aryan felt exposed. Worse, he felt vulnerable. "Shut up you swine! Shut your ugly, inferior faces!" Louder they yelled, as did the occupants of the next car down.

The last car before the loading platform was no more than twenty feet from the ground, and the Aryan knew the shouts from its occupants would be more distinct to the policemen on the ground. Fortunately, they were all yelling at once and so were the people in the crowd at the base of the wheel. He waved madly at them. "Get away, you fools!" he bellowed. "There's a maniac loose up there. I've been shot!" By now the crimson flow down his pants was clearly visible from the ground. "A berserk priest just started firing from the car below me. Only by God's grace did I escape with my life. But there are others up there in mortal danger. Is there an officer present?"

One harried policeman, trying to bring order to the crowd below the Ferris wheel, separated from the crush and called up. "Yes, man, did you get a good look at him?"

"Not with bullets flying," said the Aryan, stepping down at last, breathless from the descent. "Not everyone inside that car was moving. You've got to bring it down fast!"

Another officer, in the absence of any other plan, and with visions of a bloodbath looming, threw the lever that started the wheel moving again. All eyes were on the battered funeral car in its continued ascent to the top of the wheel.

A vanguard of police, fire, and medical vehicles sped onto the fairgrounds, the warble and wail of their sirens only heightening the pandemonium at Prater.

The Aryan faded into the background, blew a kiss to the mayhem, and melted into the rich soup of Viennese humanity.

The time for the arming of the bomb of WWRR was at hand.

Frantically, the burly Norwegian slapped Reg Danson into consciousness. "Come to, man, come to! We're about to go head over!"

The gargantuan wheel that had seemed to turn so slowly from within the observation cars, revolved with alarming speed at close hand. The girder to which the two men clung had turned from vertical to horizontal as the wheel passed the zenith of its circular swing. With gruesome deliberateness it began to slant into the descent and a plunge of certain death.

Reg lay on his back for a moment, straddled by the distracted stranger. Tony and Connie had screamed themselves hoarse, finally convincing the blond man that Reg was friend, not foe. With the realization that Danson was not the gunman, the man exerted superhuman strength to keep the unconscious Danson from sliding off the girder.

"Call the operator! Stop the wheel!"

"Can't!" screamed Tony. "The phone's ruined!"

To their horror, the men felt themselves slipping head first into a crotch of steel formed of the main outside girder and a shorter, intersecting stabilizer girder joined to one of two inner wheels that strengthened the entire superstructure.

"Oh, God!" Adrenaline pumping, the stranger flattened himself facedown onto Danson's body, grabbed underneath the girder with both hands, and pulled with all his might in an attempt to press them to the steel. Reg wrapped him in a tight bear hug. No good. Their legs began to lift and they knew they'd flip.

Connie cried hysterically.

"Jump to the cross joint!" yelled Reg, releasing the man. The stranger hesitated. "Do it, man, or we die for sure!"

The stranger pushed up, planted a foot in Danson's midriff, and made a desperate vault for the cross joint. He slammed into the girder, hitting his face, the cartilage in his nose giving way. Quickly he turned, dropped astride the girder, and caught the cartwheeling Reg Danson in an undignified embrace.

The fire battalion chief ordered the Ferris wheel halted. The lever was thrown and the colossus protested to a stop.

"Timing is everything," said Danson ruefully. With painstaking caution, he untangled himself, turned astride the girder, and backed up against the stranger who had nearly ended, and then saved, his life. For most of a minute, Reg sat with eyes squeezed shut, taking in precious, rapid sips of air. The man behind was enjoying a similar meal of sweet, delicious oxygen.

"Dad?! Dad?! You all right?" Tony's anxious voice was music.

"Are we?" asked Reg, shakily. The man at his back, nose mashed and bleeding, replied with a muffled laugh of wild relief. "Right as rain!"

For some reason, that set them both to laughing, and by the time the rescue squad got them safely inside the car below their windswept perch, the unnerved pair were roaring hilariously at anything anyone said. By the time all passengers were safely to the ground and the Ferris wheel shut down, Reg and the Norwegian were hugging like sloshed sailors.

"Sorry about the nosebleed, friend!" Reg said, slapping the man named Lars on the back. "You ever need a Siamese twin, here's my card!"

"Sorry about your jaw," Lars responded, slapping back. "I say we try out for the circus."

"You're on!" Reg roared. "But how'll we ever fit the wheel inside the tent?" That sent them both sputtering into a fresh round of laughs and slaps. By the time they had regained their composure and the police had finished their questioning, night had fallen

On the way to the airport after retrieving Reg's bags from the Rathaus Hotel—and alleviating the worried inquiries of the desk clerk—Reg, Tony, and Connie held a group hug and filled each other in on the incredible circumstances that now brought them together for a flight to Nuremberg.

"I've never seen such a cold, calculating man as that," said Reg sourly. "I never wanted you guys to come that close to evil. But then, I guess it's too late for that." He looked tenderly at the son, nearly drowned in the Potomac River, and the girl, nearly devoured by neo-Nazi monsters. How could he send them home? Home was no longer a sanctuary.

"I want you to meet Katherine von Feuerbach. Gorgeous woman. Plays the harp. She's dedicated to helping Jews return to their homeland. Her contacts think they know where Kaspar hides out. She lives in this huge old house in Nuremberg called the Gates of Hope. You'll be safe there"

Even as he said it and tightly gripped their hands in reassurance, Reg felt a shiver of apprehension. For a reason he could not name, the guarantee of safety rang hollow. With mounting fear, he wondered if within the Gates of Hope lay the jaws of hell.

He swallowed hard and held them close. There was nowhere else for them to go.

CHAPTER 19

In Rochester, New York, Fred Gaston, fifty-nine, lay beside his wife dreaming of forty-pound bass and a fishing lodge of yellow knotty pine with a jolly cook who could soak fillet of bass in a secret sauce so fine grown men cry when it's gone.

He did not hear the dog, but the dog heard the smacking of Gaston's lips and paused. The animal determined the sound was nonthreatening and resumed padding quietly from the living room through the kitchen and up the back stairs toward the Gaston bedroom.

His handler had worked methodically to disable the very expensive electronic protection system that brought a sense of false security to the senior director of international operations for GNN, the Global News Network. The estate at Pin Brook would be easy pickings for one intent on larceny. That, however, was not the purpose of the night visit by the massive German shepherd.

Again the canine paused in the doorway to the master bedroom. He saw Pauline Gaston's bare foot poking from beneath the covers. He saw the exposed smoothness of her neck and the pale thinness of arms shaped by thrice-weekly aerobic exercise. A faint whine escaped the furry throat, and the powerful chest tensed.

Fred Gaston blew a rubbery-lipped breath of air, snorted twice, tossed aside the covers, and exposed blue-checked pajama bottoms, no top, to the canine intruder. The dog registered the large expanse of bare flesh on broad shoulders made broader by thirty years of Diner's Club living. The animal's ears flicked forward, its tail went erect, its coat twitched with desire.

The primal desire to attack.

The man huffed and flopped one hundred eighty degrees. A prodigious beer belly presented itself. Growling softly, the canine rushed forward, teeth bared.

The animal stopped and gently deposited a long white envelope in the crook of Fred Gaston's arm. It smelled the man heat and whined in memory. It opened its mouth, lips curling away from pink-black gums and lethal incisors.

The dog moaned like a banshee, then broke into rabid barking.

Fred Gaston, just two years away from a catastrophic heart attack when he went to bed, now cut the time in half. He nearly fell off the bed in fright, drawing his legs up to his chin and groping for Pauline. His mouth worked but nothing came out. Pauline herself squealed enough for them both.

The noxious beast at the side of the bed roared its conditioned hate for another two minutes, lunging forward each time the man reached for the bedside phone. Then, as if by remote control, the animal stopped barking, turned, and padded from the room and out the open front door. The dog sprang through the open window of a black sedan that moved slowly down the street, lights off. The car took the first corner without a hint of screeching tires and headed for the interstate.

Fred and Pauline Gaston lay stricken for several minutes more before noticing the sealed envelope that had fallen to the floor. Shakily, they opened the envelope and read a message of horror and fascination.

David Brewster, commandant of the Iron Fist Nationalist Party, grabbed the fax, slapped his girth, and favored Peter Smyth with a self-satisfied smirk. "Twenty-four hours and counting!" he crowed. "Kaspar wants the hunting parties on alert. This time tomorrow, America will be burning—shoot, the whole world'll be burning—and all the subhumans will either die or be herded into internment camps. Once we've secured the U.S. naval vessels—and that means cleansing the crews of any 'subbies' running around disgracing the uniform—we load the sewage and haul it back to whatever dirty little hole it crawled out of!"

Smyth said nothing, and Brewster scrutinized him. "Maybe Petie's too weak in the stomach for racial cleansing. Shoot, you think I'm too much, you ought to see the Biloxi Boot Boys do their stuff! They wear special hand-tooled cowboy boots with spike cleats and razor blades between the soles and the leather uppers. Go on a stomping raid with those kids and watch a minority's ego alter right before your very eyes!"

Brewster snorted and gulped over this little play on words until Smyth had to intervene. "Because the number of brothers pledged to the Coalition is relatively small, we have to rely on the theory of chaos to pull this off," he said grimly. "That means the church firebombings, the assassinations of ethnic celebrities, the torching of minority schools—all that and more has to occur simultaneously in widespread and numerous locations. It's just too big, Herr Commandant. Too big."

Brewster looked at the thin man with the permanent frown and shook his head as he might at a mental defective. "Petie, Petie, Petie, *mein bruder.* Your vision is too small. We have been drilling for months on end. Everyone knows the plan, and defectors have not even been statistically significant in the last three quarters. Our day has come at last!" He placed a brotherly arm around his second in command.

Peter Smyth shrank from the calculated display of affection, but Brewster's grip was iron. The commandant placed his lips a fraction of an inch from Smyth's ear. "Listen, my little peon. I keep you around because next to you, I look good. But if I were to think your gloom-and-doom ways were to infect the others and weaken their resolve, I'd pull your wings off. Better yet, I'd let it out that you don't qualify under the one-sixteenth rule. A person can be no more than one-sixteenth non-Caucasian, Petie boy, to join the Coalition. Shoot, I'd hazard a guess that your pedigree's got a good one-eighth non-white Spanish, Greek, and kike mud polluting the pure white waters. Now be a good boy and repeat after me."

Smyth braced for the all-familiar litany. "The Aryan race is the noblest of all races and therefore entitled to dominate and exploit the inferior races."

Smyth repeated the line.

"All creative and heroic impulses of history were Aryan; human redemption lies in Aryan blood and the coming of a heroic leader who will establish a racially pure society which will bring about the total regeneration of mankind."

Again, Smyth parroted the prophecy of an Aryan messiah. But even as he did, he wondered why they never discussed Brewster's family tree. Could it be that the slovenly, black-haired, sweaty man before him was so far removed from the tall, blond, and blue-eyed ideal that his appearance rendered the discussion off-limits? Or could it be the fact that David Brewster was at least one-third Armenian and himself did not qualify under the one-sixteenth rule?

Perhaps there just weren't enough Caucasian gentile males to run a world.

▼

The offices of Global News Network in New York City were on red alert. Fred Gaston, senior director of international operations, arrived under police escort looking like he'd been drug behind an eighteen-wheeler over sixty miles of bad road. He hit the tenth floor of the GNN Building running, barking orders to the news anchors, the satellite feed technicians, and the camera personnel.

Up to the eleventh floor and the advertising execs, over to legal, back down to Marsh in accounting, and forty intense minutes on the phone with Louise Heidler in Bonn. By the time he landed at his own massive oak desk with the three-way view of upper Manhattan, the phone was ringing. It was CIA Director William Kesey.

"Fred, Bill Kesey. What kind of nuclear device you planning to drop?"

Gaston didn't sugarcoat the answer. "I have reason to believe that the terrorist Kaspar, whose been ripping off the treasures of the church, is crazy like the proverbial fox. He contacted me last night by German shepherd courier. A devil of a way to spend a night, I can assure you."

"Pauline, she's all right?" asked Kesey.

"Sedated," replied Gaston. "Probably will be for the next decade. The letter from Kaspar says that it's too late for anyone to prevent a global bloodbath. He claims to have unified all the Nazi nuts from here to Arabia in one cooperative international organization capable of torching, murdering, and disrupting racial minorities *at a moment's notice.* He's demanding a global television audience to tell the world of his plans. He says that if the races surrender peaceably, and go quietly into internment camps for deportation to their original homelands, the carnage will be mitigated. If he's dismissed as a crackpot or we refuse his demands for the TV press conference, he will make certain that you and I personally regret our decision. He knows Pauline's every move, Bill. He says he's sorry your daughter, Christy, was home sick from school yesterday." He couldn't hide the anxiety from his boyhood chum and didn't try. "I think this is not your garden variety wacko, Billy."

William Kesey breathed hard. His brain processed the options quicker than he'd hoped. There just weren't any. "Where's he want to hold this little town meeting of his?"

"Germany. Nuremberg. Probably right out there on the parade grounds where Hitler used to review the troops. We're supposed to stand by for further instructions."

A cracking of shells came over the line, and Gaston knew his friend was at the pistachio nuts again. Reformed smoker.

"Tell me, Freddy," said Kesey, thinking of his little Christy with her red pigtails and nose freckles that collided every time she laughed. "Do you think God punishes people infinitely for sins committed in a finite life?"

"Seems a little like overkill, doesn't it, Billy?"

"Exactly how I felt," Kesey replied. "Until now. This guy deserves perpetual hellfire."

Fred Gaston sat forward in his chair, the trappings of power in the media no longer of any importance. "I want to send Pauline to an 'undisclosed location' you government types seem to have an abundance of. Can you arrange it?"

"Done." Even as he said it, Kesey knew the absurdity of trying to hide from a mind—and a network—like Kaspar's. "We'd better not continue our conversation at this time. Call me on my secured line when you're free and we'll discuss the details. And, Freddy, you bust your backside getting this guy on TV and I'll bust mine knocking him out. Yes?"

"Sure, Billy, same as always. But you know I can't set him up for a fall. A free press demands source confidentiality. *Comprende?"*

"Yeah, Mr. Broadcast. Is that why you called for backup?"

"We never had this conversation, Billy."

Kesey laughed tightly. "Freddy, this conversation will be out on cassettes and CDs within twelve hours or I'm not king of the spooks. Watch for it on the Home Shopping Channel."

"I don't watch the competition," Gaston parried. "Dulls my edge."

This time, William Kesey did not laugh. "Watch yourself, Fred. This one stinks from here to Stuttgart. You bite it and I'm out a halfway decent golfing adversary."

They hung up. *If I bite it,* thought Gaston, staring at the phone, *a lot of people will bite it with me.*

CHAPTER 20

Lady Katherine met them in Irish lace, a tour de force in needlework, an angel radiant. Angel von Feuerbach, her Jews called her.

Following introductions and a breathless telling of the harrowing escape they'd just experienced, she applied disinfectant to Connie's cuts and together they dressed the men's cuts and bruises. But Lady Katherine seemed oddly distracted, saying only what one is duty-bound to say when a recent guest returns unannounced with more in tow, all looking as if they've eaten bad fish.

And as strangely, the deeper they went into the house, the less Katherine von Feuerbach's lacy brightness was able to penetrate the gloom, like a rapidly dimming bulb. The soberly imposing Frau Heppler came with steaming tea and sugary cookies, then took her leave as ominously as she arrived. When Katherine at last took her seat at the harp, her guests settled uncomfortably on the sofa at the foot of the painted cross. Lady Katherine looked more like a forlorn angel ornament left off a too-full Christmas tree.

Except for the pink-lacquered nails. Reg could not take his eyes off them.

"Wonderful news," she said, striking a triumphant flourish on the strings. "I've just negotiated an airlift of the last remaining Falasha Jews out of Ethiopia. They will join their brethren at a resettlement camp near Jerusalem by week's end."

Reg tried to be diplomatic. "God is good, Katherine. But we've just had a brush with Kaspar that nearly killed us all. He took the kids hostage at gunpoint and this beating was at his hands. God protected us, but not before that maniac aged us a couple decades. Did you hear from your contacts?"

"Yes."

Reg edged forward. "Where? Where is Kaspar?"

"Soon," she answered. "Any moment now, we shall know." Reg shot a glance at the phone, willing it to ring.

She leaned into a sweet melody, then began to respond to the music with a resonant thrum from deep within her throat. It was as if the notes vibrated up her arms, into her being, and out her throat back into the strings. It was a thrilling, captivating exchange that soothed their jangled nerves.

"When I was a little girl," she said, accompanying the words on the harp, deftly turning conversation into ballad, "I would tune into the Cannes Music Festival on the old cabinet radio. I listened for the harp. I would pluck the teeth of my pocket comb and dream of being one with the harp. One night the guest artist was Alfredo Romero, master of the Paraguayan harp. In the tradition of the Guarani Indians, he captured their rhythm and lyricism so incredibly that it brought the audience to a standing ovation—in the middle of the piece! My father showed me the post-concert interview in the newspaper. When asked what it was like to be given such adulation by the international community, Alfredo replied so softly, 'The people are very kind. My most important concert, however, was playing the harp in the delivery room for the birth of my little Carmena!' *That* is music, my friends, *that* is music!"

Without thinking, Tony reached out and gave Connie's hand a gentle squeeze. When she did not respond, he saw her looking past the light at the center of the room into the far shadows where stood Alois Hitler, stern and accusing. She was wan and frightened.

"What?" he whispered, but she shook her head and would not speak.

The strains of the music of the mountains of Paraguay pushed against the hulking walls of the estate, holding them back. But for the island of light centered on the lady and the harp, Tony felt sure those walls would collapse.

His father sat at the edge of the sofa, leaning into the light, drawn to its center, watching her every move. He was falling for the woman, and Tony, trying to shake the clammy chill creeping across his shoulders, didn't like it. It was all wrong. The radiant woman and the malignant house. There was evil here.

Tony looked at Connie. She knew. Lips tightly drawn and pale as paper, Connie slowly stood and brought him up with her. They moved past Reg and the harp, unnoticed, a couple of restless youths taking a little tour of the place while the grown-ups reminisced their pasts.

She tried to act the casual browser at a curio shop, but Connie lingered little at the carvings and bric-a-brac that brought her to the painting of Alois Hitler. Without her hat, hair cropped, body thin and wraithlike, she stared up at the severe countenance in the military jacket. Tony shuddered. The large, fearful eyes apprehended every crease and peculiarity in the man before her. The Auschwitz victim and the camp commandant.

"Stop it, Connie! Stop staring at him like that!" Tony whispered fiercely, taking her by the shoulders and pulling her away. But she shrugged him off.

"Demon runt!" she said acidly. "Those are the eyes of the man who nearly destroyed a people, who nearly destroyed me. This is a Hitler as sure as the sun rises in the east. This man sired a devil!"

"All right, Connie, all right," soothed Tony, arms around her, moving her through a doorway into a book-lined room. In the spare glow of a Tiffany table lamp, they idly examined the musty, aging collection.

"Must be a World War II buff." Tony ran a finger along the spines. *"The War: A Concise History. The Swastika and the Eagle. Germany and the Soviet Union. Catholic Church and Nazi Germany . . ."*

He went on for a minute, mumbling over the titles. Then he heard a loud gasp from Connie. "What'd you find?" he asked.

"Come here! Look at this. *The International Jew: A World Problem. The Conspiracy Against Hitler.* Six copies of *Mein Kampf!* Who do you know who has six copies of that? And look at this one. *Hitler and the Black Arts.* Oh, and here's a gem. *Das Buch der Psalmen Teutsch: das Gebetbuch der Ariosophen Rassen-mystiker und Antisemiten.* If my German serves me, that translates *The Book of German Psalms: The Prayer Book of Arios-Racial Mystics and Anti-Semites."*

They continued down the rows, and every title in a twelve-shelf section was of the same ilk. Hitler as savior. The Jew as parasite. Nazi apologetics and several volumes on a bizarre range of topics from racial nationalism to the historic link between motherhood and motherland. The section began with *Hitler Was My Friend* and ended with *Suicide As a Magical Art.*

"A little light reading for a winter's evening," said Tony sourly. He saw a picture frame stuck between a bookend and the side of the bookcase and started to pull it out.

Quickly, he tried putting it back before she saw. Too late. She held a shaking hand toward him. "Give."

Tony's hand shook as much. They both held the framed painting and recoiled from the gory scene. They felt the madness creep about their feet and legs. It was a terrifying portrait of a crazed huntsman on horseback, blood-red cape flying wildly in the wind. He brandished a blood-smeared sword from which dangled a human head. Wolves howled at the horse, and corpses littered the road in the wake of the murderous horseman.

Worse still was the rider's uncanny resemblance to Adolf Hitler.

The forelock of dark brown hair drooped over the left temple. The prominent nose, the trademark mustache, the moping eyes were all there. The painting was obviously very old, dated "1889" in the lower left-hand corner.

"The year Adolf was born," said Tony dully. "How prophetic."

"Mein Fuehrer," Connie said with a shudder, pressing the painting into Tony's hands. "He said he read to confirm his own ideas." She wrapped herself in a hug and looked fearfully about the walls and ceiling. "What is this place, anyway? I think we should leave."

Tony's reply never came. Distant shouts sounded from somewhere within the far recesses of the house. Male voices. Unified.

"What's that?" Connie asked, moving closer to Tony.

A snarl. A bark. An answering shout of men in zealous agreement.

The harp increased in volume.

"Come on," Tony said. "Maybe it's some of Lady Katherine's Jews." The suggestion was absurd and Tony knew it. But no way did his mind want to form the conclusion that first flickered across its screen. That was unthinkable.

The harp quieted and they heard Lady Katherine say, "Here. Tomorrow morning. Don't look so surprised. All will be made clear tomorrow at a press conference."

They passed through an archway at the other side of the library and were quickly confronted with a closed door. The ancient keyhole still held its key, and they entered a dark hallway with a faint glow of light at the far end. The closer they moved toward the light, the louder the chant became, then turned to singing:

"Though at first we are but few,
The road is broad—the aim is clear;
Forward, step by step!
Courage, come along!
Though at first we are but few,
We shall carry it off, nonetheless!"

Tony, in the lead, rammed his shin into a small table. Before he could cry out, Connie clamped a hand firmly over his mouth. She waited until he stopped rubbing the injured limb, then slowly released her hand. But not before he'd kissed it.

"Sorry," he whispered. "Wasn't paying attention. Your hand tastes like cookies."

"Didn't you get enough to eat back there?"

"Never. You've still got some crumbs on your jacket. May I have them?"

She smiled bravely and gave him a gentle shove, but he put out a cautionary arm and told her to be quiet with his lips. The chorus had stopped. Then came a lone voice, commanding and strident.

"Who—are—we?" the voice asked, spacing the words, hitting each one full throttle. They knew that voice. It was the voice of a wolf in priest's clothing.

The answer to the question came loud and virile, as one:

"We are servants of the Ideal!

"We are given to protect, to preserve, to promote the stainless blood of racial purity!

"We are the keepers of the true gospel and are sworn to apply it to all people and all times.

"True Christian faith is Aryan faith.

"True Aryan faith unfolds only within a God-created *Volkdom.*

"A God-created *Volkdom* must decisively reject the political universalism of Rome.

"A God-created *Volkdom* must decisively reject the peace-at-all-cost of international Protestantism.

"A God-created *Volkdom* must spill blood to save blood!

"We are servants of the Ideal!"

Tony felt Connie's face pressing into his back. He knew she was stifling a scream. The horror would not end. They had found the nest.

He pulled her to him and bent to her ear. "Pray with me. Lord Jesus, we don't know what to do. Should we go tell Dad or should we go on and see what this is? You saved us by your blood, now please protect us by that same blood. Let no evil harm us. Help us, please, help us!"

Connie's lips were moving too. He put his ear against them and heard, "God, if you're there, we need you bad. From what I've seen, if you're not there, then we're all condemned to die. But Tony and his dad think there's hope. Somewhere. Show us where. Please."

He kissed and stroked her head. Softly, he sang, "Jesus loves me, this I know, for the Bible tells me—"

He stopped. Connie hugged him tightly. In the near-distance, one hundred pair of boots hit the floor precisely as one. Again. Then in a steady, marching rhythm that grew ever louder.

They were coming.

Reg Danson ignored the sense of urgency that tried to steal the joy of Lady Katherine's solo. He was transported to the jungles of Paraguay, one minute tumbled in the rush and roar of a waterfall, the next resting in the delicate mist beside the churning pool. He heard the beating of hummingbird wings and the comical bleating of a flock of playful goats. Cheery birdcalls and mighty wind—he heard them all.

The harp swelled into a stunning cascade of sound that made the hair at the back of his neck stand erect.

It made a fitting sensation for the unshakable conviction that had at last wormed its way through the eerie magic casting a spell over the Gates of Hope: *She was stalling.*

He followed the swirling caress of the exquisite hands passing over the strings like butterflies, sometimes landing, sometimes hovering, very rarely staying long. The dominant hand—the left—played the melody with a feather touch. In his mind, the fingers of that same hand dipped in the communal dish, joined the fingers of his right hand.

Close as Jesus and Judas.

The rupture was complete. A thousand ugly thoughts followed. She may as well have been drawing her fingernails across a school chalkboard. She played on, but the music was gone.

He who dipped his hand with Me in the dish will betray Me.

Reg stood abruptly, spilling tea and overturning the plate of cookies. "Katherine, I'm sorry, but we haven't much time and I need to ask you something."

She stopped, opened her eyes, and gave a pinched smile of resignation. "It was nothing."

"What was nothing?"

"The music. Just a trite snatch of bar music, nothing more."

He took her by the arms and shook her gently. "It was beautiful music. And it didn't come from any bar. Stop talking as if you're always continuing another conversation. Your music is a stupefying potion that keeps me from my mission. The world may teeter on the edge of a civil war of horrendous magnitude. Neighbor murdering neighbor in Prague and Pittsburgh. What I need to know is"—he paused, heart racing, mouth cotton-dry—"are you a part of it?"

She looked at him with the same appraising stare she had leveled on Hitler's painting of Christ, trying to examine his insides. "Why do you want to know the answer? For the Vatican? Or the police?"

Reg released her. He looked down at the floor and the little pile of broken cookies. "I want to know for—for me."

She came to him and kissed him on the cheek. "Sweet Reg, you don't know how long it has been since I've heard such wonderful words from a man."

He led her to the sofa where they sat, her hands in both of his. He kissed the lovely fingers. His head came up, eyes wet with tears. "Why," he asked huskily, "why won't you answer my question?"

"Why? Undoubtedly the same question posed by the Roman centurion Gaius Cassius even as he plunged the Spear of Herod

Antipas into Christ's side in fulfillment of Zechariah the prophet, saying 'They shall look upon Him whom they have pierced.'"

Even as she spoke in that weird rote way he'd heard Connie recite the party line, Reg sensed she was listening for something. What?

"Why did they have to kill this humble and fearless man? That frustrating riddle was the thing that drove the centurion to do what he did. He did not want that holy man's bones broken like the thieves'. It was the last act of respect in the midst of the greatest cruelty."

She pressed his head against her breast. "But great as that story is, Reg Danson, a greater one overshadows it. The spear used to fulfill the prophecy of the Christ was the same spear fashioned by the ancient Phineas. It was raised in the battle of Jericho by the mighty arm of Joshua to signal the people to give the mighty shout that would collapse the walls of the city and give God's army the victory. That spear of victory became an instrument of incredible power in the hands of the centurion who became known and revered as Longinus the Spearman. It symbolizes for all time the magical powers inherent in the blood of God's chosen people!"

A steadily growing noise pierced the walls of the sitting room. From beyond, out in that hall of Reg Danson's night of terror, came the crisp slap of boot leather on wood, the approach of a legion.

Reg's head snapped up. Where had Tony and Connie wandered to? He started to rise. She held him down. "Now *we* have it, the symbol, the powerful talisman of God and we as God's chosen successors to Joshua will wield it for a short season followed by a long and glorious day of peace and prosperity!"

Reg broke free of her embrace, stood, and looked wildly at the door leading to the hall. The grandfather clock ticked like a bomb. The marching grew steadily louder, filling the house with a thick dread. It stamped along the walls of the sitting room, threatening to burst in upon them at any moment. Abruptly, it ceased.

Danson shouted, "Katherine! The Holy Lance is *here?* How can that be?"

"Because *I* am here." The sneering declaration came from the shadows at the front of the house. The young Aryan with whom Reg had so recently done battle stepped into the room, a lean, wolfish shepherd dog at his side. Danson shrank back despite himself and felt a renewed throbbing in his calf. The dog watched him intently.

The Aryan winced only slightly from his own leg wound. He was too busy grinning at the shock his entrance caused the American.

Danson moved to shield Lady Katherine. Even as he did, he knew with sinking certainty that it wasn't necessary. "Katherine," he said, "this is Kaspar, the murderer of innocents. He thinks he can start a global race war with a few trinkets of the church for a crutch."

"No, Reg," said Lady Katherine quietly. "This is my son, Frederich von Feuerbach II."

Reg choked. "Your *son* very nearly killed my son—and Miss Bird, and me."

Katherine von Feuerbach did not move. "We shall sort this out, all in due time."

The Aryan wore a curious wine-colored coat of very ancient origin. Roughly woven of a cottonlike material, it was seamless with full sleeves and extended to just below the knees. Below it were the familiar khaki trousers and shin-high jackboots.

"My bulletproof vest," said the Aryan with a loud and surly laugh. "Do you like it? I don't suppose you've ever seen the Coat of Christ before?"

Startled, Reg realized he was looking at the Holy Coat of Treves, first making its claim as the Holy Tunic in the fifth century. Katherine von Feuerbach glowed with pleasure at the sight. "Think of it, Reg Danson! The woman of the gospels with the serious bleeding touched the hem of *that* gown and was instantly healed. The power went out of Christ as if he could not refuse so strong a faith. It is one and the same power in the fighting spear of God!"

"Tradition, Katherine, nothing more," said Reg. "We cannot put our faith in objects. The power comes from the One behind the stories, the promises, the healings of Scripture. Now let's call the authorities and get your son the help he needs."

The Aryan trotted the shepherd within lunging distance of Reg Danson. "I think you are still confused on one very salient point," he said.

Reg did not like the way the dog's nerves displayed themselves in the twitching of skin, ears, nose. He thought of Maria Metternich, the guide at the Teutonic Treasury, the bloody tears in her skin, the depth of her fear. This was the dog—and the man—who had used her to get at the Lance.

"True, I am the master thief," continued the Aryan with a smirk. "But I lay those spoils at the feet of another. May I properly introduce to you, Katherine von Feuerbach, nee Kasparine, of the house of Kasparine, district of Saxony. Lady Kaspar, your liege awaits your bidding."

He bowed low. Instinctively, Reg weighed whether the greater danger sat behind him. Before he could move, however, her lacquered nails scraped lightly across the back of his neck. The hand that played the melody. The hand that signed the calling cards of death.

Dully, without turning to face her, Reg asked, "The Jewish Repatriation League, nothing more than a front for neo-Nazis?"

She stopped toying with his neck and sighed. "Nothing is ever that simple, Herr Danson. I use some of the money to help relocate quite a few Jews. But it is a very slow process. What of the other poor races needing relocation? No, a greater portion of the donations has been used to educate and fund the revolution. It is not as deceptive as it seems. We will arrive at far more sweeping results much more quickly by uniting the Aryan brotherhood worldwide. Already they are in place. Already they have the necessary weapons and troops.

They know best where the pockets of ethnic resistance are most likely to occur. Much more quickly can they neutralize the opposition and bring about the day for which we all yearn, even you. The day of no more racial prejudice because we are all in our rightful places!

"You see? I am actually maximizing the donations I receive and soon will deliver a much larger dividend than ever dreamed of by my donors."

No wonder she had been able to handle millions in contributions. Her "office staff" were the thousands of misguided bigots who thirsted to put the "mud races" firmly and forever in their place. In an inhuman, international game of Russian roulette, the unsuspecting were either saved or slaughtered at random. The smiling photos in her albums were the pictures of the few lucky pawns in her twisted version of a perfect world. The pictures of those unlucky enough to die under the auspices of the JRL weren't in the collection. They were draped in black on the pianos, mantles, and dresser tops of the shattered homes where they had once known love. And they were soon to be joined by more unless Reg, by the help of God, could somehow stop the revolution.

"You lied to me," Reg said. "About everything. About your son, about the nature of your mission. You told me that you yourself had been the target of hatred for your resettlement work." He scanned the room for a means of diverting their attention. "What of the little boy who spit on your shoes and called you a filthy name?"

"Marketing," her son replied with a satisfied chuckle. "Mother's patrons like a good overcoming adversity story. Loosens the purse strings. Keeps the police sympathetic too. You can buy a kid like that for little money."

"Don't be smug, Frederich," his mother ordered. "You know how much I dislike the smugness."

The Aryan glared at his mother. She looked as if she might strike him, then thought better of it. "We may have to force some to bend to the will of the Coalition, but that is no reason to treat them with anything other than courtesy."

Reg was incredulous. *"Courtesy?!* Katherine, people have died by your son's hand for protecting things that devout people hold in reverence. Surely you do not believe this can be a bloodless revolution? Have you seen how neo-Nazis brutalize—"

"Stop it!" Katherine shouted. "Frederich assures me that the Coalition will make every effort at restraint. If people choose to resist, there will be consequences as in all war. But the women, the children, the peaceable have nothing to fear."

"Katherine," Reg implored, "don't be so naive."

"Silence!" roared the Aryan. The animal whimpered hungrily. "Where are the other two Americans? Mother, at times you can be so careless!" With a wave of the hand, he freed the shepherd to sniff out the room. Immediately, the animal picked up Tony's and Connie's scents and padded off toward the library.

"We are about to rewrite the history of the world, Mother, and you accuse me of being smug," the son fumed. "If I swagger, it is because soon we of the clean Germanic line will no longer have to accept the charity of our oppressors. You go ahead and play on your harp and compose the music of the New Order!"

"You can be so indiscreet!" she snapped.

Reg seized on their rancor. "Have you seen your son at work, Katherine? Have you seen what he does with this dog?"

"Don't answer that, Mother. We have our agreement. I don't pry into your affairs and you stay out of mine. We may disagree on method, but in the end we shall rule as coregents."

The Aryan looked at Reg with a pitying grin. "You really are ill-equipped for this mission, aren't you? It is only dumb good fortune for you that you've remained alive this long. You cannot come between Lady Kaspar and me. She played you as proficiently as she does that harp of hers." He caressed the harp and looked at Reg.

Danson kept his fist at his side. If anyone deserved a right to the jaw, it was himself. He'd been royally duped. Not only had he placed himself squarely in danger, but the kids as well.

A shattering crash and the thud of a heavy object brought them all to their feet. Frederich ran toward the sound. "Someone's thrown a stone through the window!" he shouted from the library.

The shepherd whined and scratched madly at the closed door leading from the library into the hall. Katherine and Frederich both ran to investigate. The Aryan ordered the dog back to guard Reg. It padded slowly past Reg, ears flattened against its skull, to take up a position near the front door.

Before the dog turned to face him, Reg bolted for the door leading directly from the parlor into the hall. He nearly tore it from its hinges and slammed it in the face of the snarling canine.

Reg's heart skipped a beat. The long hall was filled with the shadowy figures of one hundred silent men with guns, two rows stretching away into the darkness. They were at ramrod attention, breathing as one.

Until Reg.

In the split second they remained frozen in surprise by his arrival, Danson plunged down the side hall from which the dog had ambushed him the night before. Halfway down he plowed into a large, soft, looming bulk that materialized out of the blackness like a freighter from the fog.

Frau Heppler.

"Oh, thank God, Frau Heppler, it's you! Help me!"

She quickly opened a door in the wall and without a word motioned him inside. *Dear old grumpy girl. Not so bad after all, are we?*

He pulled the door of the broom closet closed all but for a small crack. The cramped space smelled of floor wax and disinfectant. A metal mop pail jabbed him in the ribs.

He crouched there, watching Frau Heppler take her stand in the center of the hall, a great immovable human monolith in dressing gown. *Thank you, God, for the beautiful scowling Frau!*

The pounding of booted feet ricocheted like wrecking balls down the corridor. But the Frau did not quail before the onslaught. Steady as Gibraltar.

Through the crack, Reg watched jackboots clatter to a stop inches from house slippers. Toe-to-toe, they stood saying nothing. Then, like the center span of a drawbridge, Frau Heppler's arm slowly raised and the plump finger on the end pointed straight at the closet door.

CHAPTER 21

They crouched in the shrubbery at the edge of the estate, dreading the moment unleashed dogs hunted them down and rendered them unrecognizable to friends and family. Or storm troopers burst from the house to spray the landscape with automatic weapons fire. Tony tightened his embrace on Connie but could not still her quaking. She kissed his arm and they waited.

"I can't keep this up," Tony said at last. "I thought sure the rock through the window would bring them outside, give Dad a chance to escape. I say we go for the police."

"No way," Connie argued. "This isn't some convenience store holdup where you dial up the thief and negotiate a hostage release. There's a small army in there! These people want to rule the world. Your dad doesn't stand a chance if we force their hand."

"Oh really?" Tony lashed out. "So just where was all this sophisticated Nazi radar of yours when we went to the fair with the pistol-packing priest?"

Connie bristled. "Look, buddy, I told my life's story to public enemy number one. Who's in more danger here?"

Tony hugged her. "Hey, I'm sorry, let's not fight. I'm just a little wound right now. But what do we do? Just sit here under the stars and do nothing?"

"Shh. You pray. I'll think."

Tony gave her ear a playful twist, but she brushed him off. He kissed the baseball cap and she snuggled against him. The night wore on, the noises of restless Nuremberg gradually settling into uneasy slumber. The occasional snort of a car horn or the distant shouts of exuberant nightclubbers sounded whenever the city turned in its sleep.

Not a sound came from inside the Gates of Hope. No one moved near the dimly lit windows in the parlor or the library. It was as if they'd all left and gone . . .

. . . underground.

At length, Connie said, "It's not fair."

Tony shifted uncomfortably. His leg was asleep and he was getting cold. "That's an understatement."

"No, you don't understand. It's not fair that German youth inherit the angst of World War II. The war ended and there was little public debate over the Hitler regime. Germans were forced to bury their sentiments and press on with economic recovery. They never got credit for quickly turning a totalitarian horror into an industrious democracy. Now the kids are acting out the glory days of their grandfathers because the old problems of unemployment and the economic oppression eastern Germans brought with them into unification are bubbling over."

Tony laughed sarcastically. "Listen, dear, my father's in there with some of those poor little misunderstood Nazi kids right now. Last week they or their brothers rampaged at Buchenwald. They overturned a Holocaust display and shouted *'Sieg Heil!* Hail to victory!' You'll forgive me if I have a little trouble sympathizing with them at the moment."

She mumbled something he didn't quite catch. "Excuse me?"

This time her reply was crystal clear. "Ugly American!"

"Hey, I—"

"Don't!" she snapped, stinging him with her vehemence.

You can take the girl away from the Nazis, but it's not so easy taking the Nazi out of the girl.

She sat forward, the cool night rushing in to steal the body warmth they'd shared. "It's quite black and white for you. But soon these 'misunderstood' people are going to hold the world prisoner, never mind just your father. I suggest you make every effort in the time left to you to understand them. They could soon be your masters!"

"Never!" Tony seethed, scrambling around to face her. "I won't bend the knee to these fascists! I'm going back in that house You coming?"

In the moonlight, she studied the fierce pride and defiance in his face. Suddenly, she leaned forward and kissed him on the lips. "Dear macho Tony. Ever the white knight charging into this battle or that. And always forgetting your lance!"

He scowled. "It's the Lance that got us into this, remember? And what's the kiss for?"

"Consider it a good *knight* kiss."

"You can sleep at a time like this?"

She grinned at him. "No, blockhead. You are a good shining knight, but your tactics are all wrong. You need to be like the Free Lance, the medieval knight who instead of contracting with any particular king or government served whomever he chose." She pulled at his sweatshirt and poked him gently in the stomach. She pursed her lips. There was a glint in her eye. "Up 'til now you've been at the mercy of King Vanity and Queen Ego."

"I have not!" flashed Tony. *Yes I have,* he thought. *I don't want to take directions from a girl. I can't admit that I'm in over my head and that maybe she knows what she's talking about.* He chuckled in surrender. "Okay, okay. Sir Bullhead defers to Princess Pulls-No-Punches. What's the plan?"

"We call their bluff. Remember what you and your dad and Leo found when you researched the relics? That information's our only chance. And we've got to show Lady Katherine the full extent of her son's activities. But to pull it off, we've got to go move a little heaven and earth. You heard her, we haven't much time if it's all coming down in the morning. You game?"

He looked worriedly over at the house, then at Connie. She squirmed with an idea, eager and fully alive. To think that Hitler had reached out from the grave and nearly quenched her fire. Inconceivable. "Yeah, I'm in," he said. "Just one condition. Before we leave, we pray over the perimeter of this place, every foot of it. If there's a demon inside, I want my dad to know heaven's cavalry's got 'em surrounded."

They walked hand-in-hand, staying well back in the shadows, asking God to command the angelic forces and assure Reg he was not alone. The hulking house followed them in surly silence.

Connie watched and listened to Tony quietly and fervently beseech God to protect his father and give him wisdom and wits. He prayed for the success of whatever scheme Connie was plotting. He asked divine clemency for a world in grave danger. "And Lord," he faltered, voice cracking. "I choose to be your Free Lance, to be ever in your service only, with allegiance alone to the cause of Jesus Christ. Accept us now, feeble warriors that we are, and use us to your glory and honor. Amen."

Connie turned him to face her, wrapped her arms around him, and squeezed. "Amen," she said.

It was the dead of night in Vatican City when Father Piero Vincente's solitary cell was violated by an ungodly pounding on the door. The chief investigator for the Investigatory Council on Religious Phenomena was certain he could not stand another piece of terrible news. But what else could it be at that hour of the night but one more catastrophe in a chain of ill omens stretching from the thefts of the Coat, the Veil, the Shroud, and the Lance to the untimely death of Claudio Andone? And the wicked way between was paved with murder, attempted murder, and now what appeared to be an attempt to no less than extort human dignity from the inhabitants of earth. The Vatican had been alerted by the Italian affiliate of the Global News Network that on the morrow, the swine Kaspar would address the world with a grand plan for racial redistribution. *Madre Dios!* Mother of God! How had it come to this?

No amount of praying would dispel the devil at the door. Vincente threw a terry cloth robe over his mighty expanse and padded to the door. "Yes?" he called to the other side. He was not about to open it to any midnight messengers before they identified themselves.

"Father, Father! Come quickly! An urgent phone call. A matter of life and death."

Vincente tipped forward until his forehead braced against the door. It was Georgio, the valet, but what was the phone call? He almost preferred the seers of strange lights and tappings from heaven than the infernal reality of recent days' events.

He followed the highly agitated Georgio to the telephone. Vincente's regular secretary was ill and the valet never asked the caller to declare himself. The man hovered while Vincente took a deep breath and composed himself for whoever was on the line. He fervently hoped it was not Beatrix of Einsiedeln. The woman was a self-styled oracle who bled spontaneously from her feet and hands in conjunction with her monthly female cycle. The christological stigmata had turned tiny Einsiedeln, Switzerland, on its ear and made it a must stop on several European tours of the miraculous. Blessed Beatrix had a habit of calling him whenever her feet and hands failed to bleed on time.

He said hello in his most official bass. "Oh, yes, it is you! And your father?" He listened with widening eyes until it was necessary for Georgio to supply a chair to support the weight of what the priest was hearing. He sank into the chair, saying, "Thank you. Andone was not only a great churchman but a dear friend. Irascible, at times, but aren't we all. Small in stature was he, but such a vacuum left by his passing!"

Vincente went rigid, the bulldog face turning dark with doubt. "That is not possible! What you ask is beyond the church to grant." He listened for a moment more, the sagging jowls flushing with blood. "This is an enormous gamble! Not only have we suffered the irreplaceable loss of four treasures, you now suggest that we—"

Vincente tried unsuccessfully to interrupt the rush of words at the other end. He motioned for pen and paper, and Georgio produced them. Vincente made a notation, listened some more, and wrote again. "This is an incredible thing you ask! The church risks irreparable embarrassment." Pause. Vincente's meaty hand was a vise, squeezing the life from the handset. "No, of course I do not value things above people . . . You do not understand! These things are not mere articles of cloth and metal. They are hugely symbolic of two millennia of faith . . ." He bristled with indignation. "Yes, of course, I am aware of the relics of Buddha and Confucius and Mohammed. Two of the Islamic prophet's hairs are kept in a reliquary in the Dome of the Rock at Jerusalem. But what's that . . . Do you presume to teach me my religion?!

"Well, of course there are different classifications of relics. First-class relics are body parts of saints or objects from the Passion of Christ; second-class relics are sanctified by having touched the bodies of saints such as the instruments of torture by which the martyrs died; and third-class relics are things having been in contact with either first- or second-class relics . . . Well, I cannot say exactly what class the items you request are in, but by their very definition they would probably fall in the first . . Well, no, they couldn't *all* be, that's true, but—but . . . Look here, I—"

He quieted then, eyes shut tight, rocking slightly in the chair. Beads of sweat glistened in the whiskers of his upper lip. Then, with a sigh of enormous resignation, he said, "Yes, yes. You are right. To do nothing is to risk anarchy. I—I must act and act swiftly. I don't know how I shall get them to you in time, but the God who once made the sun stand still in a single isolated battle for Joshua can do it again for all humankind. Let us pray to that end. I hope I shall have the privilege of speaking with you again, but come what may, go with God!"

In the small hours of the morning, four related events occurred in four widely dispersed locations of Western and Eastern Europe. Under supreme orders of the pontifical offices of the Holy Roman See, keepers of the church's treasures surrendered that which they had been sworn to protect with their very lives. In Paris, France; Krakow, Poland; and St. Peter's Basilica at Rome, the guardians of antiquity hid their eyes from the unspeakable and wept tears of separation. What had once been among the possessions of Saint John Chrysostom, Boleslav the Brave, and King Louis XIV were relinquished in a modern crusade to halt an outbreak of unprecedented evil. It was perhaps to be their finest hour.

Meanwhile, at the main depot of the Nuremberg security police, photographs were gathered and placed in a large manila envelope marked "Warning: graphic contents. For official police use only."

Three jets were chartered to fly the treasures of the church to Nuremberg, Germany. That they would arrive in time was in serious doubt. All the pilots knew about their highly secretive cargoes was that time was their enemy. All the driver in the unmarked police unit knew was that only the worst cases were to be included in the manila packet.

There was one other salient point. All items were to be claimed at the airport by an earnest young man in a Notre Dame sweatshirt in the company of a young woman in a St. Louis Cardinals baseball cap and military dress.

No names were to be used. Even airport walls have ears.

CHAPTER 22

At dawn, a caravan of blue and white Global News Network and silver Nuremberg Telecommunications trucks snaked onto the grounds of the Jewish Repatriation League. Miniature satellite dishes sprouted from their roofs like shiny metal ears cocked to eavesdrop on the conversations of the heavens. Doors slid open and technicians in GNN and NT coveralls trailing thick black cable wires poured from the vehicles on sneakered feet. Cameras, light stands, spotlights, and a warehouse of ancillary gadgetry swiftly transformed the steps and veranda at the front of the estate into a studio back lot. The interiors of the broadcast vans resembled the cloistered and hardware-crammed interiors of sonar submarines, subdued lighting and colorful control panels turning the faces of the communications experts lemon yellow and lime green.

Designer-suited news personalities of French, German, Italian, Slavic, African, Spanish, Arabic, Chinese, Japanese, and British descent stepped officiously from two white four-door sedans, each door bearing the holographic image of a spinning globe held in place by the blue overlapping bars of the letters "GNN." Each newsperson had prepared scripts hastily assembled throughout the night giving what background was known from media reports of Kaspar's unprecedented string of crimes. Each also carried a copy of the same sketchy instructions and master race philosophy received from the mouth of the canine courier by Fred Gaston, GNN senior director of international operations.

But what was about to transpire exactly was uncertain in any language.

A sleek black Mercedes arrived and out stepped Fred Gaston, supreme field commander of Operation Lightning Bolt, the strictly in-house designation for this on-location "shoot." If history was to be made today, Gaston would be legal counsel, judge, and jury on what went out over the air. He could count on one hand—the hand minus the pinky finger lost in combat—the number of times he'd pulled an exclusive coup the magnitude of this one. Earthquakes didn't come this big.

Gaston, immaculate in a charcoal-gray three-piece Brooks Brothers suit, mounted the steps and stood before the grand doors of the estate, waiting as he'd been told to do. "Friggin' Kaspar had better deliver," he fumed under his breath. "This is costing GNN ten grand a minute." He patted a coat pocket and felt the reassuring bulge of the antacids. New bottle already half empty.

"As for me and my house, we will serve the Lord," Gaston read. He well knew the untarnished reputation of Katherine von Feuerbach. He also knew the heart-stopping visitation of a hound from hell. Oh yes, he'd seen it all. And to think he'd passed on an opportunity to go into produce with his Uncle Al. Next life, maybe.

The sun rose, the door opened, and out stepped a breathtaking woman in flowing silk the color of pale yellow rose petals. Like the beating of locust wings, a king's ransom of electronics started to roll. Lady Katherine, soft hair radiantly resting on pale white shoulders, offered a delicate left hand in welcome. Ambidextrous, Gaston favored his left, the disfigured one, but she took it firmly and warmly in her own. "Alexander the Great was left-handed," she said with a luminous smile.

"And Joan of Arc," he rejoined with a slight bow. *And Jack the Ripper,* his cynical muse prompted. "Lady Katherine, I am Fred Gaston with GNN, and I must ask you to honor the terms of our agreement. We have news anchors doing background for our global viewing audience as we speak, but we cannot keep the airways open indefinitely." A soft chatter of many voices and accents rose around them as the anchors updated a global audience on the coming event.

"I would dispute that," replied Lady Katherine coolly. "My son, Frederich von Feuerbach II, has asked me to make a few introductory remarks. If I may?"

He met her gaze. Fred Gaston had faced down three presidents, two members of royalty, and a mobster named Guts the Blade. But these blue-gray eyes smoked with a strange intensity. A stab of pain sliced through his entrails, and he fought to keep from grabbing his stomach. She saw him waver and held her gaze. Gaston staggered slightly and reached to steady himself. "Please do," was all he could manage before stepping weakly down the stairs. Out of sight, behind a satellite truck, he upended the bottle of antacids and chewed as if his life depended upon it.

"Men, women, boys, and girls of the world, I thank you for giving ear to this special broadcast. I am Lady Katherine von Feuerbach of Germany's house of Kasparine. You probably, and unfortunately perhaps, know me best by the code name of Kaspar."

The television crew gasped, heads rising from scripts and behind cameras as if to verify with their own eyes that the astounding confession had come from the beautiful woman in yellow silk. With jaded professionalism, they swiftly bent back to their tasks, but much more alert and sober-faced than they had begun them.

From behind the satellite trucks came a strangled cry. Fred Gaston couldn't catch his breath, and he'd run out of antacids. A couple of the startled anchors ran to his aid.

"My many benefactors have been so very kind to support me in the important work of repatriating Jews to Israel," Katherine continued. "I am happy to report that through your efforts, we have played a significant role in expediting the return. There have been five major waves of immigration to Israel since it declared statehood in 1948. JRL has been especially effective of late by helping complete the fifth wave or Operation Solomon. It began in 1971 and has resulted in the return of 45,000 Jews from Ethiopia. The sixth wave of Russian immigrants now in progress has swollen Israel's population by five hundred thousand in the past several years.

"But let us talk now of a seventh and most exciting wave that will be touched off by the events of this day. I speak, of course, of the one large pocket of Diaspora left: the North American continent. Israel desires that all Jews should come home to their rightful inheritance. They cannot be happy anywhere else in the world, not even in America, and that is why they have been so unwelcome outside their own borders. They suffer from a divine restlessness that does not allow them to put down roots and become assimilated by their adopted nations. It is not right to expect them to do so, and yet they have suffered for it."

Fred Gaston's color returned, and he brushed away any further attempts to keep him quiet. "Find me a case of German antacids," he barked at a lighting technician. "And a pound of fresh garlic. I'll be hanged if I'll be derailed by that black widow!" The technician hopped in one of the white sedans and sped off for the nearest market.

Lady Katherine smiled ardently for the cameras. Her loveliness filled television screens from Canton, Ohio, to Johannesburg, South Africa. Rowdy taverns in Albany, New York, fell silent at her words. Housewives in Glastonbury, Scotland, sent their small children outside to play and Katherine von Feuerbach filled the void. Programmers for Euro Software, welders at Ford Motors assembly plants, and clerks at Tokyo's Shimbun Department Store stopped work to gather around television sets and hear a new and chilling vision for the world.

"You know of the so-called Auschwitz lie, that the so-called Holocaust never occurred. You and I both know that statistics can be made to say whatever we want them to. No one denies that people died in the war. But that they died by the millions is highly questionable as is the degree of their innocence. Where is the objective documentation? The Holocaust has become a religion of its own when in fact the Jewish people probably owe Hitler a debt of gratitude for forcing the issue of a Jewish state."

Gaston could not get to David Levin in time. The veteran GNN cameraman ripped off the headset and stormed the stairs leading to Lady Katherine's podium. Cameras three and four zoomed in on the anguished face. "Liar!" Levin screamed, pointing an accusing finger. "You hatemongers gassed my grandparents with acid gas. In this very city the Nuremberg trials proved the enormity of your crime! Genocide claimed 5.7 million of my people and you are to blame!"

Gaston and three technicians reached Levin and pulled him back from the temporary stage. "Be gentle with him," Lady Katherine admonished. "Who can blame the man? His family suffered a great loss. I for one would like to know the truth behind the Soviet Union's complicity in the loss of life in World War II. But that is all speculative for now, and isn't it time to put the past in the past and get on with a new tomorrow?"

She brightened, the highlights in the hair, the eyes, the delicate rosy cheekbones weaving an aura of kindness and believability. She looked intently and, some would later say, *lovingly* into the cameras. Love her or hate her, two billion people were mesmerized by her delivery. "These are highly charged issues over which men and women of deep convictions differ. How could matters of the heart be any different? What we need now is a new covenant, one that will forever heal the pain that inevitably comes with forcing the cohabitation of the races. What some would label right-wing extremism is actually the saving grace for this bloodied, torn planet. Today, we restore reason to culture. Today, we declare freedom for all who live under the forced integration of democratic societies. Today is the day of your liberation!"

From up the boulevard in front of the Gates of Hope came the sound of a legion of jackboots tramping in unison and coming closer. Cameras mounted on the roofs of two of the sound trucks swung in that direction.

The wave of Aryans advanced like a column of army ants, straight ahead, unwavering. They were young men shaved bald, and they marched in a phalanx of identical manhood behind their leader. At the front of the column, sixteen men formed a wedge, each face locked in the same determined focus, each trooper in command of a matched German shepherd. At the head of the "V" strode Frederich von Feuerbach II, a smile of barely concealed contempt wreathing his lips.

The rising sea of Nuremberg residents attracted to the scene parted and allowed the powerful GNN cameras to capture the triumphal entry at the Gates of Hope.

A growing commotion at the entrance to the airline terminal's Wolkersdorf Cafe roused Connie from slumber. She slumped next to the dozing Tony Danson and clutched the manila envelope to her flak jacket tight as a skin graft. How long had they been asleep exposed for all the world to see? She smacked Tony awake with the packet.

"Hey, hey, are we there yet?" he managed, struggling up from sleep.

"Yeah, Sherlock, they defused the bomb and gave us clearance to land. We blew a tire and dropped an engine, but not a bad touchdown all things considered."

Tony struggled to sit upright. "What the heck are you—"

"What's going on over at the cafe?" she interrupted, pulling him to his feet. "Omigosh!"

She ran and he limped after, one leg numb enough for surgery. When he finally caught up she was hopping up and down, trying to see over the crowd flooding the area below the wall-mounted television and spilling out into the terminal. When he saw what she and the others saw, he snapped fully awake.

"It's him!" Tony yelled involuntarily. The crowd turned and stared at him suspiciously.

"Yes, it's Elvis!" Connie squealed, pointing vaguely in the direction of the automatic teller machine. "Quick, before he gets away!" Off they stumbled, two wacky kids in search of the phantom king of rock and roll.

"And you think I've got a mouth!" Connie whispered furiously when they were safely out of sight behind a popcorn wagon. "An eighteen-month-old Nazi in training pants could follow our trail! A bloody Panzer tank could come by and you'd flag 'em down and ask for directions to the nearest rally!"

"I would not! Everybody knows guys don't ask for directions." He grinned at her. She glowered at him.

"Hey, Miss Teen Aryan, tar and feather me later, would you?" Tony fired back, becoming just as agitated. "Our favorite priest is marching onto prime time, and we don't have all the parts for a counterattack."

"So what do you do when you don't know what to do?" she demanded, chin stuck out like a schoolyard bully.

He looked at her blankly for a moment, then smiled a little. They sank to their knees, the aroma of freshly popped corn attending their prayers.

At first they did not hear the airport page, but on the third repetition, it sank in. "Will the Vincente party of two report to airport security? Vincente party of two." Father Piero Vincente had made the sun stand still.

CHAPTER 23

Reg Danson was a prisoner without bonds, bars, or human guards. The door to the master bedroom where he'd been dumped stood wide open. Other than a seeping three-inch gash to the chin from a rifle butt, his body was whole and intact. The Aryan would return later and finish Reg at his leisure.

But by no means was Reg Danson free to go.

He involuntarily stiffened at the sound of claws on hardwood. The same sound had occurred throughout the night, every ten minutes or so. Every time he heard it he braced himself for the nightmare vision. Every time the clicking slowed and stopped just short of the open door. Then, without a sound, the hoary head and dripping muzzle would slide into view, like a wolf eel at the entrance to its undersea lair. Jasmine yellow eyes picked Reg's bones.

Again the clicking stopped just short of the door. Danson marked the wait with each kick of his heart. He dared not slumber. He could not.

The terrifying head, hairs at attention, turned the corner. The beast drew air through its twitching nostrils as if sucking Danson dry of scent. The moist yellow chips that were its eyes flashed heat.

The terrible hound would not blink.

They stayed like that, eyes locked, for long, torturous minutes until the shepherd Goebbels, tongue wrapping hungrily around its muzzle, slid back into the hall. For long minutes more, there was no sound, and Danson knew the dog waited, waited for him to wear down, get careless, make a break for freedom. Such rash action would void the master's prohibitions and allow the beast license to kill.

This silence was the worst. Danson prayed for the sound of the nails to recede back down the hall to wherever the creature kept its stationary vigil.

At last the clicking came. Relief. Another chilling wait.

It was morning. He had to make his move. Katherine and her son had made no effort to conceal their plans from him once Frau Heppler gave Reg away. A media circus was forming upstairs that would provide the global limelight an egomaniac like the Aryan would seize to take the world by the throat. He didn't know how, but Reg was not about to let that happen.

He had studied the room from his spot at the base of the big screen television that took up most of one wall. He memorized everything in the room. The dresser, the fitness machine, the huge antique bed—and on a tailor's dummy next to the bed, the hallowed Coat of Treves. The Aryan had exchanged it for a fresh uniform of khaki, flexing his impressive physique for the benefit of the captive and not wanting the Coat to detract in any way from the preeminence of the spear.

Over the headless neck of the dummy, the Aryan had draped the Veil of Veronica as if arranging his trophies for display. He lifted the Shroud from the bed and rubbed it against one cheek, smirking at the wide-eyed surprise in Danson's face.

Then the Aryan turned and lifted from the bed the Holy Lance, looking for a moment quite willing to run Danson through with it. Reg's fear was overshadowed by the presence of the weapon itself—its slender length and iron spearhead ending in a stiletto-sharp point. It was strangely unsettling and humbling. Legend said that it had pierced the Savior's side and hastened the Redeemer's death in fulfillment of ancient prophecy. Was it more than legend?

"Feast your eyes upon it while you can!" The Aryan lifted the weapon above his head and flushed with excitement. He had risked everything in the belief that the testimony of pilgrims down through the ages was true—that this was the sacred spear of Longinus the Roman; that it was, in fact, imbued with supernatural power and that he who possessed it possessed the divine.

The men who served the Aryan went down on one knee before the spear. Their master sliced the air above them with the Holy Lance in a mock knighting. Then, incredibly, he placed the Lance back on the bed, smirked at his prisoner, posted Goebbels at the door, and marched his minions from the room.

Control.

Reg decided on the oldest trick in the book. If it didn't work, he was dog food.

He wiped sweaty palms on his pants. He prayed for strength, glanced once more at the now empty doorway, and slid off his shoes. Without a sound, he crept over to the bed, and with excruciating slowness so as not to arouse the dog's suspicion, he pulled back the bedding.

He hesitated, suddenly overwhelmed by the great and timeless relics of the Passion of Christ, so near at hand. He should rescue them, not desecrate them further. Silently, he prayed. *God, what must I do?* A wave of jumbled images flooded his mind. Christ wrapped in a towel, washing his followers' feet. A sick woman touching the hem of his gown so that she could be healed. A royal robe torn by gamblers. Swaddling clothes. Empty grave windings.

I was naked and you clothed Me.

He gave thanks and stuffed a pillow in the Coat of Treves for a torso and placed it near the top of the mattress. He arranged another pillow further down to approximate the lower half of the "body." He looked about for a head and settled on a bicycle helmet which he placed at the top of the coat and half covered with the Veil. In his mind, he tried to match the Aryan's voice with the word Maria Metternich, the museum guide, had told him was the trigger command.

Nails clicked. Reg froze. *Too soon.*

Click, click, click. Wildly, Danson pulled up the covers, grabbed the Lance, and ran, stumbling and snatching up his shoes, to the walk-in closet. He ducked inside, setting the metal clothes hangers to chiming merrily. Reg tore the hangers from the bar and threw them into the center of the room.

Goebbels covered the remaining distance in a heartbeat. From between a jacket and a bathrobe, Reg watched the animal scan the room for signs of movement. It registered instantly that the prisoner was no longer in sight and that something now occupied the master's bed. In fascinated horror, Reg saw the shepherd lean into the room, its focus riveted on the bed, every nerve straining for the attack.

Danson hoped to convince. In his best imitation of Frederich von Feuerbach, he shouted, *"Vier!"*

With a guttural roar from the pit of its belly, the beast bolted forward to the bed in one mighty leap. It crashed into the headboard, turned, and tore into its prey with savage fury. A single powerful muscle covered over by skin and fur tore the history of the church to shreds.

In the split seconds before the mad dog discovered its "victim" was all cloth and no flesh, Reg slipped out of the closet and out of the room, the Lance firmly in his grasp. He knew what the great emperors and military commanders through the ages knew. There was an electricity in that grip, a palpable warming of the wood just knowing the awesome history attached to it.

Halfway along the now familiar hall, Reg stooped and put on his shoes. Before he could straighten, he heard again the dreaded sound.

The beast was coming, all of its snarl condensed into a compressed half groan, half whine, that was all the more terrible.

Reg turned to meet the black and tan body rocketing at his back. He meant to yell, *"Zwanzig!"*—the command to cease—but a survival reflex thrust the spear forward. With a sickening jolt that passed from the handle into Danson's very being, the blade sliced a deadly path through the animal's chest, lungs, and ribs before exiting midway down the backbone. The weight was too much to hold and the impaled animal hit the floor, spasmed twice, and lay still, its eyes locked open in surprise. In death, it looked almost docile, man's best friend, not at all the death machine it was in the hands of the Aryan.

"Katherine. Oh, Katherine," Reg said, backing away from the kill. He turned and ran.

He almost made it.

The attacker came out of the darkness. Strong arms locked around Danson's neck, and he was yanked backward through the door into the parlor. He managed to shout "Where are the kids?" before a hand clamped roughly over his mouth and he was wrestled to the floor.

The central command warehouse for the Iron Fist Nationalist Party was a converted barn on a remote farm a hundred miles north of New Orleans. The farm housed one of the Aryan weapons arsenals, which were scattered throughout the United States and Canada. Powerful yard lights lit the midnight scene of a civilian battalion preparing to mobilize. Banners plastered to the sides of the barn and stretched over the yard between light poles shouted venom:

"Take Back America!"
"America Belongs to White Christian Children!"
"Safeguard the White Birthright!"

"Stop Illegal Aliens—Dead!"
"God Bless America—Deport Illegals Now!"

Dozens of white supremacists loaded a convoy of vans and flatbed trucks with wooden crates of explosives, hunting rifles, and high-powered assault weapons. Exploding bullets and armor-piercing rounds would exact the greatest carnage. There was to be only one global race revolution. It would be sufficiently horrific to subdue the race-mixers for all time.

Just one massive bloodbath and the world would be safe for the white race evermore.

David Brewster, supreme commandant of the IFNP, mopped his ample neck and handed a skinny new recruit a white T-shirt, size medium. The teenager removed the "Patty Dugan's Party Bar" shirt he wore and slid the new shirt over his head, tugging it down and replacing the Budweiser hat, then tucked a metal I.D. necklace back inside the shirt. The necklace was stamped with the letters "WWRR," as was the boy's right buttock. He grinned goofily. "Thank ya, commander. I'm mighty proud to wear the colors!"

He turned and left the line, thin back now emblazoned with "Adolf Hitler European Tour 1939–45." There followed a list of nations like the concert stops of a monster rock band: "Poland, September 1939," "Norway, April 1940," "Luxembourg, May 1940"—*der Fuehrer*'s grisly itinerary of conquest.

Peter Smyth, Brewster's second in command, hurried over with a clipboard in hand, a furrow of worry between his eyes. "We should be on the road by now. Forget the lousy T-shirts. We should have been in position an hour ago!"

Brewster took the clipboard from Smyth and tossed it in the back of a battered Dodge pickup. "You know your problem, Petie boy? You don't know how to enjoy the ride. The Skins, the Boots, the Guard—all in place, all well supplied until we roll in with fresh. Meanwhile, let's relax, celebrate, and watch Kaspar touch the match to the fuse!" He looked at the closest of several television screens positioned around the farmyard and saw the Aryan mount the podium and kiss his mother on the cheek. Pandemonium erupted among the Jackboots at his side, and the GNN cameras swooped in for the broad grin of arrogant triumph that lit the Aryan's handsome face.

Midnight in Louisiana; nine A.M. in Germany.

Brewster yanked open the tailgate and released a gush of water. He threw back a heavy tarp to reveal a pickup bed full of bottled beer imbedded in ice. He raised a bullhorn and shouted, "Every Anglo-Saxon within the sound of my voice, come forth and drink!"

They rushed forward, grabbed up the brew, and gathered before the monitors to witness history.

Peter Smyth held the cold bottle thrust upon him but did not drink. He stood back and watched the profane young men joke with their women and wait for the signal from their great white hope. They were joined by a few middle-aged Klansmen who hoped mightily for a return of the glory days of the Invisible Empire. *It can't work*, he thought. *It is a hollow promise. We aren't near ready. We have not swayed enough leaders of government and law enforcement. The Pentagon is only partially turned. We lack personal discipline. This is not 1939 Germany. We will fail.*

Brewster found him and popped the top on his beer. "Drink!" he ordered, and Peter Smyth drank. He tilted his head back and drained the bottle in a single sucking swallow. "Another," he said, gasping for air. With a roar of approval, Brewster obliged. His Petie was finally coming around

The Aryan raged for twenty minutes about racial imbalance and the sins of humanity that permitted people of no common culture and interests to mingle indiscriminately. Hundreds of millions of people from Boston to Botswana listened and watched in horror as

he spun out the details of a plan to "realign" and "reassign" ethnic territory, a universal reapportionment that would halt the various "invasions" of Asians, Africans, Jews, Latinos, and other nonwhites and return them to racial "enclaves" within their countries of racial origin.

"The Semitic plot to bankrupt international government and to subvert the peace and tranquility by flooding white nations with immigrants is found out and found wanting. It will be forcefully halted and reversed. We will begin by deporting the millions of illegals that now infest Germany, Great Britain, Canada, and the United States of America. If you are one of them, I suggest you flee immediately. Tell others like you to flee. Take nothing with you, for it is your very life that is at stake.

"And I hereby nullify the seven million foreign-borns *with* proper papers. If you fall under that category, you were issued visas in error, and you should proceed immediately to the immigration office nearest you where my Aryan brothers have been instructed to grant you temporary asylum until such time as ship and air transport becomes available. A list of those immigration offices is now being shown on your television screens.

"Do not, I repeat, do *not* take more than is necessary for the journey itself. Your property, belongings, and bank assets are hereby frozen and will be used for partial restitution for the time and resources you have consumed while uninvited guests in foreign lands."

A swarm of anger and fear swept the earth at the pronouncement. Many began to sob, others to shout angrily and shake fists at the face on the television screen. Most simply stared in stupefied disbelief. It was fascism all over again.

No one in the crowd gathered at the Gates of Hope spotted the silent police vehicle pull into an alley below the estate. No one saw the officers and the two American teenagers climb the small embankment that paralleled the east side of the property.

The teenagers slipped quietly into the house. The police

stepped up beside the woman in pale yellow silk standing below the podium. The officers spoke low to the woman without turning in her direction. At first it appeared as though she might cry out in alarm, but she was too well bred to do that. She walked away with the officers.

Her confidence soon turned to shock as they forced her to look at photo after photo of tortured and dead bodies shotgunned, knifed, bludgeoned, and set afire. Each one a victim of neo-Nazi aggression; all occurring within the last two years. A bronze Star of David necklace encrusted with blood was clearly visible on one body. In another photo, a little boy with multiple sclerosis lay dead beside his wheelchair. His twisted back had been stripped bare and a crude swastika carved in the thin flesh. Lady Katherine wept.

"You cannot hope to control that kind of madness," the officer said, not unkindly.

She saw flyers and posters circulated in Germany showing rude drawings of people of color being led naked into bake ovens. The caption read: "Recipe for Aryan Domination." Others showed non-white women and children hanged, skinned, and scalped beneath the words "Earn Your Way Through School—We Pay Bounty!"

"There is nothing civilized, nothing compassionate in neo-Nazism," the police captain told her. "The Jackboots are operating on a very different level from what you may be, Lady von Feuerbach. Open your eyes. Perhaps you are sincere in your philosophical approach to repatriation, but nothing in these photos represents an intellectual discussion of human relations. It is nothing but animal brutality at its worst."

She barely heard him, the blood having drained from her fine features. Her eyes fastened on her son. The Aryan did not see the woman who birthed him, nurtured him, believed that he might actually bring order and cooperation to the racial strains of Germanic tradition. Nor did he see the tears or the trembling of the exquisite woman who once held and bathed him.

"We know that you have been diverting funds from your charity to finance a global revolution," the captain continued. "However, should you work with us, I will do what I can to influence some clemency on your behalf."

Barely above a whisper, Lady Katherine said, "I never wanted . . . *that.*" She waved weakly at the photos but refused to look at them again. "He showed so much promise, I let myself believe he would lead with a firm, yet tolerant hand. I . . . I was such a fool! All I ever wanted was to set people free from themselves. Is that so terrible a thing?"

The captain returned the graphic photos to their envelope. "Colonel Gregor Mulig of the Defense Ministry has placed the *Bundeswehr,* the German army, on full-scale alert, fully prepared to halt any insurrection. Your son will very likely lose his life and take a great many people with him."

He waited for her reply.

She remained silent.

CHAPTER 24

Reg Danson was unhurt. It seemed almost as if the big oaf all over him was a tame bear cub out for a romp.

"Pinned ya!" declared a familiar voice. The body lifted and Reg turned over to face Tony on his knees grinning at his dad like the Cheshire cat. Behind him was Connie, grinning as big.

"Where have you two been!?" he exclaimed. He hugged Connie and roughed Tony until his son cried, "Give! I give!"

"Oh, we just took a little trip out to the airport and back," said Connie mysteriously. "I got this sudden brainstorm and we had to go on an international shopping spree. Thanks to the Vatican—your name still opens doors there, you'll be glad to know—we pray we can defuse the bomb. It's a long shot, but no longer than the other ones we've taken."

Quickly they filled Reg in on the plan. When they finished, breathless, he got angrily to his feet. "That's a noble effort, guys, but it's insane we have to go through all that and then it might not work. What if it didn't? We'd be left sitting ducks. No, a good idea, Connie, but totally unnecessary. What we've got to do is unplug this idiot right now!"

Fred Gaston had died and gone to media heaven. For the first time in history, he'd bet there wasn't one TV set on earth tuned to any station but GNN. He loathed the Aryan and his dogs—both canine and human—but no rock star, natural catastrophe, political skirmish, or world sporting event could ever pull the kind of ratings they had on this one.

It was preposterous that the man at the podium could engineer the scenario he was spinning for three billion viewers. He'd better not. GNN would become the voice of the state under that regime. No, not a chance of it ever happening. So why not cash in? He was, after all, a quite stylish madman. A police sharpshooter probably had him dead in his sights at this very moment.

"Excuse me, Mr. Gaston?"

Gaston brushed Danson off. "Not now, fool. We're right in the middle of this thing."

Reg grabbed a handful of charcoal-gray sleeve and whipped Gaston around. Tony and Connie waited back by a satellite van. Several technicians stepped forward but Gaston warned them off. "Make it quick, Mr. Danson. It doesn't get any bigger than this."

"Sure it does," Reg replied caustically. "Once he gives the signal, all hell breaks loose and you've got a full-scale international riot on your hands. You might even have to run without commercial interruption!"

"Are you through?" Gaston popped another half dozen antacid tablets and a fat clove of garlic. "Our task may be slightly more altruistic than you give us credit for. If we suddenly stop the broadcast, what signal does that send this guy's thugs in Hoboken? Sorry, Danson. We don't do Mother Earth any favors except to ride this one to the bitter end."

"... Take all personal weapons of any kind to the public schools nearest you," the Aryan continued to instruct the people of all nations. "Anyone taking a threatening posture of any kind will be swiftly exterminated. All major affiliated racial intelligence agencies on earth are awaiting my signal at the end of this broadcast. Upon that signal, they have been instructed to launch Operation Cause and Effect. Those who resist—whether men, women, or children—will be killed. Make no mistake. We cannot accommodate the slightest opposition if we are to cure the ills of society. There will be pain, of course. Nothing of value comes without pain. But a spirit of cooperation will hasten the day when we can at last breathe free, each in his or her own most familiar surroundings with his or her own kind—those who look, sound, and smell alike. The grand experiment of racial tolerance has failed.

"Das tut mir sehr leid. I am really sorry about this. I see no other way."

Reg rejoined Connie and Tony. His son had never seen him so crestfallen. "I thought I could convince GNN to pull out and leave the Aryan no other forum. Their chief said that if they were to suddenly go off the air, it would mean racial suicide. I see his point, but I hate to let this guy hold the airwaves hostage." He looked at them helplessly. "I guess it's your way or the highway. Let's go!"

They rushed back through the maze of cable and equipment. Abruptly, Reg stopped. "Oh, no!" He turned pale. "You came with the police? Where are they? Quick, son, where?"

Tony waved to the east side of the property and Reg bolted.

The elite forces marksmen took up their positions on the two roofs to the direct south and west of the estate, the only directions from which an unhindered line of sight, and a clear shot, were possible. Through the scopes of their rifles they lined up the cross hairs on the neo-Nazi's face. Those to the west targeted the right temple; those to the south aimed between the eyebrows just above the bridge of the nose.

Each of them mentally squeezed the trigger and imagined the handsome head disintegrating like the meat of a pumpkin. A minimum of two other Nazis would go down at the same time, close as they were to the Aryan at the podium. It could not be avoided.

Only one rifleman would receive the actual order to fire on the speaker. All others would turn their attentions on the remaining Nazi troopers should they go for weapons. Should they order their dogs to attack, the kill would automatically transfer to the shepherds. The highly trained animals would cease the attack only upon the sound of their masters' voices. The dogs would have to be killed quickly before having opportunity to inflict maximum damage.

Innocents were bound to die whatever the melee. The charge was to minimize, neutralize, and liquidate whatever necessary within fifteen seconds.

A radio crackled softly and each man tensed for the order to fire, each hoping to lay claim to the title of supreme Nazi hunter. Not one was willing to stand down.

But their leader listened a moment to the voice in his ear. Then, hard as it was for him to say the word, he spoke into the receivers in the ears of the others. *"Nein."* They were to hold their fire.

The kill had been called off.

The Aryan paused and flashed his most beneficent smile. He had purchased the egos of the biggest names in hatred. He held the world in thrall. He was at this moment more powerful than a hundred Hitlers. The moment of triumph was at hand. Now was the time to reveal the symbolic link between this generation of young idealists and those before. Now was the time to bring forth the Holy Lance and to lock arms with the brave warriors of kingdoms past. Now was the time to ignite the Final Fire.

He stared into the cameras, and they zoomed in to capture every nuance of eye and mouth. He peered deep into the soul of every viewer, remembering how effectively Adolf Hitler had fixed his subjects with the haughtiest and most contemptuous of stares. "Do not think that I come in my own power! I have the imprimatur of heaven for what I do. In the fourth chapter of the Gospel according to Saint John we read the words of Jesus the Christ, himself an Aryan, all Jew lies to the contrary! 'Behold,' he said, 'I say to you, lift up your eyes and look at the fields, for they are already *white* for harvest!'"

He stepped back from the podium, and one of his men stepped forward from the shadows, a long slender shaft grasped tightly in both hands. He marched ceremoniously to a position facing the Aryan, placed the spear in his leader's hands, and hastily whispered something in the man's ear before going down on one knee, head bowed.

The Aryan's expression changed so rapidly, camera operators checked their lenses for malfunction. Gone was the robust light of masculine beauty. In its place was an expression so foul it made little children cry and adults cover their eyes. The Aryan raised the Holy Lance above his head, arms spread far apart. His lips parted in a sickly leer, tongue licking teeth as if to sharpen them. "Behold the spear of Gaius Cassius Longinus the Centurion, soldier liege to Emperor Herod Antipas. Behold that which pierced the side of the God-man and left wounds upon the phantom body of the risen Christ. Behold that which first shed the blood of the New Covenant. He who holds the Holy Spear holds the destiny of mankind!"

"Fake!" Cameras three and four swung to the east toward the sound of the second voice. Confusion crackled in the operators' headsets. GNN producer Gabe Rafferty came on, unable to disguise his excitement. "It's—it looks like that explorer guy, Reg Danson, and he appears to be carrying . . . *another spear!"*

Reg walked among the vehicles and cameras toward the podium. The crowd began to resonate with the news. "He has a spear too. Look, it seems identical to the other!" The crisp, uniformed neo-Nazis shifted uncomfortably. This was not in the script.

Reg stopped at the foot of the stairs and raised his spear in imitation of the Aryan. He looked the hatemonger straight in the eye. "Behold, the Spear of Krakow, Poland, venerated for centuries as rival claimant to the title Holy Lance of Longinus the Centurion!"

"What in the devil's name is going on?!" roared David Brewster, eyes glued to the television monitor over the barn door somewhere in Louisiana. The broadcast showed a preposterous scene. The Aryan and the American, spears high, facing off over who had the right spear? "Why doesn't somebody shoot that idiot?"

"Quiet!" shouted Peter Smyth to everyone's surprise. But then, he didn't normally drink beer. Good thing. Under normal circumstances, Brewster would have squashed him like a June bug for such an outburst. The thin man steadied himself as best he could on the shoulder of Sylvia Ricks, the party secretary, and pointed shakily at the screen.

"Fake!" Camera five swung to the east and picked up Connie Bird and Tony Danson striding purposely forward, an identical spear clasped in their four hands.

"For crying out loud!" Fred Gaston gobbled another handful of antacids. "Nobody said anything about a cast of thousands! Gabe, are you getting all this?"

Gabe gestured frantically from the command van like a man trying to keep a dozen plates spinning in the air at once.

Gaston's heart rate was setting a new land speed record. He didn't like it that six of his "staffers" were CIA, compliments of his old buddy, Bill Kesey, director of the agency. He liked it even less that they didn't seem to be doing a thing about anything.

Connie and Tony stood at the foot of the steps, shoulder to shoulder with Reg Danson, their spear raised high overhead. "Behold, the Spear of King Louis the Saint," they said in unison, "brought to Paris from the Crusades where it led the knights in battle victory after victory. It, too, lays rightful claim to being the very spear that pierced the King of Kings!"

All over the world, neo-fascist groups bickered heatedly over the authenticity of the three spears assembled in Nuremberg. At the Aryan Sisters League in Smyrna, Georgia, two women were rushed to Palmetto Trauma Center after nearly gouging each other's eyes out. In Moscow, Russia, the Legion Werewolf started throwing chairs and fists. Baton-wielding police were called in to quell the disturbance.

On a farm north of New Orleans, Herr Commandant David Brewster of the Iron Fist Nationalist Party debated whether or not to shut off the TVs. Maybe fake a power failure. He grimaced. He didn't like the sound of "power failure."

Maybe fetch another truckload of beer and do a postmortem in the morning.

Another five minutes. If the Aryan didn't take control by then, he was all hot air.

The Aryan straightened to his full height, raised his face skyward, and saw again the sticky blood of his beloved Goebbels staining the spearhead crimson. The man who killed the most loyal and capable creature that ever lived was less than thirty feet away, mocking the Cause before the world.

Frederich von Feuerbach, the Aryan, dropped his arms. With a venomous hiss, he plunged down the stairs to impale the despised American.

"Fake!"

The Aryan stopped dead in his tracks and watched his mother make her way over the same route taken by the Dansons and Connie

Bird. Incredibly, clutched tightly in her beautifully manicured fingers was a fourth spear.

She stood on Reg Danson's other side, spear held high, yellow silk flowing in the gentle morning breeze. The face she tilted up to her son was tear-streaked but resolute.

Fred Gaston nearly had apoplexy. He was forced to lie down in his Brooks Brothers suit across six transmission cords and a patch of faded grass. Someone splashed water in his face. He grabbed the man's lapels. "It's the CIA, I tell you," he muttered hoarsely, "The C—I—bloody A!"

"Behold!" said Lady Katherine, the declaration ringing clear and firm from the TV in an exotic pet shop in Perth, Australia, to the radio in a pink stucco duplex in Moosejaw, Saskatchewan. "I give you the spear of the Great Hall of the Vatican, long held in reverence by the pilgrim faithful as the lance that entered the body of our Lord and hastened his very death!"

Her son's chin visibly quivered on international TV.

"Frederich," she implored, "don't do this thing. We cannot slaughter the innocents. Good King Solomon includes among his proverbs of wisdom the seven things God cannot tolerate, and one of them is the shedding of innocent blood."

"Tighter, tighter!" Gabe Rafferty bellowed into his mouthpiece, and camera operators filled the screen with a mother's pleas.

The crowd from the streets and the neighborhoods of Nuremberg grew hushed. A few wept.

The Aryan stepped backward up the stairs, as if afraid to turn his back on his own mother. He tore his eyes from hers, stopped his ears against her cries, and looked again straight into cameras one and two. "Do not be fooled! You see before you the pitiful attempt of those who love the weak, the defective, the curs and culls of the human race. They wouldn't know the meaning of purebred if you stuck their noses in it. I hold the one true Spear, that which the mighty Hitler and Barbarossa and Charlemagne and so many of the greats of the

Western Empire also held and from which they derived so much of their Teutonic success and destiny!"

David Levin on camera two blew a loud raspberry and stepped from behind the camera, right index finger pointed accusingly at the Aryan. Camera three picked up the exchange. "Hitler was such a fabulous success, was he?" Levin mocked. "The man shot his own head off in a Berlin bunker and took his girlfriend with him!"

"That's a lie!" shrieked the Aryan. He grabbed the microphones as if to tear them from the podium. *"Der Fuehrer* used substitutes to make fools like you think he committed suicide. But secret German war records show that he and Eva Braun escaped by U-boat to Argentina!" Shaking, face flushed and pouring sweat, the Aryan stared into the cameras. "If you are watching, *mein Fuehrer,* know that this day we shall vindicate the Third Reich and usher in the Fourth!"

"Why don't you blow a kiss to President Kennedy and Marilyn Monroe while you're at it?" Levin jeered. Many in the crowd felt the tide had turned and joined in the laughter.

"Halt den Mund! Shut up!" the Aryan roared. He motioned to one of his men on the stairs to release a dog. With a sweeping motion of its master's right arm and a sharp *"Vier!"* the shepherd was on the cameraman in two bounds. The beast sank its incisors deep into the flesh of an upper thigh. The pants stained dark and Levin screamed.

Camera four caught it all.

A loud report snapped the autumn air. With a mortal yelp, the attacking canine somersaulted backward into a light pole and lay still in a spray of blood. The crowd shrieked and dropped to the pavement, heads covered. The sharpshooters did not reveal their locations.

The Aryan looked momentarily lost, then looked as if he might order all of his troops to release their animals on the crowd.

"No, Frederich!" Lady Katherine laid down her spear and mounted the stairs. She stopped just behind her son. He did not turn. She spoke and the world heard. "Where are the monuments to Hitler's success, my darling? Are they at Lublin and Treblinka and

Auschwitz-Birkenau? Hitler could be as physically alive as you or I, but his ideology is stone. The pride of spirit that once united this nation, perhaps it has value, perhaps we may revisit it one day and see what, if anything, may be salvaged. But never those methods, never again the end justifying the means. Reg Danson is right. Hate can never be the author of freedom. Oh, Frederich, my baby—" She reached out to touch him, but he visibly stiffened and she stopped.

Reg laid down his spear. Connie and Tony followed suit. They embraced.

Lady Katherine looked at them, took a deep breath, and stepped forward. She hugged her son from behind, laying her cheek against the strong back. "Frederich, hear me. I was wrong to encourage you in this. I have seen the photos of the maiming, the murder, all done in the name of the Cause. Your father—"

"Don't!" sobbed the Aryan, face to the sky, eyes squeezed tightly shut. "Father's 'children' were his contacts in high places, the currying of favor with the wealthy and the well-placed. I was merely the biological authentication that he was a man, that he could father a child and that he was virile enough to produce a man-child.

"Oh, I told my chums that he loved me. Look how he fed and clothed and educated me. But do you know, Mother, that I never knew what his arms felt like because they never once embraced me? Do you know that he touched me only three times that I can remember—a poke in the head when I botched a mathematics problem, an attempt to scratch a freckle off the end of my nose because he hated freckles, and a jab to the stomach to tell me when I was eight that I was getting too soft. And do you know, Mother, that I never, ever heard him say, 'I love you, Frederich. You matter to me, Frederich.' But I do recall him saying, 'Get your fat butt off the floor and disappear upstairs. Guests will be arriving shortly.'"

"No, Frederich, no. Your father cared for you. It's just that his own father never . . ."

He did not hear her. He shut her out. His mind crackled with static from a thousand raging thoughts, but only one intelligible one. *I have failed. The opportunity is past. My purpose is ended.*

The crowd, the television technicians, the police, the storm troopers and their dogs—and the billions of stunned television viewers—were silent, shocked and grieved by this most private, and public, of conversations.

The Aryan slowly lowered the Holy Lance of the Royal House of Habsburg. He stared at it and wondered if ever the immortal Savior's blood had touched the iron head. Or just the mortal blood of men and dogs.

"Let it go, Frederich," Reg Danson shouted. "It has no magic, no supernatural properties. It is merely a tool of legend, a way to stir the imagination. Where are all the great men who once held it in their grasp? They have gone the way of all men, to the grave. Their empires have come and gone. Their memories are embellished, their accomplishments padded, their glory tarnished by indiscretions. The spear is without power, authentic or not. What has power is that the Son of God came to give us that which does not die—life eternal. *His* Kingdom come. But it will only come in his time, Frederich, not by our might or force of will. The world is imperfect and cannot be otherwise until heaven."

"Listen to him, Frederich," Lady Katherine implored. "And meanwhile, we can do what we can to help those who want to go home. It is a good work, a noble purpose."

"No, Mother," Frederich grimly replied. "That takes much too long." He straightened and threw off her arms. He spoke boldly into the microphones, the tone in his voice tolerant of no opposition. "To the brothers and sisters of the Resistance worldwide, the moment you have anticipated is now come. I raise before you the Lance of the Teutons, and when I bury it deep within this man's body"—he pointed at Reg—"that is your signal to ignite the Holy Revolution, the flames of cleansing, the Final Fire!"

A collective gasp arose at the raising of the lance.

"Vier!" The command came from among the one hundred look-alike soldiers of hate. A dog hurtled through the air, knocked Katherine to the floor, and slammed into the Aryan. The spear intended to usher in the New Age clattered uselessly away.

The beast snapped and tore at Frederich von Feuerbach II. He yelled and begged and tried to fend the creature off with bleeding hands. *"Zwanzig!"* he shrieked in terror. *"Zwanzig! Zwanzig!"* But the dog ignored all but the voice of its own master.

Katherine von Feuerbach, on her knees beside the fury, screamed for mercy. "Please, someone, spare my son. Spare him, please!" Her beauty crumbling, the yellow dress torn, she stretched out her hands, imploring the troops to intervene. "Save my Frederich!"

"Zwanzig!" The anonymous command to cease attack came again from among the one hundred. None of the ninety-nine turned to betray the one who gave it. Eyes forward, countenance rigid, all one hundred remained inscrutable.

Control.

All one hundred shared in the moment of justice. But only one bore a ragged wound over his left ear from the butt of the Holy Lance. He had been ordered by the Aryan never to forget how he had earned the savage rebuke in the training chamber beneath the Gates of Hope.

He had not forgotten.

Commandant David Brewster threw the switch that blacked out the TV monitors at the Iron Fist Nationalist Party farm north of New Orleans. The beer tasted warm and flat and he pitched the half-full bottle against the side of the barn. It shattered in a spray of foam. He stepped over Peter Smyth passed out on the ground and said nothing to a dim-eyed Sylvia Ricks.

He continued down the dirt drive oblivious to the hurt and

questioning looks from the other IFNP members. They were suddenly lost, without purpose, many of them without any other home but the farm. And while each had hated David Brewster in one way or another, the loutish, unprincipled bully had been their pilot.

Their father figure now had no more substance than a stick figure.

They watched the heavy, suspendered body continue beyond the reach of the yard lights. Off the dirt road, into the cow pasture, a stout shape outlined in moonlight.

Brewster stopped. For three long minutes there was eerie silence and then a strange sound they'd never heard before.

Brewster was bawling.

Maria Metternich felt the bandages on her face. But she did not smile that an eye had been given for an eye in Nuremberg. The whimpering, bleeding man captured by the cameras bore only slight resemblance to the handsome, suave "blind" gentleman whose company and erudition she had so briefly enjoyed earlier that week in Vienna. She thought, instead, of the sympathetic American. His apologetic questioning. His kind touch on her shoulder. His words "God bless you and bring you complete healing." God had blessed her. The Aryan was destroyed.

Reg Danson gathered Lady Kaspar in his arms and sat on the porch of the Gates of Hope rocking her for a long time. Police and CIA and German Intelligence moved in for interrogation. GNN technicians disassembled the media event of the century much the same way they did the end of election day or a tennis match at Wimbledon, rewinding cable, stowing lights, depositing anchorpersons back into white sedans in the same order they had emerged.

Workers, silent and careful, removed podium and microphones from around the grieving couple.

Paramedics placed the mewling Aryan on a stretcher and inserted him into the back of a waiting ambulance. A search of the house produced Frau Heppler. "Hiding in a broom closet," said the escorting officer. Reg looked away until the frighteningly familiar house slippers shuffled past where he and Lady Katherine were sitting. Then he put out a hand and stopped them. "Just a moment, please, I have something to say to this woman."

She stood stoically, but met his gaze.

"Frau Heppler, I believe you felt trapped and that you remained loyal to your household, as twisted as it was. I don't condemn you for that."

Two tears slipped from the corners of the housekeeper's eyes.

Katherine squeezed Frau Heppler's big hand. "Thank you, Ingrid, for your years of service. Don't be afraid. You've committed no crime."

Frau Heppler's shoulders, beneath a faded brown sweater, rose and fell with a shudder of emotion. "I only ever wanted to serve, Miss Katherine." The Frau's voice was soft and deep but free of sentiment. "Still, I can tell you now that I never liked the business beyond the parlor." And then she was gone.

The crowd seemed loath to disperse, not at all certain what they had just witnessed. Days later, some would question if it had really happened at all.

"Might we start again, Reg, or have I so thoroughly poisoned the well?" Katherine tried saying it lightly, but it stabbed at Danson's heart.

"You used me, Katherine. You lied to me. You lured me into a trap. I—I can't rid my mind of two hands touching in a common bowl, one the betrayer's, the other the betrayed's. I will say that treachery has never looked as lovely."

She looked away. "It was the only way I could think to save

your life. Once you joined forces with the church, you were marked for murder."

"You didn't know me from Adam," he said bitterly. "You thought I might be trouble and wanted me out of the way so Frederich could trigger the final bomb without interference."

"No! I've followed your adventures and admired your discoveries. The world would have been poorer without you."

She was a mass of contradictions. Reg shook his head. Any way you sliced it, Katherine von Feuerbach was a dangerous woman.

For the first time, she faced her duplicity through his eyes. Still, she could not bear to call it what it was. "You don't understand. I could gain no audience for mass repatriation. Even though my husband was once highly placed, he is now forgotten and the chancellor is otherwise occupied with his enormous unpopularity and has no time for a widow and her Jewish charity. What I thought was the perfect guise for creating a new earth became an increasingly sore point with the blatant nationalists. Better I should have been rehabilitating the disenchanted German youth by creating jobs programs to keep them off the streets.

"But I thought my way quicker, more humane. I fell under the spell of expediency, and it became difficult to distinguish between acts of mercy and acts of inhumanity in the name of the New Order. I don't know if I shall ever again be allowed to rescue the displaced and take them safely home."

His hand was wet with her tears. She could be at once hard and soft. "God reconciles people to himself," he said gently. "It has always seemed like folly to beat swords into plowshares and declare the gospel of Christ, but that and only that makes friends of enemies."

"I wish I believed as strongly as you do. But I'm afraid my life's passion is ended."

"I will put in a word for you, Katherine, but trust is a difficult thing to regain. Perhaps my boss, Richard Bascomb, could use your help with his philanthropy. I don't know. But much judgment and restitution must come before then."

Katherine watched Tony and Connie, two figures in the grass among the departing vans and trucks, holding each other in much the same way as the older couple. She kissed Reg's hand. "There is our hope for tomorrow," she said. "Your son is certainly a fine and handsome young man. I envy you the love you share. Few regrets with him, I'd say."

Reg sighed and tightened his embrace. "A few. Mostly my doing. He's smart as a whip and kind like his mother was. But you're right, we do have something pretty special between us." He watched the young man kiss the red baseball cap and lay his head alongside the words *St. Louis.*

In his eyes, Connie no longer looked small in the too-big flak jacket. "It's the young lady beneath that cap who gets the medal of honor today," he said. "She was one of them once. Who can know the courage that it took for her to renounce their doctrine of hate and disarm the bomb about to explode in the world's face?"

Katherine nodded. "I'd like to get to know that one. Tell her I should like a pen pal in prison. For that matter, tell yourself the same."

She turned to look at him and closed her eyes while he wiped the tears from her cheeks. Then she reached out to pluck the strings of an air harp and heard again music from within.

Reg watched her and heard the music too. They were back in the parlor when he did not fully know her terrible secret. The music vibrated among the trees of a forest paradise. An iridescent green butterfly landed at the mossy edges of a Paraguayan waterfall. Why couldn't they have remained there?

"Have him write me sometime," she murmured, eyes still closed. "Your son, I mean. Have him tell me what a typical young man thinks about, dreams of, works toward. I should like to know.

Maybe then I can help Frederich find a new purpose and a new hope."

"I will," Reg said, brushing her hair with the back of his hand. He chuckled. "Right now, I imagine Tony's thinking of how to break the news to Miss Snow, the belle of Alexandria, Virginia."

They were silent a little longer. The shaved, uniformed storm troopers loaded their dogs into cages stacked in the back of a police semi-truck. Then, the neo-fascists themselves were loaded into black police vans for transport to temporary holding cells before transfer to Rotenburg National Prison to await trial.

"Perhaps once or twice a year, if it's permitted, you could play the harp for me over the telephone?"

Katherine laughed in regret. "Bar tune or angel's song?"

In reply, Reg softly sang into her ear. "Sacred head now wounded . . ."

"Salve caput cruentatum . . ." she sang the German equivalent.

". . . mine, mine was the transgression . . ." Reg responded.

". . . von dir will ich nicht gehen . . ." she echoed.

On the next line, their voices merged:

". . . but Thine the deadly pain . . ."

". . . wenn dir den Here bricht . . ."

Afterword

It is well documented that the Holy Lance was the object of desire for many European rulers throughout history. Adolf Hitler's obsession with the ancient spear, its brazen theft by the Nazis, and ultimate reclamation by American soldiers on the very day that Hitler committed suicide, are all a matter of public record.

Such improbable events prove once again that fact is often stranger than fiction.

Some trust in chariots, and some in horses;
but we will remember the name of the LORD our God.
— *Psalm 20:7*

To learn more about the battle against racial intolerance, you are encouraged to read the following:

A Season for Justice: The Life and Times of Civil Rights Lawyer Morris Dees by Morris Dees (New York: Macmillan Publishing, 1991)

Hate on Trial: The Trial of America's Most Dangerous Neo-Nazi by Morris Dees(New York: Villard Books, 1993)

For details on the national work of the Southern Poverty Law Center, write:

Southern Poverty Law Center
400 Washington Avenue
Montgomery, AL 36104

For details on the Holocaust and anti-Semitism, write:

Anti-Defamation League
823 United Nations Plaza
New York, NY 10017

About the Author

Clint Kelly, a publications specialist for Seattle Pacific University, is a happily married father of four. He also is a prolific freelance writer whose articles have appeared in a wide variety of periodicals, from *American History Illustrated* to *Writer's Digest.* Kelly's former occupations include teacher, forest ranger, and wilderness expedition leader.

Kelly is the author of *Me Parent, You Kid! Taming the Family Zoo, The Landing Place,* and *The Lost Kingdom.*